DARKNESS ON THE EDGE OF TOWN

JOHN BECKETT SERIES
BOOK 1

MATTHEW HATTERSLEY

BOOM BOOM PRESS

1

Heavy rain pounded on the roof of Jane Isaacs's car as it crept along London's Albert Embankment towards 85 Vauxhall Cross. As the car slowed to a stop, she leaned closer to the window, her gaze tracing up the imposing building to her right – the headquarters of Britain's Secret Intelligence Service, the home of MI6.

A Londoner by birth, Isaacs remembered the controversy that had sparked up when MI6 had moved away from Century House in the mid-nineties to this modern monolith on the banks of the river. The building – an expansive sprawl of glass and concrete – had earned itself a variety of colourful nicknames over the years. Some sneered at it as 'The Lego Building'; others referred to the bold architectural departure as 'Dubai-on-Thames'. But Isaacs didn't mind it too much. For her, it was now simply synonymous with the London skyline. A modern building, like the Shard and the Gherkin, that proved London was still at the cutting edge of design, driven by industry and progress rather than what might look pleasing to the mainstream.

The driver switched off the engine and Isaacs sat upright,

preparing herself for what was waiting for her inside. This was her fourth visit to MI6, but her first in the capacity of Home Secretary. She'd yet to be briefed on why she was being called here at 9 a.m. on a Tuesday, but whatever it was, she was determined to make a good impression on those in attendance. She was well aware that the ascension to her new role in the cabinet less than a month earlier had not been without controversy. After a swift cabinet reshuffle, she'd taken over from The Right Honourable Douglas Holmes MP, whose scandalous affairs with two special advisers had propelled him into a forced resignation and a statement read out at the gates of his Kent estate with his stern-faced wife standing supportively by his side. The affair was another grubby matter to hit an already fractious and reeling government, and there were some – many – in the party who felt Isaacs was an unfit replacement. But she'd show them. Her hope was that, under her guidance, the Home Office would reach a level of gravitas and decorum that it had been missing for the last three years.

So, shoulders back, chest out.

She could do this.

The door of her car opened, and she looked up to see Max, the head of her new security detail, holding a large black umbrella for her. It was only a ten-second walk to the main entrance, but she was glad of the cover. Glad of him. His calming presence lessened the anxiety that had been gripping her since she got the phone call at 7 a.m. this morning demanding her presence here today. It was these little things – having an umbrella held for her, being escorted places by a committed security detail – that she was still getting used to in her new role. But she wasn't complaining. She liked feeling both safe and powerful, and most of the time she did. Yet, despite her outward displays of confidence, she was still acclimatising to her new role, and today's high-stakes meeting only amplified her trepidation.

"Ma'am." Max held a large hand out to her.

She took it, offering him a gracious smile as he helped her from the car.

"Will you stay?" she asked, as they made their way to the entrance.

"Of course. I'll be right here when you're finished."

That was what she wanted to hear, but at the bottom of the steps she hesitated. The cold March air hung heavy with anticipation and tension, clinging to her like a second skin. Hard droplets of rain beat down on the taut canvas umbrella as she drew in a deep breath and focused her attention on the glass doors in front of her. Whatever this was about, she would deal with it to the best of her ability.

Gathering her courage, she slowly ascended the steps, Max's presence still a reassuring constant in her periphery. A young woman was waiting behind the sleek glass entrance, and as Isaacs approached, she leaned forward and used her ID card to open the door for her.

"Good morning, Home Secretary," she said, stepping to one side to allow her to enter.

"Thank you. And let's hope it's a good one."

Squaring her shoulders, Isaacs stepped through the door, leaving Max outside with his umbrella. Inside the building, the atmosphere was one of quiet efficiency. Decorated in a modern, minimalist style, the vast atrium was sparse except for a reception desk over to the right, which was manned by three guards who appeared to be making a concerted effort not to look her way. On either side of the space, large canvases hung on the walls, displaying famous scenes from around the capital – Big Ben, the Houses of Parliament, Nelson's Column.

"Would you like to follow me? They are all waiting for you."

The question drew Jane's attention back. "Absolutely. Lead the way."

The young woman swiped them through the security gates and then through a series of double doors. The long, silent corridors seemed to swallow Isaacs up the further they went, each step echoing like a gunshot as her heels clacked against the polished floor. She could almost feel the gravity weighing her down, sensing innumerable secrets lurking behind the closed doors and on the guarded faces of those she passed. Further anticipation coiled in her stomach as they turned a corner and she was faced with a room at the far end of the next corridor. The door was open and she could see Tristan Shepherd, the Foreign Secretary. He looked tired and nervous. At least she wasn't the only one.

Her escort accompanied her to the doorway but no further. As the woman backed away, Isaacs thanked her then stepped inside. Shepherd turned to see her enter and raised his eyebrows as if sharing a moment of grim solidarity. Glancing around the room, Isaacs recognised the director general of MI5, Emily Eastwood – who she'd met with twice since becoming Home Secretary – and also Frank Calder, the incumbent chief of MI6. She offered them both a resigned smile, and got the same in response.

There were four other people in the room, all men. Two of them were seated together at one end of a large round table in the centre of the room, talking in hushed whispers; another was pacing up and down; the fourth was leafing through a pile of papers on the table in front of him. The expression on each man's face was grave, and at least two of them looked as if they hadn't been to bed.

"What's going on, Tristan?" she whispered, as Shepherd approached her and closed the door. He stood beside her and they took in the room. "Are we in trouble?"

He cleared his throat. "I've not been fully briefed, but now you're here we'll get straight into it." He glanced pointedly at the two men sitting at the table. "But yes, Jane, from what I can gather, we're in a great deal of trouble."

They found seats at the round table as silence descended. Glancing around the room, Isaacs was surprised at how plain it looked, almost nondescript in its modernity. There were no pictures on the walls, no exposed pipework or decorative fixtures. There was just one fluorescent strip light that hung from the ceiling, casting the windowless room in a stark white glow. With no windows and only the large table in the centre, it felt spacious and claustrophobic all at once. The air was heavy with expectation.

"Robert, are you going to tell us what the hell this is all about?" the man sitting opposite her asked. "I'm supposed to be on leave. I've got a flight leaving for the Algarve this afternoon." The man looked to be in his early sixties and his features resembled those of a wolfhound. What hair he had left on his head was in direct competition with his bushy white eyebrows and visible nasal hair.

"We shouldn't need to keep you long at this stage, Brian," the man called Robert replied. "This is just a prelim. To fill you in on what intel we have. I'm optimistic we can nip this in the bud before it gets away from us."

"Before we start," Tristan Shepherd butted in. "I think it might be wise if we did introductions. I know most of you, but I'm not sure Jane here has had the pleasure."

Isaacs sat up at the sound of her name, suddenly feeling even more out of place as seven pairs of eyes all turned to look at her. "That would be very helpful," she heard herself say.

She was glad Shepherd was here. They weren't what you'd call friends, but she wouldn't have had the nerve to speak up herself amongst these titans of intelligence. The Foreign Secretary, however, was a seasoned veteran of these sorts of things and was taking it in his stride; in fact, he appeared to be revelling in the unease and chaos buzzing in the air.

Isaacs listened intently, carefully processing the names and titles as the individuals at the table made their introductions. She was familiar with Eastwood, Shepherd, and Calder, but now she added Simon Bryers, head of the NCA, and Brian Somersby, Director of GCHQ, to her mental roster. She'd yet to establish a connection with either of them but there was no time like the present. The remaining two men at the table introduced themselves as Robert Locke and Spencer Bowditch, the chief director and senior officer of Sigma Unit.

Bloody hell!

Like most people in positions of power in the British government, she'd heard the rumours regarding Sigma Unit, yet its existence had always been blurred in ambiguity. From what she'd gathered, they were a covert arm of the British Secret Service's general support branch, whose operatives collaborated not only with MI6 but also with the CIA and Mossad, and carried out clandestine paramilitary operations both domestically and abroad. They were what the Americans called a Black Ops unit – an elite group of former Special Forces operatives who were deployed mainly on 'deniable operations' in foreign territories.

On paper, Sigma Unit didn't exist. Yet here she was sitting metres away from two of its most high-ranking members. And if they were here, something big had gone down. Or was about to.

"Come on then, Locke," Bryers exclaimed, once the introductions were over. "Give us the lowdown. What have you dragged us all here for? We do have work to do over in NCA, you know?"

"Yes, this is all a bit dramatic, old boy," Somersby added, followed by a blustery laugh. "I know you secret service bods like it that way, but couldn't this have been done over the phone? Or in an email?"

Locke glanced at Bowditch, who glanced at Calder. "I'm

afraid not," Calder replied. "This is a matter of national security and we can't risk any leaks." He looked back at Robert Locke. "We can't risk *further* leaks."

"There's been a leak?" Somersby asked.

Robert Locke got to his feet and unbuttoned his single-breasted suit jacket with one hand. "We believe so," he said. "But as Frank has already intimated, we're anticipating that we can contain the problem at the source."

Locke was a tall man, with black hair parted on one side and swept back from his face. Isaacs wouldn't have described him as handsome, but there was something intriguing about him. He had a certain charm and he dressed well. He was slim, bordering on skinny; yet despite his build, he didn't seem weak. Far from it. He looked like the sort of person who was constantly wired for danger, full of adrenaline and nerves. He addressed those assembled with stern, unblinking eyes.

"Some of you are already aware that, in the early hours of this morning, one of our elite intelligence analysts intercepted clandestine communications on the dark web pertaining to a potential data breach. This breach has the potential to expose the identities and operational aliases of seven of our operatives." He paused, letting the weight of this revelation permeate the room and the ensuing murmurs to subside. "As you can appreciate, if this intel proves accurate, the security of some of our best men and women will be jeopardised."

"Is it not feasible to extract them regardless?" Shepherd asked. "Provide them protection until we can ascertain the veracity of the situation?"

A muscle in Locke's eye quivered involuntarily. "I'm afraid it's not that simple, Foreign Secretary. Six out of the seven operatives on the list are currently embedded in foreign territories, undertaking deep-cover assignments. Extracting them prematurely would result in the forfeiture of significant strategic advancements and we risk exposing ourselves exponentially."

"But if we don't pull them out," Isaacs spoke up, "their lives could be in danger."

Locke swallowed, his Adam's apple rising and falling visibly. "I believe 'could' is the pivotal term in this context, Home Secretary. Our officers' safety is of paramount importance, but we can't risk confidential information regarding Sigma Unit – as well as countless covert operations – falling into the hands of the media. Xander Templeton, the CIA section chief stationed here in London, is presently in talks with his superiors over in the States regarding the matter. Currently we are at an impasse, anticipating what happens next."

"And what are our options?" Calder asked. "Is containment viable?"

"We remain optimistic," Locke replied. "As it stands, the leaked names have surfaced solely on a dark web forum, which our analysts have already taken down. Bowditch here has just spoken with Jacob Beaumont, our chief analyst at Nightingale House. As far as he's aware, there's no indication that the list of names has re-materialised online. However, we are continuing to monitor the situation and are considering our next move."

An uneasy tension spread through the room. The idea that British Secret Service officers, already putting their lives on the line for their country, could be exposed while operating behind enemy lines hung like a dark cloud over the already charged atmosphere.

"Can you inform us of the whereabouts of the operatives in question?" Shepherd asked.

Locke fixed him with a steely glare, his expression conveying the absurdity of the question. "That information is highly classified and on a need-to-know-basis."

Shepherd bristled at the rebuff. "And don't you think *I* need to know?"

"Apologies, Foreign Secretary," Locke replied, now seemingly more cautious with his words. "However, I maintain that discussing the specifics of the operatives in question at this stage would be detrimental to national security. Many of them have been engaged in deep-cover operations for months, some even years. Which is why I'm reluctant to extract them unless absolutely necessary. Doing so would compromise ongoing missions all over the world. However, there is one name on the list that does concern me."

"Oh?" Shepherd said. "Why is that?"

"He's an exceptional officer," Locke said. "Experienced, highly trained, intelligent – one of our best assets. Yet his current assignment places him in a volatile position. Unlike the other six operatives, he's stationed here in the UK. If the leak becomes public, I'm confident we can swiftly secure the others and arrange extraction. But with this individual, I have my doubts."

Isaacs leaned forward, elbows on the table. "Why?" she asked. "Surely being on home soil makes it easier?"

"Again, I can't disclose too much information at this stage, Home Secretary," Locke replied, his expression unyielding. "What I can say is that this operative has been embedded for over two years, having secured a high-ranking position within a London-based organised crime syndicate. Our main concern is that our lines of communication have gone dark. Jacob Beaumont, whom I mentioned earlier, was acting as his handler but hasn't received any contact in over six months. We suspect the officer in question is working towards a significant breakthrough and has refrained from making contact to minimise exposure. But this also means we have no idea of his current location. If the leak becomes public and the organised crime syndicate find out, we have no means of finding him. Nor can we ensure his safety."

Isaacs stretched her neck. She didn't like the sound of this. The man in question might not have officially existed on any payroll records, but a British Secret Service officer lost on home soil following a data breach was bad optics for the Home Office whichever way you spun it.

"Will they kill him?" she asked.

"He's one of our most skilled operatives," Bowditch added. "He might be able to get to safety. We just don't know."

"And how much does this officer know?" Frank Calder asked. "If he were to be compromised, how much of a threat could he pose to us?"

Locke glanced at Bowditch, his lips pressed together in contemplation. "He's served with us for over a decade, participating in some of our most crucial missions, both domestically and internationally. He knows a lot. A hell of a lot. More than enough to undermine a decade of MI6 and CIA operations if the organised crime syndicate he's aligned with recognises his value and decides to exploit him." He surveyed the room, the weight of his words settling over those present. "But he'd never reveal anything. He's a dedicated officer and tough as hell. He'd die first."

"Can you be certain?" Shepherd asked.

"As certain as we can be about anything," Locke replied. "As you can appreciate, we are exercising extreme caution in this matter, doing everything in our power to contain this breach and prevent that list of names from falling into the wrong hands."

Isaacs nodded, catching Shepherd's eye as she did. He looked as anxious as she felt. "Do we have a name for this operative?" she asked.

Even as she was saying the words, she anticipated a sharp rebuke similar to the one Shepherd had received. Bracing herself for the terse response, she was caught off guard when Locke exchanged a glance with Bowditch, who then offered a curt nod and cleared his throat.

"The officer's name is Beckett," he told the room. "John Beckett."

2

Over in Newham, East London, two men walked along a barren concrete gangway that divided up rows of large industrial warehouses near the dockside. It had stopped raining minutes earlier, but the air was still heavy with tension, their confident strides falling in time with one another's as they approached the last warehouse at the end of the row – the one with the dark blue shutters and biometric locking system on its main entrance. Neither of the men had spoken as they walked. They didn't need to. They'd done all their talking in the car on the way over. They knew how this was going to go down.

"Just follow my lead," Rufus Delaney now rasped in a low voice as they got closer to their destination. "Everything has been taken care of. We just need to take it steady and let it play out." When no reply came, he turned to his second in command, casting him a hard scowl as if insulted by his lack of a response.

"Sure, Rufus," he said quickly. "I'm on it. Don't worry."

Delaney stopped and held his hand out across his friend's chest to halt him. "Patrick, are you sure everything is all right?"

The man nodded. "Like I told you just now in the car, I'm fine. I've not been sleeping too well lately, that's all. But you've got nothing to worry about. We've discussed the plan. It's all good. As long as Emree doesn't mess things up."

"He won't."

"Are you certain we can trust him?"

Delaney tilted his head back to take in his taller counterpart. "Why so paranoid all of a sudden? You know who we are. You know what we do. We can trust Emree because he knows what'll happen to him if he fucks this up."

"As long as there are no surprises."

Delaney laughed. Reaching up, he grabbed him by the back of the neck. "You need to get a good night's sleep, my friend. This isn't like you."

"I'm fine."

"Yea" Delaney didn't look convinced. His dark eyes were narrowed as he studied him, trying to read any signs of doubt.

"Don't look at me that way, Rufus," he said, shaking his hand away. "It's me. Patrick. I've got your back, you've got mine. The same as always."

"Okay, good. Let's do this."

Delaney strode off in front, leaving Patrick standing there for a moment with the words echoing in his head.

It's me. Patrick.

And it was. Sort of.

But not always.

John Beckett, the man who'd been living as Patrick Hamilton for the last two years, drew in a long breath. Delaney was right, this was not like him and he needed to pull himself together. But he'd also been telling the truth just now. He hadn't been sleeping well lately. And he knew why. In previous assignments he'd been able to draw a metaphorical line in the sand, leaving a part of himself back in the locker rooms of his psyche to return to once the operation was over. But two years spent as the number two of London's largest and most ruthless criminal organisation had taken its toll. The line between his own identity and that of Patrick had become increasingly blurred, making it harder to keep his moral compass intact. It was unsettling, yet he wasn't going to stop. Not when he was so close to gaining access to The Consortium. Except on days like today, he felt as if the darkness of his current life was eroding his soul.

But that implied he had a soul to begin with.

"Patrick. Get a move on," Delaney called back as he reached the door to the warehouse.

"Sure, let's get this over with," Beckett muttered to himself, shaking off his thoughts and joining Delaney.

They entered through the main door, which had been left unlocked as arranged, and walked through the dimly lit space. At the far end, they were presented with a wall of corrugated iron and a door cut into its centre. Beckett banged his fist against it, and it was opened to reveal a large, thick-set man with a long black beard and hair twisted up into a top knot. He held an assault rifle slung over his shoulder, which Beckett identified as a KORD 6P67. Russian made. Russian supplied most likely, too.

On recognising the two men, the gatekeeper stepped back from the door and beckoned them through. Beckett let Delaney go first, following him into the main space of the warehouse. This room was cold and dark and smelled of diesel and wet concrete. A fitting environment for the kind of business they were about to conduct.

Murat Caliskan was already there waiting for them. He held out his arms as they entered. "You're late," he said, his tone betraying his annoyance.

"We ran into some unexpected traffic," Delaney lied. They'd actually been waiting to get all their pieces on the board before entering the building. "But now we're here. As are you, my friend."

Caliskan grinned. He was a tall, imposing figure with a closely cropped beard and a tattoo of a serpent coiling around his neck. His black hair was slicked back and his eyes were a piercing shade of ice blue that – due to his Turkish heritage – had to be the result of contact lenses. But they only added to his unsettling appearance.

"So…? Get on with it," he snapped. "It was you who was so desperate to see me today. As I understood it, all was going well and we weren't set to meet until the end of the month. Has something happened?"

Beckett studied Caliskan's face. His unease was apparent even beneath the bravado. He raised his head and puffed his chest out regardless, one eye on his man by the door with the Russian assault rifle.

But he was correct. There was no reason for the heads of the Turkish mafia and the Delaney Crime Syndicate to be meeting today. Except yesterday The Consortium had reached out to Delaney and expressed their concern regarding Caliskan's loyalties.

"You know, Murat, I do feel your pain," Delaney began, his voice low and dangerous. "We used to run this city between us, you and I. We were the kings of our respective boroughs. But you know how it goes. Time moves on. Things change. I know the Hunger Family found it hard falling in line when The Consortium took control of London, but I thought you were a savvy old fucker like me. Someone who knew the importance of self-preservation as well as progression. I also thought you understood the potential for opportunity and growth that The Consortium's presence will provide for us all. As well, the consequences for anyone – once again, the Hunger Family, rest in peace – who goes against their wishes."

Caliskan's eyes narrowed, a flicker of doubt clouding his gaze as he shot his man on the door another glance. "Yes. Of course I do. I am on board with the new arrangement. I told them that."

"Really?" Delaney's eyes hardened with cold fury, his voice dripping with scepticism. "Because a little bird told me you've been doing a little extracurricular work over in Riyadh. Is that correct?" He stared intently at the Turk. "What was it, Murat? You thought you could get away with selling a few mills' worth of guns to the Saudis and we wouldn't find out? Tut tut. I had you down as a cleverer boy than that."

"So what if I did?" Caliskan spat back, fear flicking across his face. "What's it to you?"

"It's nothing to me, son," Delaney replied, his tone laced with a mocking bite. "But like you, I work for them now – mostly. And they've tasked me with relieving you of your duties." He lowered his head, his voice a gruff whisper. "Sorry about that."

"Fuck you!" Caliskan snarled. "You don't police me, you egotistical prick. Ozan, show our friends out…"

Three sets of eyes shot over to where the man with the assault rifle had been standing moments earlier. Only he was no longer there.

"Oops," Delaney said with a smirk. "It looks as if your men have deserted you. Clearly, they know what side their bread's buttered on."

"No way," Caliskan snarled. "You can't do this to me. If you kill me, there will be an uprising. The Turkish mafia will take matters into their own hands. You're making a big mistake. You and The Consortium. My people won't stand for this. They'll set London on fire. I tell you. My people will—"

"*Your people* have a new boss," Delaney cut in. "Patrick. Go get him, will you? He should be outside."

Beckett marched over to the door and opened it to reveal

Emree Caliskan. The Turkish mafia's new leader, as decreed by The Consortium. Murat Caliskan's younger brother.

Beckett walked with him back to where Delaney and Murat were standing, watching the elder Caliskan as his face dropped and the first realisation of his fate showed in his eyes.

"You fucking bastard," he cried out, lunging at his brother. "I'm going to kill you, you fucking piece of shit."

"No one's killing anyone," Delaney yelled, getting in between the two men. He shoved Murat back and produced a gun from out of his coat, pointing it at him. "Calm it down. Now!"

As Emree and Beckett got closer, Murat stared at his brother, those fake blue eyes ablaze with fury and betrayal. "I can't believe you're fucking me over like this."

"It's just business, brother. Nothing personal," Emree said. "The decision had already been made. I wish it was different, but this way at least we keep it in our family."

Delaney turned to Beckett and pulled a face. "Jesus. Fucking awkward this, innit?" There was mischief in his eyes. He was clearly relishing the situation. Returning his attention to Murat, his face and manner switched back to an icy coldness. "You should go, Emree. The Consortium send their thanks for stepping into the breach at such short notice. They'll be in touch."

Emree hesitated, his eyes filled with emotion as he stared at his brother one last time. Perhaps he was imagining himself in the elder Caliskan's position, Beckett thought. Or making sure he remembered this moment if he was ever tempted to stray from The Consortium's wishes. "Goodbye, brother," he whispered. "I'm sorry. But this is the life we chose."

He bowed his head and hurried away before his brother could respond. He got as far as the door when Murat called after him.

"Fucking traitor."

The younger brother paused for a second. Then he opened the door and disappeared.

"Please. Let's talk about this," Murat said, holding his hands out. He was almost a foot taller than Delaney, but the smaller man carried an air of menace that was unrivalled even within London's seedy underbelly. "I can help you. We can work together. I know you don't agree with everything The Consortium is doing. Let us work together and we can reclaim our city. Take it back from them. Please." He looked to Beckett, his eyes pleading for mercy. But Beckett could offer none. They were both trapped in the same hole and there was only one way out for Murat.

"Oh stop it, will you?" Delaney sighed. "This is pathetic what you're doing. The decision is beyond either one of us. That's the way it is now. So take it like a man, will ya?"

"Don't kill me, Rufus. I've got a wife. I've got kids…"

"I'm not going to kill you," Delaney replied.

Murat's face dropped, along with his hands. The start of a confused smile twitched at the corner of his mouth. "Really?"

"Really. I'm not going to kill you," Delaney continued, turning to Beckett. "Patrick here is going to do the honours. Right, mate?"

He handed Beckett the gun and Beckett took it without giving it a second thought. He'd suspected this was coming. It wasn't that Delaney didn't trust him – they were close friends now, as well as everything else – but if he was concerned Patrick Hamilton was faltering in his commitment, he'd want to see him prove otherwise. This was his chance to.

Beckett held the gun at waist height, the weight of the weapon familiar in his hand. It was a Glock 19 – the Gen 5 model, without the finger grooves on the handle. Beckett knew them to be good pistols, versatile and sleek. They were also a relatively new addition to the Delaney Crime Syndicate's arsenal. He knew that because he'd brokered a deal for two crates of these guns from Murat Caliskan himself not four months earlier.

The irony. Poor bastard.

He had to have realised it was one of his guns as Beckett raised it to his face, but if he did, he didn't mention it. Probably he had a lot of other things going through his mind, Beckett thought. His wife. His kids. The fact his younger brother just screwed him over and signed his death warrant. But Murat couldn't blame Emree too much. As Delaney said, the decision had already been made. The Consortium wanted a change. And what they wanted, they got.

"Come on, Pat," Delaney said. "Get on with it."

Beckett adjusted his grip on the pistol's handle. He looked into Caliskan's eyes, seeing the desperation and resignation there. He thought of all the lives that had been ruined by this man's greed, the families torn apart by addiction and crime. He thought of his mission and the greater good he was serving even as he walked this dark, twisted path. Then, in a swift, practised motion, he aimed between the Turk's eyes and pulled the trigger. The gunshot echoed through the warehouse. Murat Caliskan's head jerked back and for a moment he was frozen in a distorted tableau. Then his body crumpled to the floor.

Beckett stared at the lifeless form, feeling the hollowness inside him grow larger. He handed the gun back to Delaney.

"Good job," Delaney said, slapping him on the shoulder. "Nice and clean. We'll get Lawrence and his crew to sort this mess out and I'll let The Consortium know it's been dealt with."

Beckett nodded, keeping his expression carefully neutral. "Sure. Job done. Now let's get out of here."

3

From a casual observer's perspective, Nightingale House was but a seven-storey, eighteenth-century building nestled on the fringes of Soho, indistinguishable from countless other deteriorating office blocks strewn across the district. The signage over the entrance bore the effects of time – a faded and fraying 'N', a missing 'O' in 'House' – and the once pristine white of the glass facade was now tarnished grey, a testament to relentless exposure to dirt and diesel exhaust. If that same casual observer had been able to access the building through the main entrance – which wouldn't have been possible without a secure keycard and clearance from the highest level – they'd have entered a rather lacklustre reception area, heavy with the musty scent of neglect and featuring a pair of lifts, one of which had been out of service for more than a decade. The place seemed nothing more than a crumbling shell of a once functional edifice.

But that was the whole point.

For those who managed to infiltrate the building, using the same keycard to activate the single operational elevator, they'd discover a different reality on the third and fourth floors. Here, in stark contrast to its humble exterior, thrived the highly specialised Sigma Unit's analytical and intelligence division – a secret nerve centre, which hummed with persistent, focused activity.

Today, however, the atmosphere was even more charged than usual, teetering on the brink of chaos. Sleep-deprived operatives with frayed nerves downed copious amounts of coffee, tapping away at computer keyboards and laptops with relentless determination. Every available employee, regardless of their role, had been mobilised. All leave was suspended indefinitely.

On the desk of Jacob Beaumont's office, a phone rang. But Beaumont was nowhere near his desk. Instead, he was roaming the floor of the main space in what might have been his tenth or perhaps twelfth circuit, engaging with each analyst and meticulously examining the data displayed on their screens. His new shoes chewed at the flesh on his heels as he paraded up and down, but he hardly felt it. His mind was elsewhere. On the job at hand.

"What do you have there?" Beaumont enquired, leaning over a junior analyst's chair and scrutinising the display. "What am I looking at?"

"It's a Chinese forum, sir," the analyst replied. "Accessed through the dark web. It's a hub for disseminating disinformation and debating government policies. As you can imagine, the Chinese are not happy about it and keep taking it down, but it keeps springing back up in different guises. Whoever is behind it uses an advanced series of VPNs and cloaking software."

"And you think the list might be on here?"

"Not yet, sir. But it's the sort of place where it might appear. I'm monitoring it and will continue to."

Beaumont patted the analyst on the shoulder. "Good work. Let me know the second anything appears."

"Yes, sir."

Beaumont stood back, indulging in a brief stretch before glancing at his wristwatch. He'd been at Nightingale House since 1 a.m. and it was now closing in on noon. He'd already done a full day's work, but his duties as head analyst at Sigma Unit precluded the luxury of clocking out at a specific hour. Not in the face of an unparalleled data breach. Not when one of his best operatives – who was also his friend – was in such a volatile situation.

Beaumont and Beckett shared a history that stretched back to their service days in the United Kingdom Special Forces. Their paths had first crossed in Northwood, where they were stationed at the Permanent Joint Headquarters in preparation for a high-stakes, covert operation. The objective: to extract a group of British scientists who had been taken hostage in Libya. The situation was precarious, with the lives of the hostages hanging in the balance, and it required the utmost skill and precision.

Back then, Beaumont had been working for the Counter-Terrorism Warfare unit, a specialised team trained in both offensive and defensive strategies to neutralise threats against national security. Beckett, on the other hand, was a newly commissioned lieutenant in the SAS 22nd Regiment, having also tentatively signed to a recruitment branch of the secret service.

The year was 2008. Their mandate was to navigate through hostile territory, locate the hostages and extract them under the cover of darkness. Codenamed 'Operation Silent Storm', the mission was a testament to their combined expertise in covert reconnaissance, urban warfare and high-stakes negotiation. Beckett wasn't the easiest person in the world to get along with – he was aloof, brittle at times; and when he did speak, his attitude teetered on a knife edge between humour and hostility. But somehow he and

Beaumont, ten years his senior, got on. Beckett had a good heart beneath his steely demeanour and he was certainly a courageous bastard. Beckett had also saved Beaumont's life in Libya, risking his neck to drag the older man to safety during an ambush by a rebel militia. He'd taken a bullet in the shoulder for his troubles, but that act of selflessness had forged a bond between the two men that would not easily be broken.

Fast forward a year, and Beaumont and Beckett both found their careers taking an unexpected turn. They were singled out by the director of Special Forces and the chief of the Secret Intelligence Service and plucked from their respective units. Their exceptional performances during the Libyan operation had not gone unnoticed and they had proven themselves indispensable, catching the eye of their superiors who had a unique assignment in mind. Standing before their commanding officers, they were informed that they would no longer officially exist within the ranks of Her Majesty's Armed Forces. Instead, they were to be inducted into a new, highly secretive and elite outfit known as Sigma Unit, born from a fusion of CTW and UKSF forces. This covert team, they were told, would be responsible for executing the most delicate and perilous missions in defence of the nation. Operating in the shadows, Sigma Unit would be the last line of protection against threats that could not be addressed through conventional means.

More than a decade later, they were both still here, still serving their country from the shadows. For now, at least. Whether they would both make it to the end of the week alive hinged heavily on what Beaumont did next.

He looked up as Robert Locke appeared in the doorway at the opposite end of the room. The weariness in his posture was unmistakable – hands on his hips, shoulders sagging, and the burden of responsibility etched across his face. Beaumont could empathise. Some days the weight of their jobs felt unbearable.

Locke peered into the room, no doubt searching for him. Beaumont stepped around the side of the desk and raised his hand.

"Bloody hell, there you are," Locke muttered, as he strode forward. "Has anything shown up?"

"Not yet," Beaumont replied. "We're monitoring every forum and site that could potentially host the list, but so far we're in the clear. Have you just got back from MI6?"

Locke nodded, his eyes flitting around the room. "Yes. It's a fucking shitshow over there. No one's willing to assume responsibility for any decisions at this stage. It's like we're spinning a dozen plates and just crossing our fingers none of them come crashing to the ground."

"What about Beckett?" Beaumont asked. "He's a sitting duck out there. We need to try for an extraction before there are any further leaks."

Locke met his gaze. "It's not as simple as that. You know it isn't."

"I know he's one of our best officers and his life is in danger. If Delaney even suspects he's a mole, he'll kill him. We can't risk that."

"The leak is contained for now. We can't blow over two years of operations on a mere possibility. Beckett wouldn't want that."

Beaumont exhaled heavily. Locke was right, of course, but that didn't make it any easier to accept. "What was decided? Do we have an extraction strategy?"

Locke shook his head. "Our operatives overseas are all within reach. Only one is stationed behind enemy lines, and we're confident we can get word to them before the situation escalates if the leak goes public. Once they've reached their respective British embassies, we can reassess."

"But Beckett's situation is different—"

"Indeed," Locke interjected. "But Beckett's circumstances are also complicated by the fact he's been incommunicado for over six months. Look, Beaumont, I know you and he go way back, but it's about time we faced the elephant in the room. I didn't mention any of this at the meeting, but we must confront the very real possibility we've lost him. That Delaney has turned him."

Beaumont frowned. "No. Not John. He wouldn't."

"He could," Locke countered. "It happens. We know it happens. Operatives get embedded and they begin to sympathise with their targets." He waved a finger in Beaumont's face. "Rufus Delaney is a charismatic man with a great deal to offer someone like Beckett, a man with few ties and not much else to live for."

"Not him," Beaumont insisted. "I won't have it. Beckett is a good man. Yes, he's a little rough around the edges, but he's devoted to serving his country. That's all he is. All he's ever been. The last time we spoke, he alluded to being close to identifying key members of The Consortium, at least within London. The fact he's not been in contact for a while only points to the fact he's still on the case. He won't want to risk exposure at this critical juncture."

"That's what I told them this morning," Locke said, rubbing at his chin. "I just hope you're right."

"I am. I know it."

Locke's expression turned serious again, his eyes narrowing with determination. "That doesn't change the overall picture, though. You've got to understand the optics, Beaumont. If word gets out about the leak and our involvement in international affairs, it could create a political firestorm not just for Director Calder but for MI5 and the Foreign Office as well. They want to contain this situation while keeping S-Unit at arm's length from any discussions or enquiries regarding it."

"So we just wait?" Beaumont asked.

"Our role is to stand by and maintain operational readiness. If we get lucky and the winds blow in our favour, we'll ride out this storm and our missions remain covert. No one needs to know."

"And if Lady Luck turns her back on us?"

Locke shot him a piercing look. "Beckett's a seasoned operator, a master of his craft. He can handle himself in the field. We maintain our position and we follow the chain of command. That's the directive for now. Is that clear?"

Beaumont lifted his head, his jaw rigid with effort. "Yes, sir," he said. "Understood."

4

The biting London air coming in off the Thames swept across Pimlico, hitting Beckett like a slap to the face as he stepped out of Rufus Delaney's sleek black Jaguar.

"Are you certain you don't want to go to the club?" Delaney asked.

Beckett turned back, dipping his head into the car to glance at the digital clock on the dashboard. "It's barely past 1 p.m."

"I'm aware of that, but we've had a heavy morning, wouldn't you say? We've done some good work. I'd say a celebratory drink is in order. I'd say you need one, by the looks of you. What's going on?"

Beckett forced a smile. "Don't worry about me. Everything's fine. I just need a shower and maybe some sleep."

"If you're sure I can't tempt you."

Beckett stood and gripped the door handle. "I'm good. I'll call you later, okay?"

"Well, see to it that you do. We've got things to discuss."

Beckett eased the door shut, applying a firmer push to seal it as he closed it the final inch. Stepping back, he raised his hand as Delaney revved the engine and peeled away from the kerb. As the car disappeared around the corner at the end of the street, he turned and walked up the stairs leading to the front door of his building.

He'd been living in Pimlico for the last eighteen months, a top-floor flat in one of the large white Regency buildings that surrounded Eccleston Square. Number 72. Interestingly, from 1908 to 1913, Churchill had lived across the way at number 33; there was a blue plaque on the side of the building to prove it. Beckett had rented the place as Patrick Hamilton, choosing a high-end property in an affluent area, to fit in perfectly with the persona he'd created for his alter ego. It was a decent enough place and served its purpose.

He let himself in and hurried up the three flights of stairs to his flat. The building was also a stone's throw away from the MI6 building across the river, but the proximity to the centre of British intelligence hadn't been intentional. At least, he didn't think so. The subconscious mind was a strange beast.

Inside, he headed straight for the kitchen and opened the fridge. He hadn't eaten breakfast that morning and he was ravenous with hunger. Maybe that was it, he thought, as he pulled the remaining two chicken thighs from the fridge and placed them on the scarred surface of his butcher's block cutting board. He wasn't faltering or feeling unsettled – he was just hungry.

Yeah. Had to be it.

Beckett had made peace with who he was, and what he did, a long time ago. He'd killed people on five different continents, some for Queen and country, some for thugs like Delaney. If he'd thought about it too much it might have turned him inside out, so he didn't think about it. He hated that Delaney killed people and that he'd killed people for him. But that was his job. And most of the people he'd killed had deserved it. There'd been no women and no children. He'd made sure of that. He was a gentleman, after all.

He oiled up the chicken and rubbed each thigh with a selection of herbs before placing them on a baking sheet and shoving them into the oven on a medium heat.

Leaving the chicken to roast, he ventured into his front room. It was a space that spoke of a man caught between two worlds: one of solitude and the other of refined tastes. A dark green Chesterfield sofa took centre stage, its elegant lines and plush cushions a stark contrast to the sparsely furnished room. An old fireplace with an antique brass screen dominated one wall, but he'd never used it. A bookshelf, crammed to capacity with leather-bound classics, leaned precariously against the far wall. The Persian rug beneath his feet had seen better days. It had belonged to his family and was the only single piece of evidence in the flat that tied him to his old life. His *real* life. Its once-vibrant colours were now muted by age, the edges frayed and unravelling. There was maybe a metaphor in there somewhere, Beckett thought.

He slipped off his jacket and walked over to the record player, putting on a Chopin concerto before heading into the bedroom. As he got undressed, the soothing melodies of the great man's *Polonaise-Fantaisie* filled the space, drowning out the city below and the sound of the gunshot still ringing in his ears. Beckett enjoyed listening to Chopin and a little Bach and not much else. He didn't do modern music. In fact, he didn't do modern anything. He had no subscriptions to Netflix or Amazon Prime and certainly didn't watch any of the terrestrial channels. If he watched anything at all, it was old Marx Brothers and Fred Astaire movies on an ancient DVD player. Classics. But that wasn't to say Beckett was a Luddite. Far from it. He understood and appreciated the importance of technology. But culture was important to him, like it had been to his dad. He didn't see much culture around these days.

Once naked, he headed for the bathroom and into the shower, the hot water cascading down his muscular frame. As he washed himself, his hands ran a familiar path over the many scars and markings he'd collected throughout the years. The body of a man who had seen more than his fair share of violence. Each bump and welt told a story; each a piece of the broken puzzle that was John Beckett.

His fingers traced the jagged line scored across his chest, a lasting keepsake from a deadly knife fight in a Moroccan back alley.

The bullet wound in his shoulder, its edges slightly puckered, served as a stark reminder of one of his early missions over in Libya.

Delaney had caught a glimpse of the gunshot scar during a game of squash, but Beckett had managed to brush it off as an occupational hazard. As far as Rufus and the rest of the Delaney Crime Syndicate knew, Patrick Hamilton was an ex-Special Forces soldier who'd become disillusioned with his country after uncountable horrors faced during three tours of Afghanistan. His carefully crafted backstory – complete with corroborating records and all relevant documents – painted the picture of an educated, fearless man who'd reached breaking point and decided to carve out a better life for himself on his own terms.

The fact that most of Patrick Hamilton's past overlapped with Beckett's own had been a carefully thought-out decision and one of the reasons why he'd been tasked with the operation in the first place. Any old police officer could have gone undercover as a grunt member of the crime organisation, but the operation required someone capable of securing a top-tier position. A leader. They needed someone with intelligence, a refined background, and the ability to navigate high society. The decision-makers knew Beckett's sophistication along with his impressive stature and calm self-assurance would appeal to

Delaney, a former East End thug intent on elevating his standing.

And the strategy had paid off. After a carefully orchestrated 'chance encounter' at a boxing match two and a half years earlier, the two men had hit it off. Over the next six months, Beckett had gradually ingratiated himself not only in Delaney's business operations but also in his personal life. The two men were now friends. Beckett had met Rufus's wife and children. They'd even been on holiday together – a week in Sicily last July for the Feast of Santa Rosalia – and despite himself, despite everything, Beckett had enjoyed himself. It was a strange headspace to be in. Every day he felt himself torn between the two worlds he inhabited. It was a delicate balance of deception and danger.

He had a job to do. But to do that job well, he'd had to make himself believe he and Rufus Delaney were friends – and that he liked and respected the guy. And now, he almost did. He felt drawn to Rufus. He was charming and funny when he wanted to be.

Jesus.

Beckett shoved his head under the water to try to wash the thoughts from his head. He'd given up a lot for this job, but on days like this he prayed he hadn't lost himself in the process.

Yet he couldn't back out. He was finally on the brink of achieving his goal. Regardless of his close ties with Rufus, he was resolutely committed to his mission. As long as organisations like the Delaney Crime Syndicate and The Consortium remained active, he'd do everything possible to bring them down. Even if he had anything else to live for, he couldn't stop now.

He turned off the water and towelled himself dry, catching his reflection in the large mirror above the sink. The man gazing back at him was almost a stranger. He still had the same dark blond hair, and his eyes were still a striking blue, but recently he'd noticed a haunted quality behind them. The lines etched into his once youthful face were markers of the last two years spent infiltrating Rufus Delaney's network.

He walked into the bedroom and dressed in a black t-shirt and dark blue jeans. Delaney preferred his men – especially those operating in the upper echelons of the syndicate – to maintain a polished appearance, but when Beckett had downtime, this was his uniform. He spritzed a little cologne into his hands and rubbed it on his neck, working the residual fragrance through his hair before returning to the kitchen to check on the chicken.

The air was now heavy with an enticing aroma. The thighs were nearing completion, so he assembled a medley of vegetables for a stir-fry accompaniment – onions, peppers, mushrooms, and a few pieces of okra he found in the bottom of the fridge. He flipped the butcher's block over and prepared the vegetables, the rhythmic chopping coupled with the sizzle from the pan going some way to calming his frayed nerves. He found solace in cooking. It was a form of meditation for him, a way to focus his mind and momentarily distance himself from the tangled web of duplicity that consumed his life.

As he sautéed the vegetables in the oil and added a shake of dried chilli flakes, his mind drifted to Jacob Beaumont and S-Unit. He knew he ought to touch base with them soon. Maintaining contact during a deep-cover operation was essential – for guidance and reassurance as much as for the sharing of intel – but, as the months had gone by, he'd felt it was more important to immerse himself in the role of Patrick Hamilton.

Yet with Delaney's recent disclosure, he could sense the end approaching. Soon, Patrick Hamilton would accompany him to a meeting with the London arm of The Consortium. This was the moment he had been waiting for – the opportunity to identify key players and relay his findings. Accomplishing this could signal the conclusion of his assignment. In a few months he could be in Syria or central Africa, with a different name, on a different mission.

Could that be why he was feeling so out of sorts?

No, he told himself. Just hungry.

Because he was here to do a job and he would carry it out with the utmost proficiency. As he always did. Beckett had devoted his life to bringing down bad people, those who threatened the safety of his country and his fellow countrymen. People like Delaney, organisations like The Consortium. Once he had concrete intelligence to impart, he'd connect with Beaumont and they'd move from there. Everything was going to be fine.

He served the chicken thighs and the vegetables onto a plate and carried it through into the living area as the Chopin concerto swelled to its climax. The impassioned notes filled the room, serving as a soothing balm for his battered soul.

He sat and ate in silence.

John Beckett was a man trapped between two worlds, and with each passing day the lines between friend and foe blurred a little more. Some days he could feel the darkness threatening to swallow him. Days like today were tough. But he'd get through it. He had to. It was his job.

5

As Delaney pulled the Jag up to his four-storey riverfront townhouse, Eddie was standing on the pavement, waiting. After dropping Patrick off, he'd called ahead and instructed him to wait outside so he could take care of the car for him. Good old Eddie. Steady Eddie, they called him. He was from Brixton originally and built like a brick shithouse, but he had such polite manners and delicate ways that Delaney kept him around the house as part of his security team rather than send him out on goon work. That wasn't to say Eddie couldn't handle himself, of course. A bulbous scar running down his cheek hinted at his troubled past, as did his hands and fingers, which were thick and calloused. The hands of a street fighter.

"Afternoon, sir," Eddie said, opening the car door. "Did everything go to plan?"

"That it did, Eddie. That it did." Delaney kept the engine idling and climbed out of the car. "Park it in the usual place, will you?"

Eddie nodded and climbed into the driver's seat after him, making a show of checking his mirrors before pulling away from the kerb and heading for the secure underground garage around the corner. Delaney smiled to himself as he watched his car drive away. It had indeed been a good day. As the steward for The Consortium in London, he was already in prime position, but with Emree now in place as the head of the Turks, the power balance had shifted even more in his favour. The younger man would be easier to manipulate and control than his more headstrong brother. The Consortium knew what they were doing.

He made his way up the steps to his house, positioning himself beneath the security camera above the doorway and waving. "It's me. Open up."

The heavy oak door swung open, revealing a man almost as big as Eddie. He was wearing a tailored suit. "Afternoon, sir," he said, stepping to one side to allow Delaney to enter.

"Reginald," he intoned as a greeting. "Everything all right here?"

"Yes, sir. Quiet so far."

"That's what I like to hear." He carried on down the hallway, the scent of polished mahogany arousing his senses. A crystal chandelier hung like a crown above the black and white marble floor, a new acquisition he'd had shipped over from Italy. He didn't know how much it had cost because these days he didn't need to ask. He could afford it. He was independently solvent. Making real 'fuck you' money.

He headed up the stairs to the first-floor landing, where another guard stood stoically beside an antique grandfather clock. Delaney nodded as he passed by, heading for the master bedroom. The faint sound of soft music filtered through the closed doors, and as he swung them open, scents of lavender and eucalyptus filled his nostrils. Miranda was lying on a massage table in front of the large bay window whilst Agnieszka worked on the tense muscles in her shoulders. The Polish woman looked up and offered him a meek smile as he entered. He might as well have a massage too while she was here. Agnieszka wasn't cheap but she was a damn good masseuse and he liked the fact she hardly spoke a word of English. Not only could he enjoy his massage without the need for small talk, but there was no risk of loose lips sinking ships.

Miranda lifted her head and sighed as he approached.

"Oh, and hello to you, too, my angel," he said. "You having a nice time, are ya?"

She looked him up and down. "Do you know you've got blood on your shirt?"

"Have I?" He walked into the en-suite bathroom and checked himself. She was right. There were two spots of blood on the upper chest of his white Hugo Boss shirt. "Deary me. I must have cut myself shaving."

"Yes. You'll have to be more careful, Rufe. People will talk."

Miranda knew exactly what sort of man she was married to and what he did. But they enjoyed a certain amount of pretence in their life. It kept things interesting.

Leaving his wife to her massage, he wandered across the landing to the kids' rooms. He had two children: Rufus Junior, six, and Sofia, three. Although they were at school and nursery right now, he took a moment to survey each of their rooms, casting his gaze over the colourful toys and mobiles hanging from the ceiling. Neither of his children wanted for anything, and pride swelled in his chest as he considered how far he'd come and the empire he'd built.

Leaving their rooms, he descended the grand staircase and walked through into his brand-new, state-of-the-art kitchen, where Trey, another of his guards, stood watch in front of the French windows that looked out onto the back garden. Delaney absentmindedly emptied his pockets of his burner phones and wallet and approached the counter that ran down the length of one wall.

"I think I'll make myself a coffee," he told Trey. "Would you like a cup?"

Trey shifted uncomfortably. New recruits often did in response to his familiarity, but Delaney prided himself on maintaining a laid-back household. Albeit one where every one of his men was armed and ready to take a bullet for him or his family.

"No, thank you, sir," Trey replied in a deep gravelly voice, his eyes never straying from the back garden. "I shouldn't."

"Oh, you really should. It's fucking divine." He moved over to the colossal stainless steel 'Barista Express' machine and prepared himself an espresso, the rich aroma of bitter coffee beans filling the room as the machine hissed and steamed.

But before he could savour even his first sip, one of his phones rang. He carried two with him at all times: one for personal use, one strictly for business. The ringing phone was his personal line, but the caller ID showed it to be Max Largan, one of his lawyers. He answered after cautiously taking a sip of the hot black liquid.

"Maxwell, my old mucker. How are things? You well?"

"Good afternoon, Mr Delaney. I'm very well, thank you."

"You got news for me?"

"Indeed. As of this morning, the payment has cleared," Largan told him. "And with no hiccups on our end."

Delaney leaned against the kitchen counter, his mind racing. This was monumental. He'd been working on this deal for months and it was finally happening. He took another sip of coffee, feeling the caffeine jolt his system.

"Excellent," he replied. "And everything else is in place?"

"Yes. The funds have been transferred to the offshore account and all the necessary documents have been filed."

Delaney nodded, feeling a sense of relief wash over him. The deal was a real estate acquisition – the property in question, a massive complex near the docklands that spanned several blocks and which he planned on developing into luxury accommodation. He and Largan had spent months putting the pieces together. The stakes were high, but the potential payoff was irresistible.

"And the other parties involved?" Delaney asked, taking another sip of coffee.

"They're on board," Largan replied. "As long as we stick to the plan, everything should go smoothly."

Delaney felt a twinge of unease at the word 'plan'. Even with all his resources, this was his first foray into property development and it presented a formidable challenge. Not to mention that the current owners of the land were well-connected, with links to the Turkish mafia. It was one reason why he was so pleased to off Murat Caliskan this morning. But now The Consortium had learned of his plans and wanted a piece of the action. He would have to tread carefully.

"Good work, Max," Delaney told him. "I'll speak to you soon." He hung up and looked over at Trey, who remained vigilant by the back door.

"Everything all right?" Delaney asked him.

Trey nodded. "All good, sir."

Delaney finished his coffee, the anticipation building inside him. He knew this deal would change everything, but he was ready for whatever came next. He was about to head back upstairs to see if Agnieszka was free when his second phone rang. Trey turned as it did, their eyes meeting.

"Who the bloody hell is this?" Delaney muttered, picking it up from the kitchen island.

The caller ID showed the name *Liren Wu*. Liren was the head of the Wu Family, a rival crime syndicate based in Chinatown. Delaney and Liren went back a long way, but had never been friends. This wasn't a social call.

"Delaney here," he answered. "What do you want, Liren?"

The voice on the other end was both menacing and

mocking. "Rufus, I hope I'm not disturbing you." Liren laughed, a high-pitched chuckle that grated on Delaney's nerves.

"You're not disturbing me," he replied.

"No? But if you're answering your phone so readily, you mustn't have heard?"

"Heard what?"

Liren chuckled again. "You have a rat in your midst, Rufus. A mole, even. Either way, it's vermin."

His blood ran cold as Liren's words sank in. He shot a glance at Trey. "What do you mean?" His mind raced through the possibilities, the potential betrayals. "I know my men. They are loyal."

"Don't believe me?" Liren said. "Check 4chan. You'll find a list of current SIS officers working undercover all around the world – along with their aliases and other details. Your man is top of the list."

Delaney clenched his jaw, clutching the phone tight to his ear. "Who, Liren? What are you talking about?"

"Patrick Hamilton," Liren said, his voice dripping with malicious glee. "Your top man works for the British government, Rufus. He's a fucking rat."

6

Jacob Beaumont sat in his office at Nightingale House, caught in a silent stare-down with a greasy stain on the opposite wall. His forehead was furrowed with worry, his thick eyebrows almost meeting over the bridge of his nose. He understood Locke's reluctance to extract Beckett at this stage, but he was burdened by the idea his old friend was being thrown to the wolves.

He leaned back, his ancient office chair groaning as he did. Most of his work involved a waiting game of some sort, but today he felt entirely helpless and frustrated with it. Rising to his feet, he began to pace, an effort that was all but fruitless in the cramped room. His office was a reflection of his years of service. Piles of classified documents, battered filing cabinets and obsolete tech equipment took up the space, in glaring contrast to the cutting-edge dual monitors and computer equipment that filled the analyst station outside. The room's only light source, a dim overhead bulb, flickered intermittently, casting long shadows across the wooden floor and his time-worn desk. The old, yellowing blinds were forever closed, making the office seem even more confined.

Pacing brought Beaumont no solace, so he returned to his chair, sneering at the messy tangle of cables snaking from his computer to the outlets. His gaze settled on a framed photograph of Roni, taken on one of their holidays to Greece several years ago. In the photo she looked as if she didn't have a care in the world. Maybe in that moment she didn't. Maybe he hadn't either. But it was a long time since he'd felt that way.

His attention shifted back to the glowing screen of his laptop, feeling the pressure of time running out. Since he'd heard of the possible leak, he'd felt every second tick by. Rufus Delaney was a dangerous man, someone who wouldn't hesitate to execute Beckett if he discovered the truth about him.

Beaumont ran a hand through his silver hair. He could feel the exhaustion nibbling at him in every fibre of his soul, but he dismissed any notion of slowing down. When you were someone like him – who'd seen too much, who'd visited the darkest corners of the world – you carried the weight of those experiences with you like a second skin. The current situation was typical and uncharacteristic all at once. His mind spun as he considered every possible outcome. None of them were good. He sensed danger in the air. He hoped he was being paranoid, but he didn't think so.

He checked his phone before returning to his laptop. The monitor showed the secure messaging software commonly used by Sigma Unit for contacting deep-cover operatives. To an observer, it looked like a basic program, the coding of an archaic SMS service, but its advanced security mechanisms made messages untraceable. This was ideal for what was usually required of this system, but not so helpful when your deep-cover operative hadn't checked in for months. Beaumont knew where Delaney lived and he knew Beckett had secured himself accommodation somewhere nearby, but that was all.

He stared at the cursor blinking at the beginning of the new message box. He stared at the message thread, now blank.

For security reasons, the system automatically erased all messages after twenty-four hours. But Beaumont wondered if there was a way of recovering past data. If so, they might have a chance. For now, he typed out a message to Beckett, sensing as he did that he was likely shouting into the abyss. But he had to try. He had to try everything.

The message was brief and to the point.

Make contact. Today. Very important.

His fingers hovered over the keyboard, contemplating whether to write more. But as he was deliberating this, there was a knock at his door.

"Come in," he called out.

The door opened and Ruth Armitage entered his office. "Sorry to disturb you, sir."

Armitage had been recruited from the NCA a few months earlier after showing remarkable potential. She was one of the youngest people working at Nightingale House; likely in her mid-twenties – although Beaumont had never been adept at estimating ages - and was fast making a name for herself as a resolute and hardworking analyst.

"What is it?" he asked her, as she loitered in the doorway, her hand still clasping the door handle.

She was of slight build, with a somewhat androgynous figure. Her strawberry-blonde hair fell straight, and her complexion appeared surprisingly vibrant given her profession. The rosiness of her cheeks and the sparkle in her eyes so at odds with the pallid laptop-tan and glazed stare of most analysts.

She shifted uneasily as he addressed her. "Sir, it's live. The list. I'm afraid containment isn't going to be possible as we'd hoped."

Beaumont sat up. "Shit. You're certain of this?"

"Yes, sir. The officer names have gone public. The list has been posted to 4chan and Reddit and it's already going viral.

Someone from Al-Jazeera was lurking on the same thread I was on. It's safe to assume foreign media will pick it up imminently. Then it's only a matter of time before the BBC gets hold of it."

"Can we reach out to them and block it? Or get someone over in five or six to instigate a press blackout? This is a national security concern."

Armitage swallowed. "I'm not sure, sir. We can try but…"

She trailed off as Beaumont turned away and waved his hand at her. He was thinking hard, considering what to do. His heart felt as if it was working twice as fast; adrenaline coursed through his veins as pockets of ideas lit up across his frontal lobe.

"Come in, Armitage," he told her, pulling a chair around and positioning it on the edge of his desk at a right angle to his. "Shut the door, sit down, let's discuss this further."

Faced with the string of orders, the young analyst appeared to freeze before seemingly catching herself and doing what was instructed of her.

"What is it, sir?" she asked, sitting, eyes wide with anticipation.

"Have you told anyone else about this?" he asked.

"Not yet. The alert I created only flashed up a few minutes ago. I think I'm the first to have found it online since it re-emerged. I came straight to you."

A sinking feeling settled in Beaumont's gut. Beckett was a dead man. He had to do something. "Are we any closer to finding the source of the leak?" he asked.

Armitage shook her head. "No, sir. The document's metadata is heavily encrypted and the IP addresses of those posting it have been bounced around so much it's nearly impossible to track. Whoever's behind this is using top-tier technology, the kind only governments have access to. It could be Russia or China, but at this stage I can't be certain."

His mind raced as he glanced at his computer screen. There was no reply to his message. No sign that Beckett had even seen it. "We need to find the source of the leak. At some point, the Foreign Office will have to make a statement and we need to get ahead of the narrative."

"Understood. We're working around the clock, sir," Armitage added. "But it feels like we're chasing shadows. These people know what they're doing and they've covered their tracks."

"Yes, I'm sure. But I need our best minds on this. Can you assemble a team and instruct them to devote all their resources to this for the next twenty-four hours?"

"Yes, sir. Absolutely."

"Good. Thank you." He leaned back in his chair, rubbing at his temples. Once he was done here, he'd break the news to Locke. It wouldn't take long for him and MI6 to coordinate extraction plans for the operatives abroad. With a bit of luck, they could get through this with minimal casualties. But that just left Beckett.

What to do about Beckett?

"Will that be all, sir?"

Beaumont returned his attention to Armitage, who was now resting her weight onto her feet and gripping the arms of the chair, ready to spring into action. Once in this position, however, she remained poised, awaiting her official dismissal.

Beaumont liked that. He wasn't a stickler for tradition, or even chain of command when lives were at stake, but her actions told him she was the sort of person he needed right now – dedicated to procedure but driven by a determination to do what was right.

"One more thing," he said, shifting around in his chair to face her. "We need to get the word out to John Beckett that the leak is public and his cover has been compromised. He's in significant danger right now."

Armitage nodded. "I understand. But as far as I know, he's gone dark."

"Correct, but I recall a message from him a while back that threw up some worries because it came via an SMS message rather than the IP we had listed for his laptop. Am I remembering that correctly?"

"It's possible, sir. But, as you know, all messages are deleted."

Beaumont clenched his jaw, his frustration mounting. "Yes, I'm aware of that. But is there a way to retrieve that message? And, specifically, the phone number it was sent from?"

He watched Armitage as the implications of his request sparked understanding in her pale blue eyes. She swallowed. "Short answer – possibly. We do have a system in place that archives all incoming data using an updated government version of the Gopher protocol. The frequency of the snapshots varies from system to programme, but we hold a large cluster of Linux nodes that serve as an archive of past—"

"I don't need to know the ins and outs of the process," Beaumont cut in. "I just need to know if it's possible."

The young analyst nodded. "Yes, sir. I think so. Documents are archived with timestamped URLs, so it would help if we had a timeframe for that specific message."

Beaumont thought about it. "Start eight months ago and narrow it down from there."

"Very good. The only other issue is I'd need top-level security clearance to access the archives."

"Fine. I'll arrange for that right away." He leaned in, lowering his voice. "Let's keep this just between us for now, Ruth. I don't wish to put you in a bad position with Director Locke, but once I grant you clearance, the buck stops with me anyway. You see, as it stands, there's no direct extraction plan in place for Officer Beckett. But if we act now, we can get ahead of the curve when one is needed. You'd be instrumental in bringing one of our best men home."

The only problem was, Beaumont didn't know if there ever would be an extraction plan for Beckett. It was unusual for a Sigma Unit officer to operate on British soil. He understood why Locke wanted to avoid drawing attention if the situation went public.

However, his reasoning seemed to resonate with the eager young analyst. She tensed her grip on the chair arms and Beaumont gave her the nod. "That will be all for now."

"Thank you, sir." She rose and hurried for the door.

"One more thing, Ruth," he called after her, eliciting a pause before she opened the door. "Time is of the essence here. Once you've assembled the team to investigate the source of the leak, I want your full attention on this." He lowered his voice further as he locked eyes with her. "All our officers' lives are on the line, Ruth. But Beckett… Beckett is in the worst possible situation. We have to find him. We have to get him out of there."

7

Beckett had eaten lunch and the final throes of side two of the Chopin LP were fading into the ambient noise coming in from outside. His eyes were half-closed, the drone of a pneumatic drill somewhere below his window blending harmoniously with the last notes of the music. His mind drifted to the edge of relaxation. The past few days had been hectic, to say the least, and even someone like him deserved brief interludes of peace amidst the constant whirlwind that was his life.

But then his phone buzzed.

He sat up, scanning the room for the source of the sound. The phone vibrated again, and he spotted it lying on the tall mahogany table by the door. Getting to his feet, he shook off any lingering drowsiness, already awake and alert as he approached the table and picked up the device. He had a message. It was from a number he recognised but hadn't stored in his contact list. Lifting the phone closer, he opened the message.

Make contact. Now! IMPORTANT!

His pulse quickened, adrenaline electrifying his veins and

snapping him fully alert as his mind raced to what to do next. Delaney had given him the phone he'd been using for the past year. However, he'd once used it to communicate with Control regarding an urgent shipment arrival at the docklands. They must have stored the number in their database. That was an oversight on both their parts, but if S-Unit was reaching out through this channel, there had to be a good reason.

Protocol dictated that a burner was used for inbound communications to S-Unit. The device didn't need to be different every time, just distinct from the one receiving outgoing messages from S-Unit. It was a precaution meant to deter any attempts to track communications and it worked well. He cast a swift glance around the room, then slid open a small drawer beneath the table. Extracting a slender brass key, he made his way down the hallway.

Outside his bedroom, he stopped and clicked open the loft hatch above. The inclusion of such a space was one of the reasons why the top-floor flat had appealed to him when he was searching for a place to live. Not only did it provide an escape route to the neighbouring houses if needed, but it also housed an old lockable water tank, perfect for secure storage.

Pulling down the metal ladder, he extended it to the floor and stepped up into the dim attic. The muted light from below threw shadows across the roof beams and rafters as he knelt on the first wooden board. When his eyes adjusted to the gloom, he zeroed in on the water tank nestled in the right-hand corner. Apart from the metal tank, the room also comprised an ancient rolled-up carpet left by a previous tenant and four cardboard boxes brimming with old papers and books. The air was thick with the smell of dust and age.

Clambering to his feet, he stooped his six-foot-two frame to accommodate the sloping ceiling and made his way over to the water tank, inside which he had stashed a metal box containing essentials he might need in an emergency. Burner phone, standard-issue Sig Sauer P226 with an extended twenty-round magazine, and a passport.

He released the padlock and pried open the rusted lid of the water tank. It was empty of water and had been for years, but his fingers brushed against the cold metal box as he reached within. Lifting it out, he knelt and placed the box on the beam in front of him. He'd been trained to suppress panic, confident in his abilities to adapt and survive, but a creeping sense of dread snaked around him, twisting the muscles in his stomach. Something rotten was in the air.

He opened the box and removed the counterfeit passport resting on top. Sigma Unit had already provided him with a passport in the name of Patrick Hamilton – as well as passports in other names held in safe deposit boxes at airports around the world – but he'd sourced this one independently. It was an unsanctioned backup plan, born of the knowledge that trust was a double-edged sword and that he might need it one day. He opened the back page, reminding himself of this particular alias – Michael Day. The small photo stared back at him. In it, he looked younger and fresher-faced than he had done in years, yet he had the same intense stare as when he looked at himself in the mirror. These were eyes that had seen too much. Mirroring a soul that knew too much.

He slid the passport into his jeans' pocket and took out the pistol and the burner phone. Something told him he might need all three soon enough.

With the phone and Sig clutched in one hand, he descended from the loft and retraced his steps to the living room. Taking a seat on the couch, he laid the gun down beside him, took a moment to centre himself, and then opened up the phone. A single number was saved in the contact list. He called it.

It rang once, twice, then Beaumont's voice filled the line, deep and unwavering. "Beckett? Is that you?"

"Yes, it's me. I got your message. What's wrong?"

"I can't discuss this over the phone," came the reply. "I don't know who's potentially listening and I'm taking a considerable risk as it is."

Beckett was silent.

"We need to meet," Beaumont continued. "As soon as possible."

Beckett glanced at his watch. "Usual place? One hour?"

"Fine," Beaumont said. "And, Beckett, until then, keep a low profile and avoid contact with others. Do you hear me? I suggest you vacate your current location and go somewhere no one knows you. Where you can lay low. Understand?"

Beckett sniffed and glanced at the Sig. "Loud and clear," he replied. "I'll see you in an hour."

8

It was almost 6 p.m. The sun was setting behind the houses and tenant blocks of Brixton's Angell Town estate when Beckett reached the entrance of the dimly lit underpass. The sharp, cold air filled his lungs, providing a jolt of invigoration as he waited for Beaumont's arrival. His breath clouded in the air in front of him. He stuffed his hands in the pockets of his jacket and leaned against the wall. He was early, but he was always early. It gave him a chance to scope out the area and ensure there were no nasty surprises lying in wait.

Although, from what he'd picked up from his old friend's vague message – and more so from his troubled demeanour – Beckett anticipated Beaumont was bringing a nasty surprise with him.

He peered down the underpass. The concrete walls were adorned with layers of graffiti, a riot of vibrant colours clashing with the ambient gloom. The pungent smell of stale urine hung in the air, mixing with the pervasive dampness that seemed to cling to every surface down here, his clothes and skin included. A constant drip echoed through the narrow passage, the only sound piercing the silence. He looked at his watch –

five minutes to six. Beaumont wasn't yet late, but each passing moment ratcheted up Beckett's unease. He'd give his old friend until one minute past. Then he was gone.

From his vantage point near the underpass entrance, Beckett could see up to the main strip in front of the lowest block of the estate. Two young boys, about six or seven years old, were tossing an American football back and forth. Most children their age should be at home having dinner at this hour, but at least they were only playing sports. Still, they were young yet. There'd be plenty of time for them to get into guns and drugs and violence, Beckett thought. Which they undoubtedly would. Growing up in a neighbourhood like this, there was little else for youngsters to do.

Visiting Angell Town always got to Beckett. Growing up where he did, how he did, he knew he was luckier than most. A hell of a lot luckier than these kids. Brixton was a melting pot of diverse cultures and this estate was inhabited predominantly by Afro-Caribbean residents who had carved out a sense of community in the face of adversity. But there was only so much a community could do amongst the ever-growing threat of gang warfare, knife crimes and gun violence. Beckett knew individuals like Rufus Delaney only exacerbated the unrest. But that was why he'd been so eager to accept his current mission. London was a good city. It deserved redemption.

Rows of buildings on the run-down estate loomed over him like a series of grim tombstones, each one a monument to the struggles of the families who called the place home. The brickwork, darkened and discoloured, stood as a stark reminder of the inequality that plagued the city. Pavements and alleyways were littered with used needles and squares of burnt foil, discarded furniture and forgotten dreams. The shouts of older children echoed through the air. Off in the distance were sirens, and what might have been gunshots.

Beckett checked his phone again. 5:59 p.m.

Even with his rigorous training and wealth of experience, he couldn't suppress an undercurrent of concern as he waited. His ability to remain cool under pressure was one of his strengths, yet the prospect of this unknown threat gnawed at his resolve.

At the far end of the underpass a silhouette appeared, framed by the dim streetlights above. Beaumont, at last. As he approached, the tension in his shoulders was plainly visible, a sign that the news he carried with him was far from good. But Beckett already knew that. He braced himself for what lay ahead.

"Long time no see," he said, as his old friend got closer.

Beaumont was wearing a long beige mac buttoned up without a belt, and an expression Beckett pinpointed as apprehension. His silver-grey hair was longer but thinner than the last time they'd seen each other. He also looked exhausted, and had maybe two days' worth of growth on his chin. Beckett had never known the man to have even the slightest hint of designer stubble. If he'd not shaved that morning, it meant something big had gone down and he hadn't had the chance. Judging by his overall demeanour, Beckett concluded Beaumont hadn't been home since the previous day.

The older man gave him a long look, one eyebrow raised in mild annoyance. But a hint of warmth lingered in his faint smile. "Yeah, long time no see. And whose fault might that be?"

"I know. And I'm sorry. But I've not been turned. Don't you worry about that."

"I never thought it for a second. I told Locke as much."

"Thank you for that. I've had to maintain a lower profile than normal," Beckett explained. "Delaney and I have grown closer than ever recently – I've become his right-hand man. I couldn't risk breaking character or doing anything to jeopardise that relationship." He narrowed his eyes at

Beaumont. "But something tells me that might be inevitable now. Am I right?"

"There's been a data breach, John," Beaumont said, his voice hushed and urgent. "A list of our deep-cover operatives has leaked. We tried to contain it but we failed. I'm sorry. Your identity has been compromised. I shouldn't even be telling you this, but you need to get out of town. Fast. If – or rather when – Delaney finds out… Well, you understand the implications."

The weight of Beaumont's words hit Beckett like a punch to the guts. He lifted his head, his mind racing to make sense of the situation. "What exactly is out there?" he asked. "In the leak."

"Not everything. The list contains operatives' real names, parts of their mission history and their aliases. Your personnel record hasn't been leaked, but what has been revealed is sufficient to endanger all our operatives. Locke is working in tandem with Frank Calder to formulate an extraction strategy for our operatives abroad. But…"

"But let me guess – he doesn't want to pull me in yet and risk exposing S-Unit and their operations in the UK. He'd rather hide behind the veneer of MI6 and allow them to play the legitimate role to the world's press. Meanwhile, I'm left to fend for myself."

"It's not quite as bad as that," Beaumont told him. "But I don't think Locke got in front of this as quickly as he should have. The first we knew about the list's existence was at 5 a.m. this morning. As I say, we had hoped to contain it, but that wasn't possible." He looked away and made a sound halfway between a cough and a growl. "I'm sorry, son. I know this is hard to hear. As always, Locke has his mind on the bigger picture and hasn't decided how to handle your situation. Hopefully, that'll change in the next few hours, but I'm not sure we have the luxury of that much time. Hence why we're here. I couldn't live with myself without at least giving you a heads-up."

Beckett looked his friend up and down. A thousand thoughts and possibilities ticked over in his mind. He took a deep breath and calmed himself. He had to stay on top of this. He closed his eyes, focusing on the important questions – the who, what, why and when. "Are you compromised, Beaumont?"

"No. Of course not. Would I be revealing this to you if I were?"

"But I'm so close to getting crucial intel on the London arm of The Consortium. I don't know, Beaumont… it seems coincidental that this happens three days before I'm due to meet with them. Do we have any leads on who's behind the leak?"

Beaumont shook his head. "Not as of yet. I've got a team looking into it. Keep your phone switched on and I'll provide updates as and when we have them. But for Christ's sake, Beckett, be careful. Do you have a plan of action?"

"Don't get killed. Same plan as always."

Beaumont tilted his head to one side. "You're not concerned about what Delaney will do?"

Beckett let out a laugh that was more like a huff. A heavy silence settled between the two men. Finally, Beckett spoke. "I've got a laundry list of concerns right now, but concern alone doesn't solve anything. You know that. But I appreciate you seeking me out and giving me the heads-up. I can take it from here."

Beaumont rubbed his finger on his chin and scowled. "Are you sure you're okay, John?"

That was a grey area, Beckett thought. A moot point. "I'm fine," he replied. "Don't I look it?"

"I don't know. I can't quite put my finger on it. You just seem different. Colder. More detached."

"What? Even more than usual?" Beckett laughed. Beaumont didn't.

"Well… yes."

"Oh, come on. I've been working alongside Rufus Delaney for two years. I've had to bury most of my humanity deep inside of me. You know how it works. It's the only way you survive in this world."

"Humanity, huh? Remind me what that is again? And have you any left?"

"I certainly hope so," Beckett replied, forcing a smile.

Beaumont puffed out his cheeks. "Well, that's good to hear. For now, my advice is to pack a bag and lie low. It might be wiser to avoid your place altogether. Is there anywhere you can hide out for a few days until we know more?"

"Perhaps. It's best if I keep it to myself for now, though. You can appreciate why."

Beaumont nodded. "Fair enough."

"But I will have to return to my flat. My passport is there. Plus a few other items I'm going to need."

"All right," Beaumont conceded. "Just be quick about it. And think yourself lucky you don't have any family to worry about. Delaney strikes me as the sort of guy who would use anybody and anything to get to you if he was that way inclined. Which I imagine he will be, once he knows his right-hand man works for the British Secret Service." He glanced down and away. "Sorry, John. I didn't mean… It's been a long day…"

"It's okay," Beckett replied. "I understand. You should get going. So should I."

"Agreed. Stay in touch as much as you can. I'll do the same." He held his hand out. "And stay safe. Look after yourself."

Beckett grabbed his hand and shook it. "You too."

Turning on his heel, Beckett left the underpass behind,

stepping into the darkness that had now cloaked the city. He was done. He knew that. Or rather, Patrick Hamilton was done. Whether John Beckett would survive the next twenty-four hours depended on what he did next. He had to get home, grab his go-bag, and get out of London before Delaney sent hell to his door.

Only one thing bothered him. Beaumont had been mistaken just now. Beckett did have family. A niece. It had been years since he last saw her, and he'd never mentioned her to anyone on the current roster at S-Unit, but she'd be on his official record. In this, Beaumont had been spot on – if Delaney found out about her, he wouldn't waste a second in using her to get to him.

With a renewed sense of urgency burning in his chest, Beckett headed for his car. The clock was ticking and the game had changed. His mission now was to find his niece and get her to safety – and he had to do it tonight.

9

Amber Irving stepped back from the canvas, squinting her left eye shut. Something was off. It wasn't good. She'd been working on this new painting for the best part of a month, spending all her free time on it, but somewhere along the way her initial vision had been lost. She switched perspectives, closing her right eye to scrutinise the large canvas with her left. It didn't look any better. In fact, her left eye seemed to possess a sharper vision and the extra detail made the painting look worse.

Swirls of organic colour – browns, greens, blood-reds – looped together across the textured canvas. In some places, the paint was over an inch thick off the canvas and would take months to dry, maybe even years. She'd read that some sections of Frank Auerbach's paintings were still wet beneath the layers of thick paint he'd used in the sixties.

Auerbach was one of Amber's heroes. She loved his use of texture and the way he conjured up so much emotion in his dense, expressionistic portrayals of city scenes around London. This was what she'd been trying to emulate in this new piece – her interpretation of a photograph showing her childhood home in Primrose Hill, where she'd lived with her parents when she was young.

She lifted the photograph now and held it up against the image on the canvas. She supposed she'd *sort of* captured the scene, but she couldn't shake off the feeling she was trying too hard, forcing something that wasn't there.

Such was the life of an artist.

Amber was never completely satisfied with her finished pieces. Indeed, if she ever was, she'd probably tell herself she'd lost her critical eye and never paint again. This way, at least she kept on. Not content, but committed. It wasn't about the destination for Amber, but the journey, the process.

She let out a sigh, her muscles stretching and protesting from the strain of prolonged painting. The house was quiet, just the faint hum from the television downstairs drifting through the floorboards. She couldn't pick out the show but she didn't watch much television. If she watched anything at all, it was via Netflix on her laptop, but mostly she spent her time painting or reading.

Slumping onto the edge of her bed, she cradled the photograph in her lap. It was a creased, rectangular piece of card, taken with an old-fashioned camera, and there was a light flare coming in from one corner that was caused by the actual sun rather than a filter. Her memories of living in that house were hazy, mainly arising from stories her mum had told her. They'd moved out of London, to Chelmsford, when her grandad died and her mum wanted to be closer to her grandma. Chelmsford had been a nice place to grow up, and whilst Amber was a shy kid, she had a small but dedicated group of close friends. She'd been happy there. That was until two weeks after her fifteenth birthday when her parents were both killed in a car accident whilst she was at school.

Laughter coming up from downstairs knocked her from her thoughts. She smiled to herself, shaking her head at Carol's loud, infectious guffaws. She and her husband, Gareth, had been close friends with Amber's mum and dad, and had been listed as testamentary guardians in their will. They were nice people. They'd never had children of their own, but were kind and caring and she felt safe with them. She'd been living with them for almost a year now.

She did have an uncle somewhere – her mum's brother – but she hadn't seen him since she was nine. No one seemed to know where he was, or even if he was still alive. When her world collapsed, it was Carol and Gareth who were there for her. So moving in with them felt like the most natural transition.

Carol was a solicitor and Gareth was a detective sergeant with the Maidstone Police's Criminal Investigation Division. Amber didn't know what that entailed, but he didn't wear a uniform so she assumed he was probably quite senior. Sevenoaks was a well-to-do area, though, especially their neighbourhood, which bordered a leafy expanse of woodland next to Knole Park. She doubted Gareth ever had much crime to investigate.

She got up off the bed and returned the photograph to its place by her easel before peeling off her paint-splattered, oversized t-shirt and draping it over the back of her chair. At times like this, when fragments of her past ambushed her, summoned from the depths of a photograph or a memory that popped into her head as if from nowhere, Amber missed her parents terribly. But of course she did. They were her mum and dad, her loved ones, taken from her far too early. Yet beneath her artistic nature lay a strong, inner resilience and she was often regarded as mature and wise beyond her years.

In the weeks following the accident, she'd cried almost non-stop before deciding one day that she had to pick herself up and make the most of her rotten luck. She realised no one was coming to save her from the pain she carried, and that, if she was to carve out a life worth living in spite of the tragic loss of her parents, she had to save herself. So that's what she did. One day at a time.

Moving over to her chest of drawers, she selected a fresh t-shirt and slipped it on before taking off her leggings. She'd already brushed her teeth, but the t-shirt was one she normally wore for bed and provided decent coverage should she need to leave her room for any reason. Not that she had to worry about Gareth or anything like that. He always looked terrified, and the most uncomfortable any man could look, at the mere hint of flesh from her. She found his reactions amusing. He was sweet. Both he and Carol were. She'd miss them when she moved away to university next year, but at the same time she couldn't wait to get to London and start her new life. Amber hoped to follow in Auerbach's footsteps and study Fine Art at Saint Martin's, before progressing to the Royal College of Art to do a post-doctorate degree in painting. Failing that, she'd be happy with a place at Goldsmiths or Camberwell. Both were good art schools.

She glanced around the room. Despite only having lived here a short while, she'd made the place her own. The room was a reflection of her artistic soul, with canvases and posters adorning the walls and poetry books stacked high on the shelves. The soft glow from the fairy lights draped around her bed created a warm and inviting atmosphere, and the scent of lavender filled the air from a nearby diffuser. It was supposed to be calming and helped with sleep. A large window offered a view of the well-manicured garden and the sprawling woodland beyond with its tall trees and dense bushes.

Once ready for bed, she stood by the open window and breathed in the cool night air, stretching her arms above her head. She suddenly felt tense for some reason and wondered if she should return to the painting, try and salvage it before going to sleep. But it was getting late and she had school in the morning. Also, sometimes leaving a painting for a few days meant it looked better when you returned to it. Either way, it wasn't that important in the scheme of things. She already had her portfolio assembled, ready for university applications in a few months.

As Amber went to her bed and climbed under the covers, she heard a creak outside the room.

"Are you still awake?" Carol whispered through the door.

"Yes, but I'm going to sleep now," Amber replied. "Good night."

"Good night, darling. Do you want me to turn your light out?"

"Please."

Carol eased open the door, saw Amber in bed and scrunched up her nose. "Sweet dreams," she whispered, before switching the light off and backing out of the room, shutting the door behind her.

The room was plunged into darkness but for the dim glow of the fairy lights. Amber usually read before going to sleep, and as she leaned over to switch on her bedside lamp, she noticed her window was still open. She pondered shutting it, but the breeze was pleasant and it would aid in clearing the lingering scent of white spirit. As she reached for her book, she heard the distant sound of a car pulling up, the crunch of tyres on gravel. It sounded as if it came from the other side of the garden, from the woods. Perhaps it was young lovers – a modern-day Romeo and Juliet – seeking a private sanctuary away from prying eyes. She knew the reality was likely to be seedier if it was anything of the sort, but Amber had a poetic spirit and preferred to see the romance in life. Even when it was in short supply.

She brought her book over and turned to the page marked by her bookmark. *A Clockwork Orange*. She was working her way through an online list of a hundred must-read books and this was the next title after finishing *One Hundred Years of Solitude* a few days earlier. She'd loved that book, but found Anthony Burgess's classic novel hard going so far. Maybe it said something about her, that she preferred fantastical tales over books about violence and the breakdown of society.

But she was no quitter. She settled down in bed and started reading, when she heard a bang from downstairs. It sounded to Amber like someone slamming a heavy book down onto a hard surface. She sat up, her ears straining to hear anything else that might hint at the source of the noise. Then it came again – a muted bang. But this time a secondary sound followed, a dull thud, as though something had fallen onto the carpet. Or someone.

No, Amber mentally assured herself. It was merely her imagination running wild, perhaps exacerbated by the home invasion scene she'd just read about in her book. But then more sounds ensued. Strange noises coming up from downstairs.

She tilted her head to one side to sharpen her attention. The house remained quiet, as if holding its breath along with her. She considered calling out for Carol and Gareth, but something told her not to. One of them probably knocked something over, she reasoned, in an attempt to calm her racing thoughts. The idea seemed plausible enough. But knocking something over once made sense – twice, three times, not so much.

As the seconds ticked by, she wrestled with what she should do. Instinct had her throw back the covers and tiptoe over to the door. Gripping the handle, she edged it open, her ears alert for further sounds. And there they were. Voices, coming up from the hallway below. Men's voices. But not Gareth.

Where was he?

He was a policeman, damn it. It was his job to protect her. She craned her neck around the side of the door. Through the wooden slats that ran down the top of the stairs, she saw a figure in the hallway below. She only caught their shoulder and part of a leg, but it certainly wasn't Gareth. This individual was wearing a shiny black bomber jacket and rough denim jeans. She thought she noticed a gloved hand as well before they disappeared into the front room. She strained to hear Carol or Gareth. Where were they? Were they injured? Worse? She shook the thoughts away; she couldn't deal with them right now.

Her heart was pounding in her chest, her breaths shallow and hushed. This was a home invasion like in her book, except it was real. She had to make a break for it. If the intruder was in the living room, she could reach the front door. It would be locked, but she could unlock it swiftly. She closed her eyes, visualising the steps she'd have to take, the fastest route to exit the house. She mentally rehearsed unlocking the two deadbolts and turning the main latch. Down the stairs… through the front door… into the safety of the night. If she was quiet, she might evade the intruder's notice altogether. But she had to go now. Every second was crucial. She could practically feel the adrenaline coursing through her veins, sharpening her senses, honing her focus.

She opened the door of her room wide, ready to take the first step. But her body wouldn't do what she asked of it. She stiffened. Her pulse hammered in her ears as a man appeared at the bottom of the stairs. The sight of him turned her legs to jelly.

No!

What did he want?

He was large and intimidating, with a shaved head and a flat nose. Though his gaze was lowered, she could tell his eyes were small and cruel. He was wearing black gloves, the leather groaning and straining as he grasped the bannister to heave himself up the stairs. But it was what he was holding in his other hand that sent an icy shiver skittering down Amber's spine. It was a gun. An actual gun. It was black and shiny and had one of those elongated barrels on the end she'd seen in films. They were used to muffle gunshots. Was that the noise she'd heard before? If so, that meant…

No. Please no.

Her breath snagged in her throat. Her heart threatened to burst out from her chest. She couldn't tear her gaze away from the gun. The sight of it filled her with a deep, primal fear. Knowing it had probably killed Gareth and Carol made it even more horrific. But there was no way out now. She couldn't get past this man. She couldn't reach the front door.

It was too late. It was all too late.

10

Beckett parked his car a block away from his building on the opposite side of the street. From there, he still had eyes on the living room window of his flat, but the distance would allow him to approach on a wide arc, using a row of leafy trees as cover.

He switched off the engine and sat for a moment, watching the window. The light was on but he'd left it that way. No shadows or movement were visible. Unclicking his seatbelt, he climbed out of the car and cricked his neck side to side. He felt stiff from the drive and the tension he'd been carrying since Beaumont had reached out to him. He glanced up and down the wide avenue. The darkened neighbourhood was quiet, the only sound the distant hum of traffic and the occasional rustle of a late-night breeze. Keeping watch on his flat, now focusing on the windows of his kitchen and bedroom, he walked along the roadside until he reached the corner. There was still no movement behind the windows, but his instincts screamed of danger nearby. He needed to get up to his flat and fast, except his training told him to be cautious. Now more than ever, he couldn't take any chances.

He surveyed the area as he advanced, darting across the street and pressing himself against the side of his building. From this position, he could no longer see through the top windows, but if anyone was up there, they couldn't see him either. The streetlights cast eerie shadows on the cracked pavement as he made his way to the front door; the tall trees opposite seemed to be reaching out for him like gnarled fingers. The air was heavy with the brackish scent from the nearby river mixed in with a heady cocktail of diesel and petrol fumes. He made his way to his front door, moving silently but quickly, each step calculated to minimise the noise of his approach. As he rounded the corner, he paused. The front door of his building was hanging open.

That wasn't a good sign, but it was within his contingency plans. Steeling himself for combat, he eased open the door using two fingers and stepped inside. The hallway beyond was still, and fresh with the night air as Beckett closed the door silently behind him and made his way to the stairs. He began to climb, casting his gaze up through the winding Victorian stairwell as he went. But there was no one in sight.

He cursed himself for leaving the P226 behind. He hadn't expected to need it for his meeting with Beaumont – and he might not need it now – but it would certainly provide welcome backup. He could picture it, resting on top of his passport on the glass coffee table in the living room.

But there was no time for regrets. He had to focus on the situation at hand. With each step up the stairs, he could feel the tension mounting. He kept his body low, using the handrail for balance as his eyes darted up and down the stairwell, alert for any hint of danger. The dim lighting from the hallway below cast a sombre atmosphere over the space, his shadow spiking up the wall as he went.

Upon reaching the top floor, he paused once more. Any residual uncertainty about what might be waiting for him was now gone as he saw the door to his flat hanging open a few centimetres. He paused, straining his ears for clues of the activity within. From inside, the muted creaking of floorboards betrayed the presence of someone trying to navigate his flat surreptitiously. Propelled by adrenaline, he crossed the landing and flattened himself against the wall adjacent to his open door. Leaning around, he could see through the gap the intruders had left when they entered.

There were two men. Both big. One was wearing a denim jacket and the other a leather sports coat. Both appeared to carry Glocks equipped with suppressors, the round type; probably Illusion 9s if Murat Caliskan was the supplier. Beckett didn't recognise either of the men, but that wasn't surprising. For dirty jobs such as this, Delaney would often use local thugs. That fact was one point in Beckett's favour. They were just low-level hitmen. No real training. No class.

He bided his time at the door until the men split up. They would have ascertained he wasn't home by this point, but were no doubt planning on staking out separate rooms to catch him off guard upon his return. The man with the leather sports coat went into the living room, whilst his accomplice headed for the bedroom. Silently opening the door, Beckett slipped inside his flat and stalked the man into the living room. His gaze landed on the P226 and his passport resting on the table, but he didn't make a move for the pistol. Too noisy. Too conspicuous.

Instead, Beckett glided soundlessly towards the man. As Sports Coat registered the presence behind him and began to turn, Beckett smashed his fist into his temple, leveraging the force with a twist of his hips. It was a good punch, hard and with plenty of force behind it. You hit someone that hard in the temple, it sends a shock wave to the brain that causes immediate disorientation. You hit someone hard enough, you cause blunt force trauma and they'll drop dead on the spot. This punch wasn't quite enough to be lethal, the light in Sports Coat's eyes didn't go out immediately, but it certainly dimmed as his pupils rolled back into his skull. A bleed from a ruptured meningeal artery was most likely going to send him to the morgue, but Beckett wasn't taking any chances. As he staggered back, Beckett followed up with a swift blow to his larynx, crushing his windpipe and guaranteeing an imminent death.

Not pausing to draw breath, he now redirected his focus to the doorway as Denim Jacket emerged from the bedroom, his eyes widening in shock at the unfolding scene. Beckett reacted immediately, knowing he only had a split second head start on the guy. Charging, he stomped down with force on the man's kneecap, shoving him against the wall before his startled brain could send a message to his trigger finger. He hit the wall with a thud and it sounded as if all the air had been knocked out of him.

Seizing the gun, Beckett wrested it from Denim Jacket's grasp and smashed his elbow into the bridge of his nose. As he howled out in pain, Beckett tossed the gun and reached for the lamp near the door. In one fluid motion, he yanked the cord from its socket, manoeuvred behind his assailant and looped the cord around the man's neck. As Denim Jacket struggled, Beckett pulled the cord tight. At the same time, he forcefully yanked the man backwards, positioning his hips low against the man's side to leverage his own body against him. This allowed Beckett to easily hoist the man off his feet despite their similar height and build. The makeshift garrotte bit into the flesh on the man's neck as Beckett leaned over and maintained pressure. Denim Jacket kicked and struggled for a few moments, but Beckett held firm until he felt his body go limp and heard a final, desperate exhale.

Letting the lifeless body slump to the floor, Beckett brushed himself down and scanned the room. The curtains were open and the lights were on, but the fighting had taken place at the far side of the room. Unless the people across the street had a particularly keen interest in the comings and goings in his flat, he wouldn't have been seen. Regardless, he moved over to the window to check. The lights were off in the flat opposite. All was good.

He headed straight for the bedroom and opened up his wardrobe to reveal a small metal safe on the bottom shelf. Kneeling, he dialled in the combination and swung the door open. Inside were two more passports, both 'official' ones supplied by S-Unit – one for Patrick Hamilton and a German-issued passport for Bruno Hartmann, an alias he often adopted when working overseas.

He pocketed both passports, then lifted out the only thing left in the safe. A small A5 notepad. Flipping it open, he flicked past the initial pages, which contained the names and contact information of the many assets he'd employed over the years. He found what he was searching for on the second-to-last page – the address of Carol and Gareth Ford. Amber's guardians. He saw they lived in Sevenoaks. Not too far away. But – damn it – he'd hoped there might have been a contact number, too.

Not a problem, he told himself. But that meant time really was of the essence.

Pulling his go-bag out from under the bed, he unzipped the grey canvas holdall and threw the notepad and passports on top of the minimal selection of clothes, underwear and toiletries already inside. Underneath these, a fake bottom concealed two clear zip-lock bags containing five thousand pounds in used notes and the equivalent in euros. He carried the bag into the living room and tossed the other passport inside. Moving over to the fallen men, he checked their pockets and found a set of car keys in Denim Jacket's trouser pocket.

An Audi, if the keyring matched the car. It wouldn't have been his first choice of vehicle, but it would be fast enough.

"Much obliged, gentlemen," he muttered to their lifeless bodies.

Then he stuffed the Sig down the back of his waistband and got the hell out of there.

11

Spencer Bowditch clutched the cardboard file to his chest as he navigated the low-lit corridors of the MI6 building. The echo of his polished leather shoes bouncing off the walls punctuated his stride. The faint hum of the fluorescent lights overhead did little to alleviate the stress bubbling inside of him. He passed two women coming the other way, both attractive, both sporting dark ponytails. Neither of them looked his way but he glared at them all the same, silently coaxing them to reciprocate until they disappeared from his field of vision.

Bowditch, a wiry man with a receding hairline and sharp, rat-like features, often felt he didn't get the respect or acknowledgement he deserved, especially given his rank and experience. He'd served at Sigma Unit for six years – almost on par with Locke – and had held the position of assistant director for the last three. Before that, he'd worked at MI6 and then at UKC, a highly specialised surveillance unit run by the SIS with the same classified status as Sigma Unit. Bowditch knew he could be hard to work with, but that was only because he expected the same commitment from his colleagues as he himself always gave. The lack of acknowledgement irked him. The sidelong glances from analysts when they thought he wasn't paying attention were not lost on him. Some days the paranoia ate at him, leading him to question the loyalty of his co-workers. Other days it felt as if he was the only person who gave two hoots about the security of his beloved country.

He arrived at the door of the conference room, inhaled deeply and pushed it open. It was a different room to the one they'd used that morning. It was larger, more stately. The lion's share of the space was dominated by a gleaming mahogany table, and sitting around the edges, the same stern-faced individuals from the previous meeting. The upper echelons of British intelligence, Calder and Eastwood, the heads of MI6 and MI5, sat side by side at the far end, their piercing gazes locked on Bowditch as he entered. The Home Secretary and the Foreign Secretary sat opposite Bryers and Somersby all of their expressions unreadable. Nearest the door, Locke sat with his arms folded, whilst across from him, Beaumont nervously tapped a pen against his notepad.

Bowditch nodded at Locke before taking his place at the head of the table, striving to project an aura of confidence as the eyes of everyone assembled turned his way.

He cleared his throat and began. "Good evening, everyone. I appreciate your presence at this late hour. As you're aware, we're dealing with a critical issue, and we deemed it crucial to keep you updated on any developments."

"Again, though," Somersby piped up, "couldn't this have been addressed over the phone or email?"

"I'm afraid not," Bowditch replied, the muscles across his shoulders tightening as he addressed the old man. "Our top priority is confidentiality and the safety of our operatives in the field. But I'm very relieved to announce that, just a few minutes ago, we received confirmation of the successful extraction of our intelligence officers who were on deep-cover operations overseas. Five out of the six are now securely stationed in British embassies and the sixth is en route to France as we speak. That leaves us with one officer from the list still not accounted for, and I put it to you all that our primary focus in the coming hours should be to locate John Beckett and ensure his safe retrieval."

Beaumont coughed and furrowed his brow. "I was under the impression that we were to hold off on searching for Beckett. That it was too complex a situation and we couldn't risk exposure."

Bowditch's eyes narrowed. Jacob Beaumont had been a thorn in his side ever since he started his tenure at Sigma Unit. Bowditch was of the opinion that the man was too chummy with some of the operatives. And he was a pain in the arse, to boot.

"As you're well aware," he countered, "the situation has evolved rapidly. We now believe it's in our collective best interests to retrieve the officer in question."

Just then, the door swung open and a towering figure entered the room. Xander Templeton, the London-based CIA section chief, whose team had been working in tandem with Sigma Unit for some months. All eyes were drawn to him as he crossed the room, leaving the door open in his wake. He was a physically imposing man with a wide, chiselled jaw and piercing blue-grey eyes that held an intensity no one could ignore. His neatly tailored dark trousers and snug, three-button burgundy sweater emphasised his solid build, while his thick white hair gave him the air of a Hollywood silver-screen icon. He exuded authority and power and his unexpected arrival appeared to have unnerved everyone present – a fact that brought a smug smile to Bowditch's face as Templeton took up position at the table's end, hands clasped behind his back.

"I assume you've all heard the news?" he asked, his deep, gravelly voice commanding undivided attention. "The swift extraction of your compromised agents overseas is commendable. However, that means many of our co-ordinated missions have been forced into hiatus as a result." His penetrating gaze swept the room, finally settling on Locke. "With the leak about to be public knowledge, we need to seize control of the narrative as soon as possible. It's critical we determine who's responsible, where the leak originated from, and how we can prevent a similar occurrence in the future."

Beaumont shifted in his seat. "What about our assets in Russia and China? Can we reach out to them? Surely they have some inkling as to who might be behind the leak."

Bowditch responded with a derisive snort. "We can certainly try. But even if they know something, they might not be inclined to share it with us. You know how these things work. It's best we keep this in-house as much as possible. This remains a highly sensitive and precarious matter." He savoured the flicker of uncertainty in people's eyes as the weight of his words settled. "Mr Templeton and I have conferred prior to this meeting and we share concerns regarding the intelligence officer currently unaccounted for on UK soil. John Beckett."

The sight of Beaumont's smirking at this announcement stirred Bowditch's ire. He wished he had the wherewithal – or the authority – to walk over and slap the smug expression off his face.

"So it's the two of you who've decided we should now look for Beckett?" he asked.

"And bring him home," Bowditch added.

Beaumont turned to Robert Locke. "This is the first I've heard of this. How about you?"

Locke raised an eyebrow. "Yes, but I'm receptive to the proposal. If we can retrieve Beckett and bring him home without any major fallout, that would be the ideal situation. I don't like the idea of leaving our man high and dry, regardless of his reputed capabilities. But it won't be simple. For starters, we have no idea where he is or how to contact him."

A hushed murmur spread across the room, reflecting the escalating tension as discussions deepened. Bowditch shifted restlessly in his chair, perspiration dotting his forehead as he strained to pick up every overlapping conversation. The consensus in the room seemed to be they were playing a high-stakes game of chicken with fate – but also that there was little else they could do at this stage.

As the realisation dawned on everyone, an uneasy silence descended, punctuated only by the sporadic tapping of pens and rustling of papers as the attendees pondered their options. Bowditch sat upright, his leg jittering nervously beneath the table.

It was Templeton, his fingers drumming an impatient rhythm on the tabletop, who broke the silence. "Enough," he growled. "We're going around in circles here. I don't know how much any of you are aware of Beckett's history, but he's been involved in missions involving the CIA over in the Middle East, in Russia, and on American soil. It puts me in a very fucking precarious position. And I'm not the only one. From what I see from his file, he pretty much knows the colour of all our panties." He paused, his icy blue eyes scanning the room, sizing up each person present. "We can't have him in the wind. That's a fact. We need to pool our resources, share intelligence and work together. The clock is ticking and we're all aware of the stakes."

Jane Isaacs shifted uneasily in her chair. "But if we're perceived to be collaborating too closely with the Americans," she began, her voice faltering, "it could provoke the very suspicion we're attempting to allay."

Bowditch was glad he wasn't on the receiving end of Templeton's gaze as it bored into the woman. "Would you rather risk our collective security, Home Secretary?" he asked. "This is bigger than politics or public relations. We need to act, and we need to act now. It's been relayed to me on more than one occasion that Beckett would never break under duress, and from what I've heard about the guy, I'm inclined to believe that. But, unlike my daddy, God rest his soul, I ain't a gambling man. I don't want to take that chance. So our priority now is locating Beckett. Sure, he might be able to handle himself against the guy he's been working for these last two years, but with his identity exposed, others could now be hunting him, people who want to harm us. In the wrong hands, Beckett is the ideal asset – a potential weapon to be turned against both our countries. We cannot risk such an outcome. We cannot allow that to happen. We need to get to him before any of our enemies do."

Tristan Shepherd spoke up next, his voice firm. "Mr Templeton is right. We must work together covertly to retrieve this Beckett fellow. The alternative sounds unthinkable."

The room fell silent once more. Bowditch cleared his throat. "Very well," he said. "We will establish a joint task force and share intelligence. Our operatives in the field will coordinate their efforts to track down Beckett and bring him in."

Locke, his face set in a grim expression, nodded. "Fine. But we'll need to move fast. Beckett is a highly trained operative and a master of evasion. He won't be found easily."

Beaumont nodded. "And we should also consider the possibility he's already aware of the leak and is taking steps to cover his tracks."

"That's precisely why we need to act with urgency," Templeton boomed, his voice cutting through the air like a razor. "If Beckett goes to ground, we may never find him."

Bowditch stiffened as Beaumont leaned into Locke and whispered something in his ear.

"You got something else you want to add?" Templeton asked him.

Beaumont sat back and folded his arms over his stomach. "Only that I'm not particularly comfortable with some of the language being used." He glanced at Calder and then the Foreign Secretary. "Let me remind you, Mr Templeton, that John Beckett is one of His Majesty's Government's top operatives – one of the finest we've ever had. If we are bringing him in, it has to be alive."

Templeton gruffly cleared his throat and flashed Beaumont a broad smile. "Naturally we bring him in alive; what else?" He shot Bowditch a look and then glanced at his watch. "Now, I've got a video call I need to be on. If anyone needs me, you know where I am." He strode towards the door, but stopped and glanced back. "Hey, don't all look so worried, guys. It's going to be fine. This is what we do all the time, right? We're the best at this." And with that, he opened the door and left the room.

12

A mere ten minutes later, Robert Locke found himself on the second floor of the MI6 building, en route to Frank Calder's office. Clutched under his arm was a sheaf of papers; a classified dossier hastily printed at the request of the Foreign Secretary. His instructions: to deliver it 'as soon as humanly possible'. Any second now.

As Locke reached the end of the corridor, his eyes were drawn to a window overlooking the Thames. He paused for a moment, allowing his gaze to wander over the dark waters. It was just past ten, the night sky seamlessly blending into the inky river. Narrowing his eyes, he could distinguish the lit silhouettes of the Tate Britain and the Chelsea College of Arts on the far bank. To his left, on this side of the river, was Battersea Power Station, while the London Eye and Palace of Westminster graced the skyline to his right. All timeless British institutions, all vulnerable if the information held in Beckett's head fell into enemy hands.

Locke pulled the papers out from under his arm and knocked on the door with a firm hand. "Locke," he announced.

A momentary silence greeted him from within. Then the door opened, revealing Frank Calder standing in the doorway. On seeing Locke, he lowered his chin and gave him a look that seemed to say, "I'm sorry about this," and, "It wasn't my call." Behind him, Tristan Shepherd, the Foreign Secretary, was pacing restlessly in front of a large window. He'd taken off his jacket and tie, and his hair was ruffled as if he'd been running his fingers through it.

"Ah, Locke, there you are," he said, walking over as Calder shut the door. "Do you have any news for me?"

Locke deliberately avoided Calder's gaze. "Not yet, sir. The joint meeting only just concluded. I've yet to be briefed. However, I do have this for you." He held up the stack of papers. "Beckett's file, as requested."

Shepherd glared at the document as it bowed in Locke's grip. He snatched it and began to flip through the pages. "Is this it?" he asked. "It's not very extensive."

Locke straightened his back. What Shepherd held was far from the complete file, but it was all he was prepared to share with anyone outside Sigma Unit. He had hoped it would be enough to satisfy Shepherd's curiosity. But perhaps not. "You must understand, Foreign Secretary, John Beckett doesn't officially exist. His file is heavily classified and meticulously redacted."

Shepherd's lip curled as he continued to skim the pages. "This doesn't offer much insight about the man." He glanced at Calder. "Do you know him, Frank?"

Calder cleared his throat. "I know of him, sir. Naturally. But Beckett and I have never actually crossed paths in person. He was already deeply entrenched in his work for S-Unit when I assumed the role of chief. Nevertheless, I've heard nothing but glowing commendations of him as a top-notch operative and a decent man."

"Yes, yes, I'm sure he is, but that doesn't offer much

context, does it?" Shepherd snapped. He moved away from the two men, carelessly tossing the papers onto Calder's desk before resuming his position at the window. Once there, he turned back to Locke. "What else can you tell me about him? Off the record."

Locke moved closer. He'd been awake now for over twenty-one hours and his patience was frayed and his skin felt like paper. He needed a shower, a strong coffee, and something sugary – in that order. What he didn't need was a testy interrogation from an irritable politician.

"I'm not sure how that would be beneficial, Foreign Secretary," he replied.

Shepherd rounded on him. "I need to know what I'm dealing with here, Locke. If this man poses a threat to national security, I need to know. If the shit hits the fan, this looks bad on all of us. I'm sure you're aware of the recent turmoil within the government: infighting, betrayal, duplicity. With local by-elections looming, we can't afford any further damage to the party. So, I say again, I need to know what I'm dealing with."

Locke didn't move. He'd suspected this was behind the Foreign Secretary's insistence to meet, and he was damned if he'd be drawn into playing politics when so much else hung in the balance.

"Xander Templeton certainly seems concerned that Beckett is still out there and an unknown quantity," Shepherd went on. "If he's worried, then so am I. That is, unless you can convince me otherwise."

Locke raised his head, his voice resolute. "Might I remind you both – Chief Calder, Foreign Secretary – that our operative's life still hangs in the balance. His real name and alias have been revealed whilst embedded in deep-cover surveillance, working for one of the city's most ruthless crime lords. Our primary concern is to extract him from that danger and transport him to safety."

"Yes. Mine too," Shepherd said, casting a meaningful glance at Calder. "So let's collaborate on this. Tell me more about this man. You seemed happy to let him fend for himself this morning, arguing that his extraction might compromise Sigma Unit. What's changed?"

Locke hesitated. It was a good question. One he didn't really have an answer for. It was true that he had initially resisted the idea of extraction, fearing the potential fallout for Sigma Unit. But that was him purely with his chief director hat on. There was still a heart beating beneath the heavy layers of protocol and procedure.

"Earlier today," he began, his tone measured, "our perception of the threat level was different. We believed Beckett's cover was still intact and that we might contain the leak. Even then I believed, given his exceptional skillset and adaptability, he could weather the storm and possibly even return to Control himself." He paused, his jaw tightening. "However, I am now in agreement with Templeton. If our enemies have seen the leak, which we have to assume they have, this revelation puts not only Beckett's life in jeopardy but also our entire operation and every asset connected to it. We're now dealing with a potential breach of national security, a complete compromise of our covert operations. Beckett's extraction is no longer a matter of choice but of necessity – a tactical manoeuvre to mitigate collateral damage and protect the integrity of our intelligence network."

"So get word to him," Shepherd said. "Tell him to get his arse back to Control immediately."

Locke nodded. "We're trying, sir."

"Good. Now give me something I can relay to the Prime Minister about this national bloody threat. Anything. Who he is. Where he grew up. What his favourite colour is. I don't care, but I need something."

Locke and Calder exchanged uneasy glances. Calder gave

him a reassuring nod. At least, that's what it looked like.

Locke drew in a deep breath. "Fine. But let me remind you this remains top secret, Foreign Secretary. Between the three of us and the Prime Minister. It goes nowhere else."

Shepherd's countenance shifted to one of seriousness. "Naturally."

"From what I can recall, Beckett was born in Chelmsford," Locke began, his voice tinged with uncertainty despite having scrutinised Beckett's entire file just minutes earlier. "His age is nebulous, but somewhere in the region of thirty-five or thirty-six. He comes from a military family. His father was Hugo Andres Beckett, a name you might recognise. He was a highly decorated and very well-respected general. Fought in the Falklands and then in the Gulf. Tragically, his plane was shot down over Afghanistan in the summer of 2002."

"It rings a bell," Shepherd said, though his eyes betrayed his ignorance.

"John was boarding at a prestigious private grammar school at the time. Boreham, I think," Locke went on. "Then in 2005, he enrolled at Oxford University to study Politics, Philosophy and Economics. Initially, he aspired to a career in finance, as that was what his father had wanted for him. However, once there, he chose to follow in his father Hugo's footsteps and joined the Training Corps as an officer cadet. Reports from the time describe him as highly intelligent and athletic yet somewhat solitary. By all accounts, his father's death rendered him insular and quiet."

"But clearly a brilliant man," Shepherd said. "I had no idea he was… well, that he was so well educated."

Locke smiled, casting a glance at Calder. He suspected what Shepherd meant to say was that he had no idea Beckett was someone like him – upper-middle class, Oxbridge-educated. Privileged. Not that Beckett, or Locke, saw it that way. Beckett and Shepherd were not the same.

He cleared his throat and pressed on. "Whilst at Oxford, he caught the eye of a visiting SIS officer, and after graduating, he tentatively signed to a recruitment branch of the secret service. The same year he became a lieutenant in the SAS, being deployed to Helmand where he was involved in Operation Eagle's Summit, and Operation Shahi Tandar the following year. In Afghanistan he earned a reputation as a fearless and formidable fighter. In 2010, he was pulled out of action and offered a position with Sigma Unit. Julia Sanderson, my predecessor, oversaw his initial interview and the enrolment process."

Shepherd gave a low whistle. "That's quite the résumé. So, when you say this chap can handle himself, you aren't exaggerating."

"Indeed, sir. Beckett is proficient in all aspects of intelligence operations and direct action – from agent handling, unarmed combat, surveillance and counter-surveillance, to advanced driving, infiltration and exfiltration techniques, as well as handling small arms, explosives and covert communications." He paused to catch his breath. "The list goes on. His impressive skills have been widely deployed both domestically and internationally. He typically works alone, but has significant experience of working with highly specialised units of the SAS, the SBS, and – as you're now aware – the CIA."

Shepherd nodded. "And his ongoing assignment involving this Rufus Delaney person – Delaney would be ready to kill Beckett if he found out he was a mole?"

"Unequivocally, Foreign Secretary," Locke replied. "We also believe Delaney now serves as steward for the London arm of an organisation known as The Consortium."

"The… who?" Shepherd looked from Locke to Calder and back again. "Why have I never heard of them?"

Locke coughed, attempting to clear the persistent lump in

his throat. "We have limited information on them at present, Foreign Secretary. They're an elusive organisation, using proxies like Delaney to carry out their underhanded operations across diverse sectors. Our current intel on them is patchy and unverified. What we do know is that for the past three years they've been gradually seizing control of the city's criminal underworld. However, we suspect their insidious influence extends far beyond that. High-rise developments, banking, and even law enforcement, both here and internationally. This is why I was hesitant to extract Beckett from his deep-cover assignment unless absolutely necessary. During his last check-in, he hinted that he was getting closer to uncovering crucial information on The Consortium."

Tristan Shepherd rubbed his chin, seemingly deep in thought. "I see." He was quiet for a long time, then he burst into action, striding towards the door and wagging his finger in the air as he went. "Excellent work, gentlemen. I've decided I'm going to lead on this case as much as possible. So the minute we have any new information on Beckett or his whereabouts – or these Consortium people – I want to know about it." At the door he stopped. "You must call me the minute you get any new developments, Chief Director Locke. Day or night. Understood? I want to be kept in the loop."

With that, he yanked open the door, and after bidding the men good evening, exited the room.

Calder ambled over and shut the door, his eyebrows arched and his cheeks bloated in an exaggerated sigh as he turned to face Locke. They were both visibly exhausted, and Calder's expression said all that Locke was feeling. With everything else at stake, they now had to navigate a rambunctious Foreign Secretary who seemed keen to interfere and potentially take the credit for any wins. It was a problem.

And right now, it was the last thing they needed.

13

Beckett's grip tightened on the wheel of the stolen Audi A8 as he sped down the M25 towards Sevenoaks. The car was old and hadn't been looked after. A cluster of colourful, tree-shaped air fresheners hanging from the rearview mirror did little to mask the stench of dirt and cigarettes. However, it was fast and had almost a full tank of petrol. Plus, now he knew Delaney was most definitely coming for him, driving his own vehicle was out of the question.

Leaning over, he switched on the radio, flicking through the channels in rapid succession as soon as he heard any kind of electronic beat booming out of the speakers. He couldn't find anything he wanted to listen to so he switched it off again, settling for the relentless purr of the engine instead. The dashboard clock read 22:29. He'd been driving for over half an hour and, by his reckoning, he had another hour to go before he reached Amber. A mixture of frustration and concern swelled within him as he bore down on the accelerator, the needle of the speedometer rising through the eighties to hover just shy of ninety.

There was no way Delaney could know about his niece, he told himself. But he also knew there were no absolutes in this life – failing to prepare for all eventualities could be the last mistake you ever made.

As he sped on, his mind churned with other questions.

Why had this happened now?

Who stood to benefit from such a data leak?

His knuckles paled on the steering wheel, the road ahead blurring into insignificance. The leak could have been the work of nihilistic hackers, the type who revelled in global chaos, yet something about that theory didn't ring true. It seemed too convenient, too orchestrated, to be the work of anarchists or mere activists.

A quick glance at his reflection in the rearview mirror revealed wide, luminous eyes; but rather than feeling alert and ready, he felt wired. An edgy restlessness pulsed within him. Though given the day's events, it wasn't surprising. That morning he'd been on the brink of a significant breakthrough, the situation with Murat Caliskan a necessary evil on his path to success. Now, just hours later, he found himself condemned once more to a life in the shadows. Shedding the alias of Patrick Hamilton wouldn't trouble him, but the problem ran deeper than that. John Beckett had to vanish, and his niece, Amber, along with him. At least for a time. Rufus Delaney would be ceaseless in his desire to execute the man who'd betrayed him and would exploit every resource to get to him. With Delaney's alliance with The Consortium and their potential ties to the police, it was only a matter of time before Amber's existence was revealed. They had to disappear.

The notion of taking Amber to S-Unit and asking them for assistance had crossed his mind, but there was something about the way Beaumont was acting earlier that troubled Beckett. He trusted his old friend without question, but Beaumont didn't call the shots and Beckett could predict how his precarious situation might be perceived by Sigma Unit and the SIS as a whole. To them he was unpredictable. A weapon, potentially, in the wrong hands – a ticking time bomb that could detonate any moment and wipe out everyone he'd ever come into contact with.

For the next twenty-four hours, at least, he could trust no one. His priority was to retrieve Amber and ensure her safety. Then he'd consider his situation more thoroughly. But a gut feeling told him he couldn't go back. That he was now a ghost.

Yet, what had really changed? he thought to himself. Most of his adult life had been spent as a shadow, not ever truly existing anywhere. John Beckett was someone who lived on the dark side of the street. He no longer knew how to be any other way.

As the Audi powered on, eating away at the miles, his thoughts turned to Amber. Despite not really knowing her, she was the last remaining member of his family, a living reminder of a time when he was more than just an asset to be used and discarded. The last time he saw her she was just nine, and her mother, Rebecca – his sister – was still alive. He remembered her as a good-natured, friendly child, full of joy. Whether she was still all those things, after losing both her parents at such an impressionable age, he wasn't sure.

He knew what it felt like to lose a parent. He didn't know teenagers.

Amber must be almost eighteen now. She had her whole life in front of her. So, no. He didn't know her at all.

But he would tear the world apart to keep her away from the kind of people and things he had been involved in.

As Beckett entered Sevenoaks, the world outside the car seemed to slow down. Stopping at the first set of traffic lights, he pulled his phone from his jacket, securing it in the plastic holder already attached to the windscreen with a suction cup. Opening up the maps application, he keyed in the postcode of the Fords' house. He was only ten minutes away. The time on the dashboard showed 23:10 – late in the day for an unsolicited visit, but he reckoned he had a good excuse.

Grove Road was long and curved around the side of a large golf course, its boundaries marked by dense foliage. There were only a handful of residences along the road, each one a lavish property set within its own grounds and with two cars parked in the driveway – invariably a high-end Range Rover and something sporty for the weekends.

The Fords' house was on the crook of a bend by a fork in the road. Beckett was glad to see the lights in the front room were on as he pulled up, choosing to park a little further down on the roadside, facing away from the property for ease of getaway. Also, he didn't want to worry the family unduly before he could explain himself.

He killed the engine and regarded the house. It was set back from the roadside, surrounded by a high wall, but the gate looked to be open. It was a grand place, similar in size and locale to where he'd grown up. It was the kind of home where one could escape the chaos of the world, and for a fleeting moment he envied the Fords' seemingly idyllic existence. Shaking that thought away immediately, he shifted his attention to the windows, looking for any sign of movement. All was still.

He climbed out of the car and eased the door shut, making sure not to let it slam. The sparse streetlights revealed a dark grey Mercedes parked further up the road near the woods. It struck Beckett as peculiar. Why not park in a friend's driveway if visiting? But the vehicle looked abandoned. He entered the property and approached the front door, his hand instinctively hovering over the Sig Sauer in his waistband as he scanned the shadows for potential threats. At the door, he knocked once and tested the handle. It was unlocked. Unusual even in such a safe area, especially this late at night.

"Hello?" Beckett called into the silent house. "Carol? Gareth? Are you there?"

No response.

Holding his pistol with both hands, he cautiously stepped into the hallway, leading with the weapon. The quiet within the house was unnerving. He stealthily moved towards the end of the hallway, finding himself in the kitchen.

Clear.

He retraced his steps silently, pivoting his weapon as he moved into the front room. There he was met with a grim sight. The bodies of Carol and Gareth Ford. There was no need to check their pulses. Carol was seated in the armchair facing the door, eyes open, a precise bullet hole between her brows. Gareth lay sprawled on the floor next to the fireplace, a flowery cushion beside him. Blood had pooled around his body, already saturating the thick cream carpet. Beckett's guess was he'd risen from his seat as the gunmen burst into the room and was taken down instantly. He'd tried, the poor bastard. Two innocent people – dead. Collateral damage in a game they'd never asked to play.

He swallowed the bile that rose in his throat and pressed on, senses on high alert. The house remained eerily still and his instincts told him there was no one else here. No one alive, at least. He moved from room to room, his gun trained on every shadow, but there was no sign of his niece.

Making his way upstairs, he moved at a measured pace despite the inner rage twisting at his abdominal muscles. He swept each of the four bedrooms in turn but they were all empty. No other bodies. No sign of a struggle. It was a small mercy, but he knew Delaney would want Amber alive – to use as leverage against him. He searched each room for clues, every passing moment weighing heavily on him.

How had Delaney discovered his connection to Amber so rapidly?

Beaumont had seen the contents of the leak and it hadn't mentioned his niece. *Think yourself lucky you don't have any family to worry about.* Those were his exact words. So it was safe to say she wasn't mentioned in the same document.

Beckett drew in a sharp breath.

The Consortium. It had to be.

And if they were already involved at this level, the situation was worse than ever.

14

Beckett glanced around Amber's room, trying to get an impression of the niece he no longer knew. She appeared to be well-read and artistic – like her mother. There were books and paintings on every available shelf and surface. An artist's easel stood in a corner, a fresh canvas showcasing her evident talent. Beckett had never been particularly artistic himself, that was Rebecca's forte, but he thought the painting was excellent. The colours and the texture. She was good.

He looked around for a photo of Amber. In his day, teenage girl's bedrooms would always have a noticeboard, overflowing with snapshots of themselves and their friends. But it was all online now. It was a shame, but Beckett didn't buy into the older generation's obsession with wilfully misunderstanding the youth. Times had changed, that was all, and you had to keep moving in this life. Adaptation was essential. Besides, there were bigger battles to set your sights on in the world. Much bigger.

As he turned, he felt a draught coming from somewhere. Turning towards the source, he drew back the curtain to discover the window was open. Wide open. Not the way you might have it if you wanted some fresh air – but as if someone had used it as an exit. He leaned his head out. The cool night air was invigorating, and as he looked down he saw the roof of an extension, low enough to jump onto. Peering out into the darkness, he noticed a flicker of light over in the woods. A torch. Possibly two torches.

He left Amber's room and bounded down the stairs, taking them three at a time. Heading straight for the kitchen, he yanked open each drawer in turn, finding a substantial kitchen knife on his third try. He grabbed it and held it aloft. The six-inch blade melded seamlessly into a steel handle, providing a reassuring weight. It was an all-purpose knife and more than suitable for his purpose.

Returning to the front room, he stepped over Gareth's lifeless body and spotted a silver-framed photograph on the hearth of a young girl. It had to be Amber. She looked just like Rebecca when she was that age. Smashing the glass off the corner of the mantlepiece, he pocketed the photo and made his way through to the adjoining dining area. A large bi-fold door stretched across the expanse of the back wall, and as he approached it he noticed it was slightly ajar. Pushing it wide open, he slipped out, running down to the bottom of the garden where he'd seen the lights.

Holding the knife's blade with his teeth, Beckett scaled the garden wall and dropped down into the dense woodland beyond. The scent of damp leaves and earthy soil filled his nostrils, but the trees and shrubs provided excellent cover and the ground was spongey with moss, perfect for stealth movement. The torchlights were more discernible now, their beams slicing through the darkness like twin lances. One was roughly a hundred meters ahead, while the other was deeper in the woods, about three hundred meters to his left.

Beckett moved like a shadow, his senses sharpened by the

urgency of the situation. The soft ground meant his footsteps were all but imperceptible as he pursued the first torchbearer. Each step was calculated, his body gliding smoothly between the trees, his eyes never leaving the moving light beam. He gritted his teeth. He had done this countless times before – stalking a target, closing in for the kill – but this time it was personal.

The moonlight filtering through the trees cast shifting silhouettes that merged with the darkness, but as he drew nearer, the outline of the man holding the torch became more distinct. Beckett observed his lumbering gait; completely unaware of the danger in his wake. He saw the weapon in the man's hand, a glint of metal in the moonlight, the attached silencer. The adrenaline coursing through Beckett's veins fuelled him on as he closed the distance, approaching the man from the rear. His grip on the knife tightened, the blade facing downward, an extension of his body, ready to strike with lethal precision. With every silent step he closed the gap.

One second. Two seconds.

On three he reached out and grabbed the man around the throat, pulling him backwards and disrupting his balance. At the same time, he drove the kitchen knife upward against the man's weight, straight into the kidney, inducing an immediate shock response. The man let out a gasp but nothing more. Taking advantage of his adversary's falling momentum, Beckett twisted away and sliced the blade across the man's throat with surgical precision, severing both the trachea and carotid arteries. The man slumped to the wet ground. Dead before he got there.

Beckett went still, listening into the darkness as his eyes darted up ahead. The second torch continued its erratic dance, the bearer seemingly unaware of his partner's fate.

Wasting no time, Beckett set off in pursuit, moving rapidly but with stealth. His path straightened as he drew closer, weaving around trees towards the remaining light. This guy was bigger in both bulk and height than the other one, but still no match for him. Beckett was six feet two and usually weighed in at around a hundred and ninety pounds. He'd been working out a lot lately, too, so it was almost pure muscle. More importantly, he had the element of surprise, along with over fifteen years of elite military experience in deadly close combat techniques. And he had a knife.

Staying low and in the shadows, he approached his prey. As he got closer, a tree branch snapped beneath his feet, but he ducked behind a thick tree trunk in time as the man whirled around.

"Johan?" he hissed into the darkness. "Is that you?"

Beckett held his breath, rotating the knife so its blade pointed upward. He waited. Eventually, the torch beam dipped as the man turned back the way he'd been facing. Stepping out from behind the tree, Beckett covered the space between them in two silent strides. Once in striking distance, he raised the knife and, leveraging the heavy base of the handle and his own body weight, struck with force at the man's stellate ganglion, a nerve cluster at the top of the pectoral muscle. Executed correctly, as it was now, this stun technique could silence and immobilise an opponent for a few seconds. That was all Beckett needed. He followed with a deadly thrust of the knife into the man's subclavian artery at the point where his neck met his clavicle bone. After such a strike, death was inevitable within five to ten seconds. Beckett lowered the man to the ground and peered around him.

No more torches. Snatching the one from the dead man's hand, Beckett held it aloft with his left hand, swaying it around in front of him.

"Amber," he whispered. "You're safe now. I'm here to rescue you."

Taking a few cautious steps, he turned slowly, the beam of light dancing on the dense woodland surrounding him.

"Amber Irving," he tried again, his voice louder this time. "Please don't be scared. My name is John Beckett. I work for the British Secret Service. I'm here to help you." He paused briefly before continuing. "I'm also your uncle. Rebecca's younger brother. It's Uncle John."

The term 'Uncle John' felt cloying and awkward in his mouth, but his efforts were rewarded a moment later when he heard a rustling sound over to his left. He followed the noise to an area that was heavy with tree cover, the sinewy branches twisting around each other to form an organic cage of leaves and wood.

"Amber. It's Uncle John."

He focused the light on a spot where the leaves parted just enough for a person to enter the woody confines beyond. There was more rustling and stirring from within the thicket and then a figure slowly emerged. A girl, or rather, a young woman. Her face was pale, her eyes wide and darkened with fear. Her bottom lip trembled as she looked up at him.

Summoning a smile, perhaps the hardest thing he'd done in the last few minutes, Beckett nodded. "Yes. It's me."

Amber was wearing an oversized white t-shirt that hung down to just above her knees. Red scratches from the vegetation crisscrossed over her arms and legs. There was a thick streak of mud across one cheek and her blonde hair, almost the same colour as his, was tangled and dishevelled from her panicked escape through the woods. But she'd done well. She was alive.

"You're really my uncle?" she asked. By the way she was looking at him, he could tell she recognised him – and that her adrenal system was no longer telling her to flee. He nodded again, before her eyes fell on the bloody kitchen knife in his right hand. He quickly hid it behind his back, but the return of fear in her eyes made it clear she'd seen it.

"The men who murdered Carol and Gareth are both dead," he told her. "I'm sorry you had to get caught up in this. They were going to use you to get to me. But you were brave. Clever, too."

Amber still hadn't blinked. "Yeah. I heard noises and then I saw one of them coming up the stairs so I climbed out of my window and made a run for it," she explained before looking away, tears welling in her eyes. Losing your parents and your surrogate family all within five years – it was a lot to take in for a young woman.

"You aren't safe here," Beckett told her. "Neither of us are. We need to leave."

"Where to?" Amber asked, her eyes darting nervously around the woods.

Before Beckett could answer, he felt his phone vibrating in his jacket pocket. He took it out. The caller ID showed a number he recognised. Giving Amber another reassuring nod, he flipped open the phone.

"Good evening, *John Beckett*," Rufus Delaney said, his rough East London drawl even more sinister under the moonlight. "What a bloody shame it's come to this."

15

Beckett raised a hand, signalling Amber to pause as he turned away and focused on Delaney's call. "It was always going to happen eventually," he said into the phone. "But whatever your plan is regarding my niece, you need to forget about it. Four of your men are dead. You don't want to lose any more."

Delaney went quiet. Beckett glanced back at Amber. She was still staring at him with her mouth open. Her resemblance to Rebecca was unnerving. But it also tightened his resolve.

"I mean it, Rufus. Leave Amber alone. I'm with her now. Your plan didn't work."

"Jesus Christ! After everything we've done together," Delaney snarled back. "I took you into my life. Into my family. You ate at my fucking table, mate. You played football with my boy."

"It's nothing personal," Beckett told him.

"Oh, it bleeding well is, son. Fuck me. Patrick Hamilton. I trusted you with my life. You were my top man. My friend. You killed for me. On more than one occasion. Do your superiors know that?"

Beckett didn't answer. He knew better than to jump into an aggressor's sphere of reference. Instead, he answered the question with another. "Why are you calling me?"

"I was hoping we could make a deal, but it sounds like my bargaining chips have not landed well for me. Bugger." He laughed humourlessly. "Still, I wanted to hear your voice. To hear for certain that you aren't Patrick Hamilton. My man. My friend."

Beckett did a full three-sixty turn, scanning the area for danger. He saw no more torches and heard no sound except for the static on the line and Amber's shaky breaths.

"Well... I'm not your friend. I'm not Patrick Hamilton. So what now?"

"Come in and see me."

Beckett held the phone away from his ear and looked down at the glowing green screen. He considered Delaney's request. For all of one second.

"And if I don't want to do that?" he said, returning the phone to his ear.

"Then I won't rest until you and your pretty little niece are in the ground. But you have my word, Patrick, *Beckett* – whatever your fucking name is – if you give yourself up, she won't be harmed. She's nothing to me, is she? She'll go free. She'll be safe."

Beckett's gaze fell upon his young niece. She was a mess, dirt-streaked and terrified, her eyes glassy. Yet beneath the facade of shock, he saw a glimmer of resilience. A spark of determination. She was a fighter, this one. But she'd had to be.

"I'm not going anywhere," he told Delaney, but his eyes were fixed on Amber. "She's already safe."

"You think you can protect her forever? From me? You do know who you've been working for these past two years, *mate*, don't you?"

"Do you know who was behind the leak?"

Delaney's laughter crackled over the line, louder this time. It sounded like genuine amusement. "Do you think I'd tell you if I did?"

Beckett knew it was a long shot, but he remained quiet, allowing Delaney time to continue.

"No. I don't know who was behind the leak," he said eventually. "All I know is you were on it and it's made me very upset. You've embarrassed me, mate. Made me look a fool in front of a lot of powerful people. I can't have that. You know that. You're going to have to pay for what you did."

Beckett's jaw clenched. "You didn't need to involve Amber. Or the Fords. They weren't a part of any of this." He watched her as he spoke. He saw her lips tighten into a determined line, her gaze never leaving his.

There was another pause, and then Delaney's voice came back, laced with menace. "It is what it is. You know what you have to do. You know what'll happen if you don't. You have twenty-four hours, *John Beckett*. Then I won't be asking so politely."

Then the line went dead.

16

Beaumont was in his office, making a cup of strong black coffee from the battered old kettle he kept in the corner of the room, when he heard a knock. Leaving what he was doing, he crossed to the door rather than call out an invitation to enter. Opening it, he found Ruth Armitage loitering meekly in the doorway. She couldn't have looked more suspicious if she'd tried.

"Armitage, I didn't know if you were still here," he said, stepping aside and gesturing for her to come in. "You do realise it's almost midnight? You've been here as long as I have."

"Yes, sir," she replied, her voice low and anxious. "I'm going to go home shortly for some rest, but I wanted to see you before I did."

She was about to continue but Beaumont held a finger up to her and she fell silent. Stepping around the side of her, he shut the door with a decisive thud.

"Do you want a coffee?" he asked, as the kettle clicked off and steam filled the corner of the room.

"Not for me. Thank you."

"Yes," he agreed, considering his own caffeine

consumption. "I should probably leave it. I've had far too many today. Please, sit." He beckoned her over to his desk with a flick of his hand. She followed him and he pulled a chair out for her before settling into his seat opposite. "What brings you here this late?" he asked, observing her closely.

Armitage's eyes darted between her hands and the ceiling as if seeking answers from both. Then, finally, they rested on him. "I didn't know what to do for the best, sir. I know you asked me to keep this between the two of us, but I was unsure if it was the right thing to do. Director Locke was very clear – any new intel is to be reported directly to him."

Beaumont laced his fingers together, resting them on the desk as he leaned forward, his face dropping into a serious expression. "But you haven't been to Director Locke?"

"No. Not yet."

Beaumont leaned back. It was a tricky play. He'd worked alongside Robert Locke for many years and he trusted the man. Hell, he even enjoyed the man's company on those rare occasions they weren't both up to their elbows in grave national security crises. But Locke was a man who played everything with a straight bat. He was a stickler for procedure and had the added pressure of Xander Templeton and the Foreign Office breathing down his neck. Not that Beaumont thought Locke would do anything to jeopardise Beckett's safety, but he had a bad feeling about Templeton. He'd never taken to the fellow.

"You've made a discovery?" he asked Armitage.

"Possibly," she said. "I mean, I think so. Yes."

"Good. You did the right thing coming to me first. Despite Director Locke's instructions, he can't be everywhere all at once. Currently he's tied up at MI6, so I'll relay your findings to him when he's available. It might sound like we're circumventing protocol, but it's just practicality." It was a paltry explanation, but the best he could do off the top of his head and it seemed to placate the young analyst, at least for now.

"Okay," she said, nodding eagerly as if to convince herself. "The thing is, sir, I've been doing some deep digging into the metadata pertaining to the leak and I've reason to believe the origin is much closer than we initially assumed."

"How close?"

"I've not been able to pinpoint the exact location yet, but definitely within Europe. Maybe even the UK." She gestured at his open laptop. "Can I show you?"

Beaumont pushed back from the desk, the casters on his old chair squeaking as he did. "Please, be my guest," he told her, angling the laptop in her direction as she shuffled her chair around to sit in front of it.

She removed what looked like a fashion bracelet from her wrist, made from intertwined threads of orange and blue coloured string. Beaumont would have mistaken it simply for some trendy emblem of modern-day activism. But as he watched, Armitage snapped open the bracelet's plastic clasp to reveal a USB plug.

"Ingenious," he muttered under his breath, as she inserted the device into the side of his laptop and focused on the screen.

After a flurry of keystrokes, she leaned back and swivelled the monitor around so they could both see the screen. It displayed a map of the world, with flashing dots in various locations indicating responsive IPS and VPN networks. A search window on the left-hand side of the screen showed a list of associated links for the last 30 days; and on the right, a table labelled 'Critical', 'Warning', 'Routine' and 'IP Ranges' charted a series of database server attacks.

"What am I looking at in particular?" Beaumont asked.

"Here," Armitage said, typing an IP address into the right-hand table and hitting enter. "Whoever leaked the document was using an elaborate hop sequence to throw us off the scent.

But after running a bespoke traceroute program, I was able to get a more accurate reading. It's not China. It's definitely not Russia. Look."

She hit enter again and Beaumont's eyes widened, taking in the large red circle that now engulfed the whole of the UK and most of mainland Europe, going down as far as central Spain and spanning across to Germany's border with Czechia.

"The leak came from somewhere in that circle?" he whispered.

Armitage nodded, her eyes not leaving the screen. "Yes, sir. I'm certain of it."

He sat back and folded his arms, mulling over the implications of this information. "So it could have originated from somewhere inside the UK?"

"There's every possibility, sir," Armitage said. "But why? What would anyone here stand to gain by exposing our operatives?"

A heavy silence hovered between them. Beaumont had no immediate answers to these questions, but he needed to find them. And fast. Every possibility, no matter how unfeasible or disconcerting, demanded scrutiny.

He adjusted his position, rocking his weight forward and leaning closer to the young analyst. "This is great work, Armitage. Your diligence is commendable and you were right to bring this to my attention." He paused, his gaze wandering towards the encrypted world on the monitor, a world fraught with flashing lights and virtual threats. "But for now, this information must remain between the two of us. Don't mention anything to Director Locke. Not yet. Let me discuss your findings with him initially and I'll include you in any subsequent meetings. Clear?"

Armitage nodded. "Yes, sir."

"Good. We're still in a high-risk, high-pressure situation. If there's even a remote possibility that someone within S-Unit or

SIS is compromised, we must exercise extreme caution. With Officer Beckett still missing in action, our operational security measures need to be robust. At this stage, we can't afford to take any risks." As he spoke, he rotated the laptop around so it was facing him and pulled the brightly coloured USB bracelet from out of the side. For a moment, he considered holding onto it, but handed it back to Armitage. She'd already proven herself more than trustworthy and a valuable asset. "Here. Keep this safe. Don't share it with anyone else."

"Absolutely, sir," she replied, taking the bracelet from him and snapping it back onto her wrist. "Is there anything else for now?"

Beaumont exhaled, sinking back into his chair. "No. You go home, Armitage. Get some well-deserved rest. Once you're back in tomorrow, come and find me and we'll take it from there, see where we're at. But I'll want you to keep digging. See how close you can get. We need to find whoever did this so we can ensure it doesn't happen again." Satisfied he'd said all he could for now, he nodded at the door. "Can you see yourself out?"

"Yes, sir," she said, rising from her seat. "Thank you, sir."

Beaumont watched as she hurried for the door and exited the room. Once alone, he let out a long sigh that seemed to drain him of all his strength. He looked over at the kettle. Maybe he would have that coffee after all. It was going to be a long night.

17

Beckett was no stranger to the world's darker corners, but the damp, cold woods of Sevenoaks suddenly felt alien to him. He placed his phone in his pocket and gave Amber what he hoped was a reassuring smile. She stood a few paces away from him, trembling. Her eyes, wide as saucers, were filled with fear, shock, and a glimmer of bewilderment. Over the years, Beckett had learned to push any feelings of regret or remorse aside – they weren't helpful in the world he inhabited – yet seeing Amber now, a sensation that felt a lot like guilt burned in his chest. He was a soldier, conditioned to cope with terror. She was a seventeen-year-old, thrust into a world she was wholly unprepared for. All because of him.

"Amber," he said, trying to sound soothing. "We need to go back to the house. You need to get changed and pack some things. We need to leave."

She stared back, her lip trembling.

He realised he was still holding the knife, wet with the blood of the men who'd murdered her new family. He carefully laid it on the ground and approached her, grasping her upper arms and bending down to make eye contact.

"Amber, listen, I know this is a lot to take in. I know you're scared and confused and don't know what to think, but I need you to do this for me. I'm your uncle and I'm on your side. But I'm also an officer of the British Secret Service and I've been compromised. My cover's been blown. Unfortunately, that's put you in direct danger also. I'm very sorry about that. I thought I'd put enough distance between us both physically and digitally that it wouldn't happen, but obviously it wasn't enough. Now I need you to do as I say. Do you understand? It's the only way I can assure your safety."

She sniffled. "Where will we go?"

"First, back to the house," he said, releasing her arms and straightening up. He positioned himself beside her, guiding her forward with a gentle hand on her back. "Let's move."

He guided her through the woods towards the roadside, carefully avoiding the corpses of the men he'd killed minutes earlier. From there, they hurried back to the Fords' house, Beckett scoping out the area as they went, paying close attention to the connecting roads. But there was no one in sight, not even a passing car.

Once they were inside, Beckett shut and locked the front door behind them.

"Get dressed and pack a bag. Essentials only," he instructed, leaving Amber at the bottom of the stairwell and making his way into the kitchen. In the doorway he paused, waiting until he heard the sound of footsteps on the stairs before walking over to the sink and twisting on the hot tap. He scrubbed the blood and dirt from his hands with soap, then splashed water on his face.

He dried off using a tea towel and then tossed it onto the kitchen table as he surveyed the room. He was leaving DNA and his prints all over the house, but it didn't matter. The local police would probably find the two bodies tomorrow or the day after and his prints would be on the handle of the knife they'd find nearby. They'd search their databases and draw a blank – his details didn't exist anywhere except on one database, only accessible by those with the highest security clearance in the country. However, once his biometric data was entered into the Kent Police's database, a sophisticated algorithm would likely trigger an alert at Sigma Unit. But that wasn't a problem either. He'd be long gone by then and he wanted Beaumont at least to be aware of the unfolding situation. This way was safer than contacting him firsthand.

He gravitated towards the kettle, finding it already half full of water, and switched it on. Three metal storage containers stood on the counter beside it, labelled, 'TEA', 'COFFEE' and 'SUGAR'. Sliding the coffee canister towards him, he removed the lid, the harsh, dusty aroma of instant coffee wafting out. He wasn't a fan of instant, but he was unsure when he'd next be able to sleep and he needed the caffeine.

Opening cupboards, he found the coffee mugs in the third unit along. Selecting a red one that had a small chip on the rim, he placed it next to the kettle. There was a porcelain spoon-shaped dish resting beside the wall with a tea-stained teaspoon lying on top, which he reached for. He scooped two spoons of coffee into the mug and poured in the boiling water, followed by some cold water from the tap to temper it.

Taking a sip of the hot, bitter coffee, he leaned against the countertop. The cool granite seeped through his clothes as he let the steam and heat of the drink revive him. He was already thinking ahead, calculating the next move.

"Amber," he called up the stairs. "Do you have a passport?"

"Shit! No! I don't!" she called back. Her voice was shaky, like she was barely holding it together.

Beckett thought some more.

"Do you have an official ID of any kind – with a photo?" he replied. "A driving licence, for instance?"

"I've only just turned seventeen," she yelled, her voice steadier now. She'd come to the top of the stairs, so didn't have to shout so loud. "Gareth was going to teach me but… I've got a provisional licence. It arrived a few days ago."

Beckett took a gulp of coffee. That could work. Pushing off the counter, he walked to the doorway. "Go get it," he said. "Bring it with you and hurry up."

Amber did as she was told, moving now with an efficiency that belied the fact her world had just been flipped upside down. Beckett leaned against the kitchen doorframe and finished his coffee in two more gulps. Amber having a photographic driving licence meant they had options, but it would take time. They would need to lie low for a few days. Somewhere safe, where Delaney couldn't find them. It was a tense situation but there was nothing else he could do.

"Ready!"

He looked up to see Amber standing in the hallway at the bottom of the stairs. Her transformation was striking. In the woods, just twenty minutes earlier, she'd seemed like a vulnerable little girl. Now a young woman stood in front of him, scared but strong. Her eyes still possessed a certain glassiness that could be attributed to trauma or fear, but the determined set of her jaw suggested she was coping better than he had dared hope. She had cleaned the dirt from her face and arms and pulled her hair back into a ponytail. She even looked to have applied a little mascara around her eyes.

He glanced at the rucksack at her feet. "What did you pack?"

"Clothes, mainly. Some books. My laptop and phone."

He shook his head. "Sorry, you can't bring those. They can be traced."

"What? Are you serious?" She wrinkled her nose. "How can I keep in touch with my friends?"

"You can't. Not right now. When we get to wherever we're going and you're safe, we'll reassess. I know it's hard but that's how it has to be."

Amber started to protest, but a stern look silenced her. Reluctantly, she unzipped the rucksack and removed the electronic items, placing them on the sideboard at the bottom of the stairs.

"You'll need a proper coat," he told her, assessing her attire.

"Won't this do?" she asked, tugging at her grey hooded sweatshirt.

"No. Something warmer."

Amber nodded and retrieved a green wax jacket from a cupboard next to the front door. "This?"

He nodded his approval and she put it on, sliding out the hood of her sweatshirt and draping it down the back of the jacket. She was also wearing black jeans and brown hiking boots. Good choices, Beckett thought. She'd grasped the circumstances and dressed accordingly. It was another reassuring sign they might get through this.

"Where are we going?" she asked.

"You'll see," Beckett replied, setting his mug on the counter and walking towards her. "Time to go."

As he neared, Amber hesitated, looking around the house as if she were trying to memorise every detail.

"Do you think they suffered?" she whispered.

Beckett could sense her fear and uncertainty but didn't have time to comfort her. They needed to leave this house and disappear before any more of Delaney's men showed up.

"No, they didn't. They're at peace now."

"Can I just go and—"

"No, Amber. It's not advisable."

He took her hand, and she allowed him to lead her outside.

Closing the door behind them, Beckett guided Amber over to the car. Neither of them spoke as they settled in their seats and he started the engine. When they drove away, Amber turned and looked back at the house, possibly mourning the life she was leaving behind. Still, Beckett was glad to see she'd found some semblance of composure. Once the house was out of sight, she shifted around and settled in her seat, her gaze fixed on the passing trees.

"Are you going to tell me what's going on?" she asked, after they'd been driving for a while.

Beckett didn't respond, his eyes focused on the dark road ahead.

She persisted. "Don't you think I deserve an explanation? Gareth and Carol are dead. I was about to be as well if you hadn't shown up. What's going on?"

"Those men wouldn't have killed you," he said. "They need you to get to me."

"Oh, wonderful. Should I be grateful?"

Beckett gripped the steering wheel.

"Why are these people after you?" Amber asked.

"As I said, I work for a branch of the British Secret Service. I've been undercover for two years, but this morning my details were leaked online and now the head of the crime syndicate I'd infiltrated wants me dead. He wants to use you as bait to get to me. So that's why I'm here. That's why we have to get you far away. Somewhere safe."

He hoped that would be enough, but Amber continued to stare at him. "And...?" she said, drawing out the vowel sound. "Where have you been for the last ten years or however long it's been? Why did you never contact me? After Mum and Dad died, I had no one. I needed you."

Beckett chewed on his lip. "I couldn't have been there. I was working."

"You were working? Wow."

She scoffed loudly and turned back to the window, shaking her head in disbelief. It was her way of dealing with it, he told himself.

"I'm sorry," he mumbled.

"Yeah, me too. So what am I supposed to call you? Uncle John? Just Uncle?"

Beckett would do just fine, he thought, but he kept quiet.

"Why aren't you talking to me?" Amber asked.

Beckett grunted. He wasn't one for lengthy conversations, especially during high-pressure situations. He expressed himself in actions, in decisions, in the way he could read a room or take down an enemy.

"Look," he started, his voice gruff. "I'm not… good at this. I'm not used to interacting with… teenagers."

Amber snorted. "That's the understatement of the century. And I'm not a teenager. Not really. I'm almost eighteen."

"You've only just turned seventeen. You said it yourself."

"Oh, you were listening? But no birthday card, though. Ever."

He shot her a glance. She was looking at him with a strange expression on her face. Despite her annoyance, there was a hint of amusement in her eyes. It was a rare moment of levity in a world turned upside down, and Beckett found himself smiling despite himself.

They drove on in silence, the car's engine humming a steady rhythm as Beckett ran through plans and backup plans in his mind. His soldier instincts were in full swing, but there was also a nagging feeling at the back of his mind, a sense of responsibility for the young girl sitting beside him. He was her only hope. Her only family.

"Are you going to tell me where we're going?" Amber asked. "Do you even know?"

Beckett glanced at her, then back at the road. He exhaled slowly, the tension in his shoulders easing a fraction.

"Don't worry," he told her. "I've got a place in mind. We'll be safe there."

18

Locke was keeping it together. But with minimal sleep, Sigma Unit's reputation and the life of one of his top operatives hanging in the balance, it wasn't easy. Whilst he was used to the chronic stress that came with leading an elite team, the current situation demanded all his tactical dexterity and diplomatic acumen, as much as any high-stakes military operation ever had.

As he exited his office, his normally confident stride was more of a defeated trudge, his footsteps echoing off the cracked, yellowing walls. A decorated soldier – having received the Distinguished Service Order as acting commander of 22 SAS in Afghanistan – his posture generally reflected his solid military background. This evening, however, his shoulders sagged with the weight of responsibility. A relentless headache persisted no matter how many painkillers he consumed.

As he approached Beaumont's office, he saw the light was off and a rush of frustration tinged with anger blossomed in his chest. Even though it was past midnight, he expected his chief analyst to still be onsite. He began to curse him under his breath but was interrupted by a tonal beeping sound – the room's alarm setting itself for the night. That meant Beaumont must have left seconds earlier.

Locke hurried down to the end of the corridor, and as he rounded the next corner, he found Beaumont standing on the landing waiting for the lift. He turned when Locke approached.

"Robert, there you are," he said. "I'm getting off home for a few hours. I need a change of clothes and a shave at the very least. Did you want to see me?"

Locke got up to him before he replied. "I wonder if we can have a quick chat."

Beaumont glanced around. "Here?"

"Is anyone next door?"

"A couple of my techies. Not many. They can't hear through here."

Locke surveyed the area, tucking in his shirt as he did so. "Fine. It shouldn't take long."

Beaumont squared his shoulders, his brow furrowed as he took in Locke's dishevelled appearance. "What is it?"

"I wanted to know, between you and me, what's your take on the Beckett situation?"

Beaumont hesitated, his eyes flickering with an unreadable emotion. "You mean with Delaney or…..?"

"Everything."

Beaumont clicked his teeth. "It's… complicated. As you know, when we first became aware of the leak, I was all for locating Beckett and bringing him in as soon as possible. But now, I'm not so sure."

"I see." Locke had so much more he wanted to say but he stopped himself. He needed Beaumont to elaborate, to explain his position further. He held his gaze. The unspoken tension in the air was palpable.

"We should assume Beckett is now aware of the leak," Beaumont continued. "If that's the case he'll have gone underground. He's more than capable of evading capture and staying hidden. If so, locating him will be even harder and will consume significant resources and time."

Locke rubbed his upper lip. "Is that what you really think?"

"How do you mean?"

"Well, you know Xander Templeton and the Foreign Office are now breathing down our necks to bring Beckett in? At any cost. Templeton believes him to be a threat to both our nations' security."

Beaumont maintained eye contact, not giving anything away. "Is that what you think, too?"

"I don't know." Locke leaned back as if seeking answers in the polystyrene ceiling tiles above. They had none to offer him. "From Templeton's perspective, Beckett is a liability, an unpredictable element that could jeopardise multiple joint operations. But, he's one of us. He's our operative. And I'll be damned if I'm going to let Templeton and Shepherd dictate our actions."

"That's the spirit."

Locke sighed. "Are you making any progress sourcing the leak?"

"We're working on it." Beaumont shuffled his feet as the elevator signalled its arrival. It was clear he wanted to leave, but Locke wasn't finished yet.

"You know Beckett better than anyone," he said. "In your opinion, is there anything we should be concerned about? Could he turn? Could he roll on us?"

Beaumont shook his head. "Never, sir. Beckett's loyalty is unwavering. We have to ensure Templeton understands that. The last thing we want is the CIA getting antsy and taking matters into their own hands—"

"That won't happen," Locke cut in, his voice resolute. "I won't let it."

"Well... that's good to hear," Beaumont replied. Behind

him, the elevator doors slid closed and he squared his stance. "But I also wonder if we're focusing our attention in the wrong direction. Do we currently have eyes on Delaney?"

"We're monitoring his residence," Locke said. "There's been no sign of him. Not surprising, really. We know he never gets his hands dirty. But he's got men all over the city and if he knows the truth about Beckett – and we should assume he does – then our man is in serious danger. No matter how capable he is of handling himself."

"One other thing I realised," Beaumont said, glancing over Locke's shoulder. "If Delaney is now aware of S-Unit's existence, he could create additional issues for us."

"Shit." Locke clenched his teeth. "What a fucking mess."

"You said it."

A tense silence fell. Locke knew he had to tread carefully, to balance the needs of his country with the life of a man who had given everything for it. His thoughts drifted to Grace, waiting at home, the seventeen missed calls and countless texts on his personal line signalling the impending uncomfortable conversation. His poor wife had been cooped up in the house all day with Poppy. Her first child. His third. He thought of all the promises he'd made to himself when they got married – that this time around things would be different, that he wouldn't let work take precedence over his home life, that he'd be a better husband and father.

"Robert? Are you all right?"

Beaumont's question pulled him back to the present. Locke blinked to refocus himself. "Yes. Fine. Listen, if Beckett reaches out to you, let me know immediately. Regardless of our concerns, we need to bring him in."

"Yes, sir." Beaumont's voice was steady but his eyes betrayed a flicker of doubt.

Locke stared back, searching for more in Beaumont's gaze – a glimpse of hesitation, a touch of fear, a hint that Beaumont knew more than he was letting on. Had he already heard from Beckett? Was he withholding critical information?

"Go home, Beaumont," he said. "Get some rest. We'll regroup in the morning."

Beaumont nodded, but as he turned to summon the elevator, he paused. "Sir, I have faith in Beckett, just as I have faith in you. S-Unit will get through this."

Locke managed a tight smile, but it only masked his growing concerns. He watched as Beaumont pressed the call button and waited while the elevator doors pinged open. As he stepped inside, he turned back and their eyes met. He offered a reassuring nod before the doors slid closed, leaving Locke alone on the landing with nothing but the crushing weight of his decisions for company.

He waited for a second more, then he trudged back to his office to call Xander Templeton.

19

Rufus Delaney stood in the seldom-used front room of his opulent London home, trying to make sense of what was happening. The expansive floor-to-ceiling windows framed a breathtaking view of London's familiar skyline, but the spires and towers of Westminster, bathed in a silvery glow, only served as a stark contrast to the darkness that brewed within him.

He leaned forward, pressing his brow against the window, the cold glass grounding him momentarily. He felt as if he was the centre of a spiralling maelstrom of hate and confusion. Although he had battled mental demons in his youth, he had always managed to claw his way out of despair by focusing on external accomplishments or goals. He'd focus on the next job, the next rung on the ladder, the next person he had to destroy on his way to the top. Tonight, however, he felt trapped and unable to climb anywhere. There was no escape from the chaos within. It might have been because now he was the top man, there was nowhere left to climb. But if that was the case, where did it leave him?

People often spoke of the walls closing in on them during

times of extreme stress, but he never understood the visceral reality of that concept until now. Except it wasn't just the walls. It felt as if the entire world was tightening around him, threatening to suffocate him. He was drowning in a sea of turbulent fury, only some of it directed outwards. Burning indignation coursed through his veins, fuelled by the knowledge that someone he'd trusted had betrayed him and eluded capture not once, but twice.

The bastard had killed four of his men. Fucking amateurs. He was paying these people a lot of money; how could they not carry out a simple task?

He glared at the phone clenched tightly in his fist, the facial recognition software unlocking the screen to reveal the last thing he'd looked at – John Beckett's file. One of his tech experts had got hold of a heavily redacted copy and forwarded it to him twenty minutes earlier. It appeared the man he'd known as his friend, Patrick Hamilton, wasn't just a traitor but a formidable adversary. A highly commended SAS soldier and Special Forces officer. It was grim reading, but no man was invincible. Beckett had to be eliminated. And soon.

Delaney stepped away from the window as a fresh wave of anxiety hit him. Beckett wouldn't be so foolhardy to attack him at home, but it was better to be safe than sorry. That was what his old man used to say and the old dog lived until he was ninety-three. Not bad going for an East End thug who smoked filterless Woodbines, drank six pints of Guinness a day and had once worked as a fixer for the infamous Kray twins. Rufus always maintained he was from good stock. That he'd live to a ripe old age if circumstances allowed. But that meant nothing if someone was gunning for you.

He walked across the room, taking in his surroundings as he did. Normally when he took stock of his immediate accomplishments – his house, his furniture, his top-of-the-range kitchen and sound system – he was filled with a sense of pride and achievement. But tonight these symbols of his hard-won victories only served as reminders of the fragile empire he had built. The plush carpet underfoot, the priceless art on the walls, the bespoke furniture, it all seemed utterly meaningless as the realisation he could lose everything hit him like a punch to the guts.

Because it wasn't just Beckett he had to worry about.

"Rufus? Where are you?" Miranda's voice interrupted his thoughts. He opened the door to find her standing in the hallway. "Oh, you're in there. Well… we're ready."

There was no love or even affection in her eyes when she spoke, but why would there be? Rufus had assured her time and again that his business would never encroach on her or the children's safety. And now here he was sending them fleeing in the night from their home. He looked down at his children. At Rufus Junior and Sofia clinging to their mother's legs. Their innocent faces were drawn with sleepiness and maybe fear as well. A lot had been said in the last few hours and kids were perceptive. It was naive to think they didn't pick up on things.

Rufus walked over to his wife and placed a hand on her shoulder. "It's only for a week or two," he told her. "Just until everything blows over. Which it will. I promise."

He'd had Eddie book the three of them on the next flight to the south of France. Their plane departed in two hours. One of his men would meet them at Marseille airport and drive them to his villa in Le Rouret, Côte d'Azur. It was a nice place, near the sea and with fields all around. He'd also had Eddie call in a favour with a firm he knew over there to provide twenty-four-hour security. His family would be safe there. So would he when he joined them. But he had work to do first.

"What's going on, Rufus?" Miranda asked. "I know what you've told me about Patrick, but there's more, isn't there? Something you're not telling me."

Delaney pulled her to him and kissed her on the top of her

head. "Miranda, don't be daft. You know I wouldn't keep anything from you, my sweet. This is just a precautionary measure. I'm sure everything will be fine. And you love it at the villa. You'll all have lots of fun, won't you, kids?"

He leaned down to ruffle his son's hair, but the children clung tighter to their mother, their eyes full of suspicion. Delaney knelt and pulled each one to him in turn and kissed them on their cheeks. "You'll all be fine. I promise. And I'll be with you before you know it. Now, you need to leave. You'll miss your flight."

He stood and clocked Eddie, standing in the dining room on the other side of the hallway. As Miranda helped the kids with their coats, he gestured for the big man to join him at the front door.

"I want you to take them to Heathrow and park up in the long stay car park," he told him, lowering his voice so Miranda couldn't hear. "Stay with them until the very last moment. Accompany them as far into the airport as possible and then wait until you see the plane take off. I want you to confirm they're safely in the air. Then return here."

Eddie nodded. "Yes, boss. Understood. Don't you worry about a thing."

"Good man." Delaney slapped him on the shoulder and put on a wide grin as his family joined him at the front door. As Eddie turned to unlock the door, Delaney caught Miranda's eye, mouthing, "Don't worry." And then, "I love you."

All he got in return was a roll of the eyes, but he understood. She was scared and angry and probably annoyed that her life had been unceremoniously thrown into disarray. For a woman who didn't work and didn't seem to do anything but drink gin and have massages, Miranda got awfully irate if her routine was changed in any way.

"I'll see you all soon," he called after them as Eddie helped them into the waiting car. He stood at the door and waved until Eddie had started the engine, then glanced up and down the road and closed the door.

Once back in the house, the hallway seemed far too quiet. But with his family's safety secured, a cold, hard determination now settled over him. He walked into the dining room and through into the open-plan kitchen where two more of his men, Harris and Ahmet, were waiting in silence, their faces grim with anticipation.

"We need to find Beckett," he told them. "Tonight. I want every man and every resource we have at our disposal working on this. Even if he is as good as they say he is, he's not fucking Batman. I want him brought to me – alive. Understood? I don't care what you have to do, what favours you have to call in. I need Beckett found."

Harris and Ahmet bowed their heads in unison. "Yes, boss."

"Good men. Now go. I want at least one of you to report back every hour on the hour. Keep me updated. We need to get on top of this. That man has pissed me off royally and he needs to pay for what he's done."

The two men exchanged nervous glances before nodding in agreement. "We'll find him, no matter what it takes," Ahmet replied.

Delaney dismissed them with a wave of his hand and they disappeared into the shadows of the house, their footsteps fading down the hallway. Alone once more, he realised his heart was beating at a rapid rate. It felt as though he was on some kind of strong stimulant, but he'd taken nothing. Just full of adrenaline and rage.

And perhaps anticipation, too.

His reputation, and more importantly his survival, depended on him finding Beckett and making an example of him. This man, this traitor, had made him look weak and it couldn't have happened at a worse time. Delaney was currently standing on the edge of greatness. Acting as The Consortium's steward in London was set to propel him to bigger and better things, but that would all be in ruins if he couldn't look after things in his own backyard. He had to regain his status. He had to show The Consortium – and the world – he wasn't a man to be messed with.

Making his way upstairs, he mentally prepared himself for the task ahead. Once in his study, he shut the door behind him and walked over to his desk. From a hidden drawer under the desktop, he retrieved a small burner phone and, with a steadying breath, flipped it open and called the only number he had saved on this particular device. A direct line to The Consortium.

Because the time had come. With Beckett still in the wind, he needed to inform them of the situation. Their potential reaction was daunting, but the alternative – staying silent and allowing the situation to spiral further out of control – was worse. The Consortium would not react kindly to the news that he'd let him get away not once, but twice. But with the right spin, by employing his famous cockney charm, he might ride this out. If he took out Beckett in the next twelve hours, he could regain his footing. Time was against him, but the game wasn't over.

He held his nerve as the ringtone chirped ominously in his ear. Finally, the phone was answered and a deep voice echoed down the speaker. "Mr Delaney, what can we do for you at this time of night?"

He inhaled deeply. "We need to talk," he replied. "We might have a slight problem."

20

Sitting at the bar of the Star Hilton on Albert Embankment, Frank Calder was nursing his second double scotch. It had been a gruelling day and rather than drive back to Cambridge tonight, he'd decided to get a room in the city. It was a familiar midweek routine for him and Angie understood the need. She was a good woman and had stood beside him his entire career. She couldn't have been prouder when he moved from his role as director general for political affairs at the Foreign and Commonwealth Office to become chief of the Secret Intelligence Service six years ago. But there was a limit to how much he could push his wife's loyalty. After his stupid indiscretion last year, he was aware of how crucial it was to avoid temptation.

He'd finish this drink, then retire to his room and call her. Though it was well past midnight, a message left would calm her worries and assert his solitude. Even if his call woke her, he was sure she'd prefer that to a morning filled with doubts. Plus, it was going to be another long demanding day tomorrow. He needed rest.

He was preparing to down the last of his scotch when he

became conscious of a large presence beside him. Assuming it was another hotel guest, he turned casually, ready to extend an acknowledging nod and a smile. However, his cordial expression faded as Xander Templeton's commanding features bore down on him.

"Oh. It's you."

"It's me," Templeton replied, speaking from the side of his mouth. "And it's you. Who'd have thought it."

The burly American turned away and squinted at the rows of liquor bottles displayed on an illuminated plinth at the back of the bar.

"Are you staying here also?" Calder asked.

"Nah," Templeton drawled, his eyes still scanning the bottles. "I've got an apartment over in Kensington. I came to see you."

Calder nodded, already suspecting as much. He hadn't noticed anyone tailing him on the walk over here and normally he kept a keen eye on his surroundings. He took a moment, composed himself, then adjusted his position on the stool so he could take in his new acquaintance without craning his neck.

"What can I do for you, Mr Templeton?"

Templeton leaned back as the young woman behind the bar came over. "I'll have a club soda," he told her, then frowned. "Umm… soda water?"

The woman nodded and hurried away to fetch his drink.

"Nothing stronger?" Calder enquired.

Templeton fixed him with a hard stare. "I don't drink. Not when I'm working."

Well, that told him. Calder put down his glass of scotch. "We have to switch off now and again, though, don't you think? Downtime is vital in this job. It can drive you mad otherwise."

Templeton emitted a low growl. "The enemy never sleeps, Mr Calder."

"So why are you here, Mr Templeton? I assume it isn't to give me advice on how I conduct myself."

"No. It's not." An uneasy silence fell as the barmaid returned with a small bottle of soda water and a heavy-bottomed glass containing ice and a slice of lemon. Templeton thanked the woman before scooping out the slice of lemon with his huge fingers and placing it in one of the black square napkins stacked on the countertop.

Calder watched as he slowly poured out his soda water, letting it gush over the cubes of ice, the sudden temperature shift causing them to crack and splinter. Was this some sort of act, he wondered; a power play from Templeton?

Still staring forward, the brusque CIA section chief took a sip and smacked his lips. "Tell me what you know about this John Beckett guy," he said.

Calder's throat tightened. "Have you spoken to Locke? He's Beckett's commanding officer and—"

"Yeah, I spoke with Locke twenty minutes ago," Templeton interrupted. "It was like getting blood from a stone. He gave me all the official stuff, of course, stuff I already know. But I sensed he was reluctant to give me anything else. I don't know, Calder. I'm sure Locke is a good man, but I feel like he's got too much skin in this game. You know what I mean?"

"I don't know about that," Calder replied. "He's committed to his men and wants to bring Beckett in as quickly as possible and without harm. The same as we all do."

Templeton emitted another low growl. "You know, Beckett's been on a lot of highly classified missions involving my people, but I've never actually met the guy. All I want to do is get a feel for who he is – as a man and as a soldier. The more we know about him, the easier it will be to find him." Templeton turned and made eye contact. Despite his large cranium and thick-set brow, his eyes were small and close together. The effect did nothing to diminish his arresting demeanour. If anything, it only added to it. "Because I want the same as you, Frank. We all want that."

Calder held his gaze. If that was the case, he wasn't entirely convinced their goals were aligned. He was far less invested in Beckett's safe return than in weathering the storm with his reputation intact. In whatever way that could be attained. The last thing he wanted was for the press to get wind of Beckett's situation and it all blow up in his face. The next thing would be him having to explain to the PM why the British Secret Service had been caught with their pants down. He felt like he was currently balancing on a high wire above his life, precariously swaying between safeguarding his career and doing what was right.

"Come on, Frank," Templeton said, waving his hands in the air. "Completely off the record. I just want to know where you stand with this guy."

Calder picked up his glass and drank back the last of his scotch. "He's the best we've got," he said. "But I never really took to him. He's difficult to work with. He can be abrasive, aloof. I was involved more closely with him on his last mission, the one before this one. I can't go into any detail, of course, but it was like pulling teeth getting him to follow orders. Don't get me wrong, he made some good decisions that meant the operation was a success, but those decisions were not authorised via the proper channels."

"That's what I thought," Templeton said. "Doesn't play well with others, huh?"

Calder nodded, relaxing into the conversation more as a thought hit him. "Actually, I do have some concerns about the current situation." He glanced over his shoulder and lowered his voice, the two double scotches spurring him on as he leaned in. "Between you and me, Mr Templeton, I don't think it'd be the worst thing in the world, given the circumstances, if our mutual friend was lost in action. Permanently."

Templeton leaned back, closing one eye as he surveyed Calder. He turned his head slowly from side to side, letting him know he was trying to get a read on him. "Is that so?"

Calder shrugged. "A clean slate, before the press picks up on anything too damaging, would be on my wish list."

Templeton stuck out his bottom lip, nodding, thinking to himself.

Calder leaned in closer. "But like I said, that's just my personal opinion. Of course, as head of MI6, I'll do everything in my power to make sure Beckett is recovered safely," he said, maintaining a facade of professionalism. "But if something were to happen to him, I can imagine with everything that has gone on, there wouldn't be too many questions asked."

Templeton raised his head, peering down his nose at him. "I appreciate your honesty, Frank. And don't worry, this will stay between us." He took a sip from his glass, his gaze hardening as he looked away. "But Beckett's life is not a bargaining chip for your reputation or anyone else's. He's a soldier who put himself on the line for his country."

A frown creased Calder's brow. "Excuse me?"

Templeton grinned. "I think we should leave it there, Chief Director. Don't you?"

Calder sat back, battling the sense of confusion that had suddenly overcome him. Templeton continued to glare at him until the penny dropped. "Oh. I see. Yes. Quite." He glanced at the clock on the wall, realising it was way past midnight, closer to 1 a.m. "I should get to bed," he said, pushing off from the counter. "I'll see you tomorrow."

Templeton nodded, finishing off his soda water. "You take care, Frank."

As Calder got up from his stool, he felt his legs give way a little and it wasn't just from the scotch.

What the hell just happened?

He took a deep breath, trying to steady himself as he made

his way towards the exit. The hotel lobby was mostly empty as he passed through; a couple of foreign businessmen waited patiently at the reception desk, but that was all. He tried not to make eye contact with anyone as he called the lift. He was tired. He needed sleep. Hopefully, he'd wake up to some good news. Either Beckett had been brought in or he was dead.

Right now, either option would work.

21

Jacob Beaumont was also nursing a large scotch. But rather than propping up an expensive bar in the city, he was at home in Crystal Palace in his favourite armchair. Not that he was any more relaxed there. If anything, being at home surrounded by the mundanities of domesticity only raised his stress levels. He had intended to go to bed and get some sleep and had even turned in for the night. But once there, he'd found it impossible to settle, and rather than toss and turn and keep Martha awake, he'd got up and fixed himself a drink. He'd hoped the scotch would soothe his frayed nerves. It hadn't.

He'd spent close to thirty minutes in the dimly lit living room, just gazing at the muted news channel, his mind a whirlpool of disjointed thoughts. The leak, Armitage, Beckett, Locke, all the secrets he was shouldering regarding the mission – each aspect was a burden he was struggling to bear.

He wondered if he should speak to Locke in the morning, come clean about tipping off Beckett and inform him of what Armitage had uncovered. But a nagging voice in the back of his mind urged him to be cautious. Locke was an honourable man and under different circumstances – if Sigma Unit had been managing the matter internally – Beaumont would have confided in him as soon as he'd had the idea of how to contact Beckett. The same with Ruth Armitage; Locke would have been included in any meetings between him and the young analyst. But Sigma Unit weren't leading on this. Not anymore. There were so many volatile pieces on the board right now, one wrong move could prove disastrous. Not only for Beckett but for himself. Beaumont knew he was risking his career going down this particular path, but he'd come too far now to turn back. A win was his only option.

A sudden yawn overtook him, his body demanding rest. It was late, too late for such ponderings. He'd sleep on it and hope for a clearer perspective come morning. As he drained his glass and fumbled around in his chair for the remote to switch off the television, his phone vibrated on the coffee table.

He reached out for it. No caller ID, but his gut told him it was Beckett. "Jacob Beaumont," he said, answering.

"Thank God I've got you. You're still up then?"

Beaumont sat back. He was right. He was also surprised just how glad he was to hear his old friend's voice. "Where are you, John? In fact, no, don't tell me that. How are you?"

There was a crackle on the line, but he hoped it was just static. Beckett was silent a moment, then spoke. "I'll be honest with you, I've had better days."

"I'll bet. You do know everyone is looking for you?"

"Everyone?" He sounded distracted. Like he was driving.

"Yes, everyone. Us. The M's. The CIA. We all want you home."

"I see. So they've changed their minds about bringing me in?"

"Seems that way." Beaumont spotted the remote control lying on the carpet under the table. He leaned down and picked it up.

"You don't sound convinced," Beckett said. "Talk to me."

Beaumont switched the television off, plunging the room into darkness save for the light seeping in through the curtains and the faint glow from his phone's screen.

"You need to come in," he told Beckett. "I can protect you."

"I'm with my niece. I'm driving us somewhere safe. Somewhere Delaney won't find us."

"Your niece? I didn't know you had a niece."

Static filled the line once more, and Beckett's reply was lost. When he spoke again, his voice was clearer. "No one did. Or so I thought. I knew she could be used against me if the wrong people found out about her. Well, that's what's happened. So now I need to make sure she's safe. After that, maybe I'll come in. Do you have any news on Delaney's whereabouts?"

"Not entirely. Locke has a unit stationed outside his house and we're continuing to monitor the situation, but you've got to appreciate that it's a total shitshow around here. People are losing their heads over the leak and the implications. That's why I urge you to come in. It's the only way we can guarantee your safety. And hers." Even as he spoke, Beaumont knew he didn't sound entirely convincing.

Beckett swerved the suggestion. "At some point in the next day or two, the police are going to find two dead bodies at a flat in Pimlico. They'll also find two more in the woodland next to Knole Park in Sevenoaks. All Delaney's goons. At 17 Grove Road in Sevenoaks, they'll also find the bodies of Gareth and Carol Ford."

Beaumont cleared his throat. "Were those you as well?"

"No. They were looking after Amber, my niece. Sort of foster parents. Her parents both died a few years back. Car crash."

"I'm sorry to hear that," he said, but Beckett grunted as if it was a pointless thing to say. Maybe it was. "So Delaney's men are responsible for the civilian deaths?"

"That's right. They were there to kidnap Amber, to use her as leverage against me so I'd turn myself in to Delaney. But they didn't get the chance. Amber's a tough one. She's definitely my niece."

Beaumont heard a girl's voice in the background but couldn't tell what she was saying.

"How old is she?"

"Seventeen."

"And she can handle herself on the run?"

"She'll have to."

Beaumont nodded, his mind racing. He understood Beckett's reluctance to come in at this stage. Everything was uncertain and precarious and Delaney was still a threat. Yet he also suspected not coming in would bring even more trouble his way.

"Did you leave prints or anything at the house?" he asked.

"Yes. At the time, I was reluctant to use this phone to call you. I reasoned one of your analysts would be alerted when my prints flashed up on some database and once you knew who lived at the property you might piece together what had happened. But now I need your help, which is why I'm calling."

"Oh?"

Beaumont leaned forward, resting his elbow on his knee. Beckett's plan had been a good one, but it worried him. If his old friend could be placed at the crime scene, it was an open goal for anyone who wanted to use it against him to cover their own backs. He could already envision the headline:

Rogue agent – possible Russian spy – murders Sevenoaks couple before fleeing the country.

Shaking the thought away, he returned his attention to the call. "What do you need from me?"

"A passport," Beckett said. "Do you have a pen to hand?"

With his eyes now accustomed to the gloom, Beaumont got up and crab-walked over to the far end of the coffee table to retrieve the pen and notepad he kept there. "Hang on a second," he said. Returning to his seat, he cradled the phone against his cheek and shoulder, flipping past the first few pages filled with Scrabble scores between him and Martha. "Okay, I've got one. Go."

"All right, it's Amber Irving. Date of birth: January twenty-eighth, 2006. She's got a provisional licence, so she'll be in the database. Use her details to pull her photo but she'll need a new identity. I know we can't get one through the normal channels, but I was thinking about the guy we used a few years ago when we had to go into Syria at short notice and Locke didn't want to wait for clearance from MI6. That Albanian fellow? What was his name?"

"Krista? Kriska? Something like that? But yes, I know who you mean. I've still got his details somewhere. I can give him a call."

Beckett exhaled, the relief in his voice was unmistakable. "Thanks, Jacob. You're a star."

"It's going to take me a day or two to sort out," he said. "And it's going to cost you."

"That's fine. I've got money." Beckett paused, and for a moment Beaumont thought they'd been cut off. But then his voice returned, low and serious. "Also, I need to know – in your opinion, who can I trust right now?"

Beaumont curled his lip. Now there was the big question. "You can trust me."

"I know that. Anyone else? Locke? Calder?"

"I'll be honest with you, John. I don't know how to answer that question at present. There are a lot of people involved in this situation with a lot of conflicting ideas and differing objectives. It's hard to say." He considered revealing what

Armitage had discovered about the source of the leak, but decided against it. "All I would say is be damn careful."

Beckett laughed. "Aren't I always?"

"I'd like to think so, but with you I'm not so sure." Beaumont laughed too, but it sounded forced and only made him feel worse.

"Okay. Thanks, Jacob. I'll keep this line open as much as I can. Only you have this number, so it should stay secure. Let me know when the passport is ready."

"Will do. But like I say, it could be tomorrow, it could be the day after."

"Fine."

Beaumont raised his head. "Are you going to be able to stay alive that long?"

"Looks like I'm going to have to." Beckett laughed again but stopped abruptly. In the ensuing silence, Beaumont felt a sudden desperation. "I'll speak to you soon," Beckett added. "Bye for now."

He hung up, leaving Beaumont alone in the darkness. He sat in his chair for a minute longer, then got up and went into his study. He had an expert forger to look up. And a call to make.

22

Beckett could feel Amber's gaze boring into the side of his cheek. He gripped the steering wheel tighter, trying to ignore it. A minute ticked by. Two. Three.

"What is it?" he asked finally.

"Excuse me?"

He glanced at her. She'd shifted around in her seat and was facing him. "What are you doing?"

"I'm not doing anything."

"You're staring. It's not helpful."

Amber scoffed. "Oh, I'm sorry. Is it not helpful? I do apologise." She shunted around in her seat. "Do you know what else isn't helpful? Having two men with guns kill your new family before chasing you through a damp forest. Then for your long-lost uncle to turn up and kill them, before whisking you away without any real explanation of what the hell is going on."

"I told you. I'm a—"

"Yes. You're an officer of the British Secret Service and you've been compromised. I get that bit. Thanks. It's every single other thing I'm having a problem understanding."

Beckett drew in a deep breath. Seventeen-year-old girls were just as hard to get on with as he'd imagined they would be. But she did have a point. He cleared his throat. "What do you want to know?"

"Where we're going, for a start."

"A place outside of Bentworth, near Winchester. An old farm. We'll be safe there." He checked the petrol gauge. They'd been driving for over forty-five minutes and had about the same distance left to go. He'd taken the lesser A25 rather than the M25, to avoid CCTV, but so far they'd had a good run and traffic had been sparse. They were approaching West Clandon, where they could merge onto the A31 that would get them most of the way there. After that, it would be a mix of country roads and dirt tracks.

"Who owns this farm?" Amber asked.

"It used to belong to your grandfather."

"Oh." The news seemed to stun Amber more than satisfy her curiosity. As he peered over, she sat back in her seat and turned to look out the side window. Her hand moved to her eyes, brushing away a tear.

Oh bugger, Beckett thought. That was all he needed.

"I'm sorry," he muttered, the words like cotton wool in his mouth. "For everything. Carol and Gareth… your mum and dad." He reminded himself to breathe; thought about cranking open the window. "You'd have loved your grandad. He was a good man."

She sniffed and nodded and forced a smile as she glanced back. "Yeah, Mum said. I never knew you lived on a farm."

"We didn't. It was more of a… summer residence I suppose you could call it. A retreat for my parents when life got a bit much." He laughed silently to himself. He supposed the old place was still fulfilling that purpose.

"Who lives there now?"

Beckett's hands tightened on the steering wheel as he

pulled the car around a large roundabout to join the A31. "You ask a lot of questions, you know that?"

"Yeah, and you don't speak, so maybe I have to."

He smiled. Fair enough. "A man called Nigel Davis."

"Who's he?"

"An old friend. Sort of."

"Sort of? Can we trust him?"

Beckett raised his head. "Yes. We can."

"How do we know that the same people who are after you won't come looking for us there?"

"No one knows about the property. Or my links to it."

"I heard you on the phone before. You said no one knew about me. But someone clearly did."

Beckett tensed his jaw. "It'll be fine. Trust me."

"Trust you? Okay, cool. I'll trust you. Why wouldn't I? You seem like such a trustworthy guy. Very open and empathetic, too. Do people tell you that?"

"All right, Amber. Let's have less of the sarcasm, please."

She snorted again. "At least you picked up on it. I was beginning to think you were autistic or something. Or a psychopath."

Beckett didn't respond, but had to stifle a smile all the same. His young niece was certainly bold, but he supposed that was better than her being so riddled with trauma and panic he couldn't get her to cooperate. She was strong. A Beckett through and through.

And he wasn't a psychopath. Or autistic. He'd had enough tests and trials throughout his career to know that for certain. Rather, he was composed, meticulous, and strategic, traits that would ensure their safety until Beaumont came through with the passports.

Amber reached over and switched on the radio, filling the car with the heavy throb of electronic music.

"No!" Beckett snapped, turning it off.

"Aw, come on. I like that song. Please."

"No. No music. Especially not that."

"*Especially not that*," Amber repeated, aping his deep voice. Out of the corner of his eye, he saw her hand snaking back to the radio controls.

"I mean it, Amber. Stop."

She huffed and sat back. "Fine."

"Fine." He rolled his shoulders back. There was a lot to deal with in terms of his and Amber's new relationship, but for now he just had to survive the next few days. Once they were safely out of the country, he'd have time to consider their next steps.

"Where are we going once we have passports?" Amber asked, as if reading his mind.

"I'm not sure yet. Somewhere far away. Somewhere no one will ever find us. I have contacts in Europe." He looked at her as he spoke. "I know this is hard for you, Amber, and you've already been through so much in your young life, but I can't give you any reassurances at this time. All I can say is that I'm here to protect you and I will do that. But you have to trust me. Okay?"

She held his gaze for a moment, then nodded. "I do trust you, Uncle John."

He forced a smile and Amber did in return. Good enough. He checked the dashboard clock. It was a few minutes after one. They'd be at the farm before two. He put his foot down and refocused his attention on the road ahead.

23

Nigel Davis lay wide awake in his expansive double bed, far too big now for one person. Especially one who had shed considerable weight in the past year. It was worry that had done it as much as not eating. Stress and grief, too. Plus the booze. He never needed to eat when he was drinking, but he never remembered to, either. The bed sheets were ice cold from the chill that seeped into the stone farmhouse at this time of night. It was a welcome respite in the summer months; not so great in late March. He adjusted his position, did breathing exercises, worked on consciously relaxing each body part in turn like they'd taught him in the army. None of it worked.

Conceding to his insomnia, he threw back the duvet, swung his legs over the side of the bed, and planted his feet on the worn wooden floor. At this time of night, the old house seemed to magnify his loneliness. The heavy silence that hung in the air was a cruel companion – and not much of one at that. Everything was a constant reminder of the void left by Kate.

He shuffled across the room and grabbed his dressing gown from off the back of the door. After flipping on the landing light, he made his way over to the stairs, which creaked and groaned as he made his way down. His eyes lingered on the selection of photographs lining the stairwell – him and Kate on their honeymoon in Mauritius; the two of them out horse riding; one of Kate slightly tipsy and beaming at the camera with so much love in her eyes it always crushed his heart a little to look at it. To say Nigel had struggled since her death three years ago would be an understatement. Some days he thought he was doing better. Other times, the void in his heart felt like an abyss that could never be bridged.

Kate had been strong until the end, fighting a valiant battle against the bone cancer that relentlessly and eventually claimed her. Nigel had watched on, helpless, as his vibrant and loving wife withered away in front of him. Her eyes, once so full of life, grew dull and resigned. Her body, once fit and energetic, became nothing but skin and bones. He felt as though he had aged decades in those three years, his youthful spirit sapped away by the cruel hand of fate. He was thirty-seven, but most days he felt closer to ninety-seven.

He shuffled through the dining area and into the adjoining front room. The old farmhouse was a model of rustic charm, with exposed wooden beams, a brick fireplace, and furnishings that whispered of bygone eras. Yet everywhere he looked he saw memories of the life he'd shared with Kate. It wasn't upsetting to him that everything reminded him of her, but it wasn't reassuring either.

Searching for a distraction, Nigel flicked on the television. The flickering screen cast shadows up the walls, illuminating the worn leather armchair that stood as a silent witness to the many nights he'd spent wallowing in his misery. He took in the empty bottles, the takeaway cartons, the surfaces coated in a layer of dust. The once-plush carpet was now stained with the remnants of spilt whisky, and the stale scent of tobacco lingered in the air. But so what? There was no one he needed to impress.

He sank into the armchair, trying to lose himself in the monotonous hum of the twenty-four-hour news channel. Yet even the familiar drone of the television couldn't keep the demons at bay. He sighed and rubbed a hand over his face, feeling the rough stubble fast becoming a beard. His mouth felt like sandpaper. He reached out for the pint glass half full of water on the coffee table. He didn't know how long it had been there. He didn't care.

Lately, he had been trying to stay sober, though he wasn't entirely sure why. Perhaps it was an attempt to stay of sound mind, should the unbearable weight of his grief finally push him over the edge. He stared at the television set. The news anchor was talking about some protest that had broken out in London that day. Eco warriors, or something. He wasn't really paying attention. Not for the first time, he thought about moving away. A fresh start in a new town, or even a new country. It was what Kate had urged him to do before she died and he'd sort of promised her as much. But he didn't think he could bring himself to actually do it.

A noise outside jolted him from his introspection. It sounded like a car going past further down the lane. But at this hour?

A rare burst of energy propelled him out of his chair and he headed down the corridor towards the small room next to the front door. He hadn't entered this room for weeks, but the monitors were still working. There were three in total, each depicting a grid of four images from various cameras installed around the property. It was an archaic system, installed long ago by the previous residents, Kate's ex-husband's family. They'd been a lot more security-conscious, perhaps with more to protect than he and Kate, but when the two of them had taken over the property, they'd kept the cameras on regardless.

He leaned on the desk and examined each screen in turn, but the feeds revealed nothing out of the ordinary, no speeding cars. The only movement came from the leaves rustling in the wind.

Here at the front of the house, though, he was closer to the road, and as he listened he heard another noise. Not a car engine this time but a bang. His fatigued heart raced. He reached up to the shelf above his head and pulled down his old stack-barrelled shotgun, a Browning B25. Back in the day, he'd used it for shooting game – rabbits and the odd pheasant if he was lucky – but he hadn't used it in years. Still, you never forget. Nigel had joined the Royal Regiment of Fusiliers as a rifleman straight from university. The Fighting Fifth. He'd done two tours before realising the military wasn't for him. It turned out that leaving the army was the best decision he ever made. When he returned from service, he reconnected with the newly divorced Kate – the rest, as they say, was history.

He retrieved a box of shells from the shelf, loaded the shotgun and stuffed a handful of extra shells in his dressing gown pocket for good measure. Then he made his way to the front door, sliding his feet into an old pair of slippers as he went.

Switching off all the lights, he eased open the front door. Visitors were a rare occurrence these days, so if someone was here, they might well be seeking trouble. And if so, they'd certainly find it. Nigel knew every inch of these grounds and he was prepared to defend them – and the memories they held – with everything he had. He stepped out into the night, a chill breeze sending a shudder down his spine.

The shadows seemed to shift and sway as Nigel prowled across the garden and headed in the direction of the noise. He moved with purpose, his senses on high alert, the weight of the shotgun a comforting presence in his hands.

"Who's there?" he whispered into the darkness. "Show yourself."

There was no response. No further sounds, either.

He inspected the outbuildings and sheds, but found nothing out of the ordinary. Even the chickens in their coop appeared unperturbed. Frustration and anxiety mingled in the pit of his stomach, the tension mounting with every step.

Had he imagined the noise, he wondered; was his mind playing tricks on him now?

Circling back to the house, he caught a glimpse of movement in the kitchen window. Someone was there. A man, judging by his height. Nigel's heart leapt into his throat as he tightened his hold on the shotgun. The back door opened into the kitchen, and he approached it on a wide arc, preparing himself to confront his uninvited guest. He couldn't see a weapon on the man, but that didn't rule out the possibility he was carrying one. Nigel crept up to the door and stopped, his heart pounding in his chest as he reached for the handle and eased it open.

"What the hell do you think you're playing at!" he yelled, as he pushed the door open and raised the shotgun. "Stop what you're doing or I'll…" The words died in his throat as he saw the man and the teenage girl standing in the kitchen before him. They both had bags with them. And he recognised the man.

"Beckett?" he gasped.

The man smiled. "Good evening, Nigel," he said, his gaze sweeping over him with an unsettling intensity. "I do hope we're not intruding."

24

Beckett held his hands up as Nigel stared at him open-mouthed. "Are you okay, Nigel?" he asked. "You look like you've seen a ghost."

"I feel like I have," he replied. "What the bloody hell are you doing here, sneaking up on me in the dead of night?"

Beckett put his bag down and stepped forward, placing himself strategically between the shotgun's muzzle and Amber. "I'll explain everything. But can you lower your weapon first? It is rather off-putting."

Nigel complied, resting the shotgun against the kitchen counter, the barrel facing the ground. He rubbed at his face. "What do you want, John? I haven't seen you in five years."

"Has it been that long?"

"I'd say. I did wonder whether you might turn up to Kate's funeral. But no." His eyes flashed with indignation. "I assume you know."

Beckett nodded. "Yes. My condolences. She was… She was a good woman."

"She was the best," Nigel snapped. Then, nodding at

Amber who was cowering behind Beckett's back. "And who's this?"

He stepped aside. "This is Amber Irving. Rebecca's daughter. My niece."

"Hey," Amber said, offering a timid wave. "Pleased to meet you."

Nigel gave her a brief, strained smile before returning his attention to Beckett. "What the hell is going on?"

"I was wondering if we could stay the night," he replied. "Maybe two nights. We need to lie low for a while and we've got nowhere else to go. I'm sorry to impose, I really am, but we're in trouble and this was the only place I could think of that might provide us sanctuary."

"*Might?*" Nigel repeated. "What sort of trouble are you in?"

Beckett glanced at his niece. "Amber, do you think you could make us all some tea?" he asked her, gesturing at the kettle on the worktop.

"Tea? At this time?"

"Yes."

"Fine. Whatever." She shucked her rucksack off her back and walked over to the counter. "Does everyone want a cup?"

"Not for me, thanks," Nigel replied.

"Let's go through into the front room," Beckett told him, attempting to regain control of the situation. "I'll give you the lowdown."

Nigel had resignation written all over his face, but he nodded and shuffled past him into the front room. Beckett followed and, once they were seated, spent the next five minutes briefing him on everything that had transpired over the last twenty-four hours – his deep-cover operation, the leak, rescuing Amber from Delaney's men, plus his reluctance to return to S-Unit while the situation was so volatile.

"So that's where you've been for the last few years," Nigel

said, once he'd finished. "Working for some fucking crime lord in London. Jesus, John."

"Yes. And now he wants me dead. Knowing Delaney, he won't rest until one of us is six feet under and will exploit anyone or anything to get to me. Which is why I need to get Amber out of the country."

"And then what? What will you do?"

"I haven't thought that far ahead. My priority is securing Amber's safety."

Nigel leaned back in his chair and rubbed at his face. "This is some heavy stuff, John. How can I help?"

"You're already doing it, providing us shelter. That's enough."

"Where are you planning on taking her?"

Beckett shrugged. "I've got a contact in Spain that might be able to help out. I just need to speak to them."

Nigel snorted. "Yeah, that might be a good idea. Most people don't take too kindly to acquaintances just showing up on their doorsteps, you know."

Beckett smiled. "I knew you'd missed me."

That one almost got a genuine smile out of Nigel. *Almost.* The two men sat up as Amber entered carrying a tray of drinks. "I made one for you anyway," she told Nigel. "But leave it if you want." The mugs clinked together as she set the tray on the coffee table.

"Thanks, that's kind of you," Nigel said, giving Amber a grin that faded almost immediately. "Gosh, you do have a striking resemblance to Rebecca, don't you?"

"You knew my mum?" she asked, her interest piqued.

"I did. Your uncle and I go way back. *Way,* way back."

Amber glanced between the two men, her attention resting on Beckett. "Why didn't you tell me that?"

"I didn't think it was important."

She rolled her eyes and addressed Nigel. "Has he always been this difficult?"

"Oh, absolutely," he replied. "But somehow he gets away with it. People often mistake good looks and eloquence for charm."

Amber laughed. "But you've known each other a long time?"

"Nigel and I grew up together," Beckett told her. "We lost touch for a while when I went to boarding school, but then we both turned up at Oxford University in the same year and rekindled our friendship. That's where we met Kate."

"Kate?" Amber asked.

Beckett glanced at Nigel, giving him the option to continue the tale. But he shook his head.

"Kate was my ex-wife," Beckett continued. "We were both doing the same degree. She was great. The three of us became inseparable. We had some amazing times. Kate and I married right after graduating. Nigel was the best man at our wedding. But she and I were already different people by then. I'd just signed to a recruitment branch of the secret service and my heart was set on making a name for myself there. We made it work for a year, but the strain of my work became too much for her. For us both. We divorced two years later."

Amber's expression contorted, deep in thought. "So… then you married her?" she asked Nigel.

He smiled. "That's right. My time in the armed forces had just ended and I was at a total loss with what to do with myself. My family owns a manor house in Nottinghamshire, so I was never going to be worried about money, but I had no clue where I was going in life. Then, one day, I was in London and I bumped into Kate in Covent Garden and everything changed. I don't think we left each other's side from that day onwards. Until…"

Beckett tensed as Nigel looked away, his voice wavering.

Amber glanced at Beckett. "Oh, she's…?"

He nodded solemnly.

"Three years ago now," Nigel continued, his voice steadier. "Bone cancer. A terrible disease."

"I'm so sorry," Amber told him. She reached for her mug as the room fell silent, only broken by the sound of her sipping the warm, milky tea. "But you two stayed friends?"

"I wouldn't go that far," Beckett said. "I wasn't the best man at Nigel's wedding, let's say that."

"But how come you're living here, Nigel?" she asked, glancing around the room. "I thought the house belonged to my grandfather?"

"By the time Kate and I divorced, both my parents had passed away," Beckett explained. "I talked to your mother and she agreed to let Kate have the farmhouse. She didn't have anywhere else to live at the time and I was working overseas mainly. I didn't need it. Plus, there were no hard feelings when we split up. We both knew it was over."

"And you're sure none of these people who are after you know about this place?" Nigel asked.

"I'm fairly confident. We transferred the deeds to Kate's name when I joined Sigma Unit and most of the details from my past were redacted or wiped clean from my record. Me having an ex-wife and an old family home might still exist in the memory of the person who conducted one of my initial briefings, but not in any file."

"Let's hope not."

The room fell silent again. Beckett stared at the mug of tea on the table in front of him.

"Hey," Nigel whispered. "Look."

Beckett followed his eyeline. At some point in the last few minutes, Amber had succumbed to sleep. Her head lolled onto her chest, occasionally jerking up as if trying to wake herself but failing. Beckett reached over and took the mug of tea she had clasped in her lap.

"She's had a tough day," he whispered. "I'll take her up to bed. Is she okay in the spare room at the back of the house?"

Nigel nodded. "There's a stack of boxes against the wall. Kate's clothes, mainly. But the bed is clear."

"Thanks. One more thing. Is my father's security system still in working order?"

"It is," Nigel replied. "I checked it earlier. Although, I'm not sure why he ever had it installed. There's never been much need for it around here, I'll be honest."

No, Beckett thought to himself. But there might be.

There really might be.

"I'll get Amber settled and I'll be back down," he told Nigel. "I wasn't followed here, but I'm going to stay up, just in case."

Nigel smiled. "No. You get some sleep. I'll keep watch."

"Thanks, but this is my problem. I've put you out enough. It's on me—"

"Don't argue with me, John. This is my house now, remember? I can't sleep anyway these days and you look as though you could do with a few hours at least. When did you last sleep?"

Beckett thought about it. "Seems like a long time ago now."

"Exactly. So get some rest. You can take the spare room opposite the stairs. There's nothing in there but a rickety old cot bed, I'm afraid."

"That's fine. I've slept on worse."

"I believe it."

Beckett let out a sigh. "All right. Thank you, Nigel. For taking us in. I appreciate it."

Beckett stood and carefully lifted Amber off the couch

before heading over to the stairs. She felt light in his arms and looked so vulnerable now in sleep.

"Oh and Nigel," he said, pausing with one foot on the bottom step. "I know I haven't said it yet, but I'm sorry about Kate, and that I wasn't at the funeral. Hell, I'm sorry about everything."

"Yes." Nigel sighed. "Me too."

Beckett gave him a terse nod, then carried Amber upstairs.

25

They were gaining on him.

He didn't know who they were or what they wanted. All he knew was they were in pursuit and if they caught him he was a dead man. Time was running out. He needed to escape. The intensity of his heartbeat was suffocating, but he pushed on. It felt as though he was running through treacle or quicksand, each step causing him to sink deeper into his own personal hell.

A twisted labyrinth of demonic shadows and nightmarish visions spanned out in front of him. Visions of bloodied battlefields and terror-stricken faces. The screams of fallen comrades and the dying breaths of insurgents filled his ears as he stumbled on through the hellscape, pursued by faceless adversaries. He tried to call for help, but he had no voice.

He had to escape.

He had to find refuge.

He had to reach Amber.

Amber…

Beckett's eyes snapped open, his heart playing a prestissimo beat against his ribcage. A figure stood over him, shotgun in hand. Disoriented, Beckett blinked rapidly, his surroundings coming into focus.

"Nigel?" he rasped.

"They're here, John," he said. "I don't know how they found you, but they're here."

Beckett bolted upright. "Shit. What time is it?"

"Almost a quarter to six."

In an instant, Beckett flung the covers off and was on his feet. He'd slept in his clothes as he always did in situations such as this. Pulling on his old boots, he hurried down the landing to the room where Amber was sleeping. He pushed the door open and approached her bedside. "Amber. Wake up. We need to leave. Now."

She stirred and mumbled something he couldn't make out, still lost in the throes of sleep. Beckett tapped her gently on the cheek with the back of his fingers, trying to rouse her without causing unnecessary panic.

"Amber. Wake up!"

It did the trick. She sucked in a sharp breath and sat up abruptly.

"What's going on?" she asked, peering up at him, the whites of her eyes glowing in the dim light of early morning. "Where…?"

"They've found us," he said. "Get up. Get dressed. Come downstairs. Now. And don't turn any lights on."

Leaving Amber to ready herself, he met Nigel at the top of the stairs.

"How many?" he asked.

"Not sure. They're in two black SUVs. They turned onto the track from the main road about thirty seconds before I woke you. They'll reach the house in the next minute. You need to go."

They descended the stairs in silence, and as they reached

the ground floor, Beckett could hear engines growling in the distance.

"Amber," he called up the stairs. "Get down here. Now."

She appeared on the landing and hurried down. Beckett guided her through to the kitchen, where they grabbed their bags before assembling at the back door. Nigel was still holding the shotgun steady at waist height, but Beckett noticed the beads of sweat on his forehead and the rapid rise and fall of his chest.

With one hand, Nigel reached up and unbolted the door. "Go," he said, opening it. "Quickly."

Beckett stopped. "You're coming too."

"No." Nigel shook his head. "I'll hold them off so you can escape."

Beckett stepped closer and lowered his voice. "But that's suicide."

"Maybe." Nigel didn't blink as he held his gaze. "But it'll also give you a fighting chance of getting away. And what have I got to live for?" He grabbed Beckett around the back of his neck. "I mean it, John. Go. Save your niece. Save the fucking world. It's what you do."

Beckett glanced at Amber. The engine noises were getting louder. Ten seconds away. He gave Nigel a solemn nod, then grabbed Amber's hand.

"Let's go," he told her. "Move fast and stay low. Follow my lead."

They dashed from the kitchen in a straight line, heading for the cover of an avenue of apple trees lining the east side of the garden. Beckett had intimate knowledge of the property and planned on navigating around the edge of the grounds in a wide arc, using trees and the garden as cover.

"Two big cars have just pulled up," Amber whispered, glancing back at the house.

"Don't worry about it," he told her. "Just focus on getting to the car."

Their breaths came in swift, shallow gasps as they skirted the perimeter towards the dirt track where Beckett had hidden the Audi out of sight from the road. While they made their way to the far side of the grounds, he slowed his pace and steered Amber ahead of him. Peering through a thicket of dense evergreens, he saw a group of men surrounding the house. Six of them. Their faces were obscured in the murky light of near-dawn, but the silhouettes of their assault rifles were unmistakable. He pressed on, catching up with Amber who'd stopped to wait for him.

"Nearly there," he whispered. "Keep your head down. Don't look back. No matter what."

The crack of gunfire reverberated through the air as they reached the dirt track. Glancing back, he saw Nigel leaning out the window of one of the upstairs rooms, shotgun at his shoulder. Still an excellent shot, he took out two of the intruders, one after the other. But that still left four of them and he needed to reload.

Beckett's heart raced as he guided Amber through the trees towards the car, but at the next clearing his gaze was drawn back to the house. Just in time to see Nigel take a flurry of bullets in the chest and stumble backwards into the darkness of the room. Beckett clenched his fists, but he couldn't deal with the loss of his old friend right now. Besides, Nigel had accepted his fate; he knew what would happen by staying. Cursing under his breath, Beckett turned and ran after Amber.

"Is Nigel okay?" Amber asked, when he caught up with her halfway down the track.

"I think so," he lied.

It took them another five minutes to reach the car. Once there, they tossed their bags onto the back seat and climbed in. Beckett had parked at the top of a steep incline, anticipating the need for a stealthy exit. He released the handbrake, allowing the car to roll silently down the slope before starting the engine.

As they sped away, Amber turned to him, panting. "What now?" she asked. "Does Grandad have any other country houses we can hide out in?"

Beckett sniffed. "There are actually three more properties in the family name. But I'm now banking on them serving as suitable diversions."

"What do you mean?"

As they reached the main road, Beckett shifted gears and took a right, heading north. Delaney, despite being a ruthless man and a savvy criminal, was also impulsive, often allowing his emotions to override his judgment. Beckett was now counting on this fateful flaw. He anticipated Delaney would spend the next day or so hunting them down in the countryside around Kent and Essex. Meanwhile, they would retreat to a place he would least expect. That was the hope, at least – the gamble.

"Uncle John?" Amber snapped. "Where are we heading?"

"Back to London," he said. "We'll find a secure place to lie low until your passport is ready. Somewhere we won't be found."

"That's what you said about the farmhouse."

Beckett didn't respond. He was all too aware of his previous reassurances.

"And then what?" Amber asked.

Beckett met her probing gaze. "Then we get out of England," he told her. "Perhaps for good."

26

Rufus Delaney stepped out of the rear of the SUV, gravel crunching underfoot as one of his men approached. The gunfight had now ceased, but the air was heavy with death.

"Is Beckett here?" he asked.

"Not that we can see, boss. There was a lone shooter upstairs but we've taken him out." He frowned. "Not before he shot two of ours, though. Coyle and Nash."

Rufus sucked his teeth. "Both dead?"

"Yes."

"Fucking hell."

He glanced around, surveying the run-down farmhouse before him. The first light from the new day's sun was appearing over the horizon, casting long shadows across the desolate property.

"You and Trey search the grounds, cover every available route out of here. We have to find Beckett, today. It's vital. Do you understand?"

"Yes, boss."

"Okay, then, what are you waiting for?" Delaney shooed

him away. "Fuck off. Bring me back a dead traitor."

He watched the man lumber away, then puffed out his cheeks. He didn't like losing his rag, especially not in front of his men. Yet the gravity of the situation was escalating.

A chill wind whipped at his face, amplifying the unease that had been brewing since he discovered Patrick Hamilton's real identity. He gritted his teeth, fighting to keep his anger in check and remain focused. The Consortium had a low tolerance for failures and he was well aware they would soon be seeking reprisals. He was determined not to be another fallen pawn, like Murat Caliskan, but it now felt as if he had a ticking clock hanging over his head.

He entered the house through the front door, finding himself in a dim utility room that smelled of dampness and decay. The main living area was no better, with old, yellowing wallpaper and sparse, dust-coated furniture illuminated by a few functional lightbulbs. The house was lifeless, devoid of any warmth. Delaney shuddered, and not just from the cold.

Harris stood on the far side of the open-plan living area, weapon at the ready. He greeted Delaney with a curt nod as he approached. As part of Delaney's inner team, Harris – along with Ahmet, Trey, and Eddie – had weathered many storms with him. All of them were competent, sturdy, and loyal, yet Delaney questioned whether even they could protect him if he failed to deliver Beckett to The Consortium. It was The Consortium that had provided him with the information about Beckett's niece. Consequently, they would expect him to have this pathetic mess cleaned up by now. On the phone earlier, they'd been explicit. No more fuck-ups. He had to find Beckett or it was his head on the line.

"The house is clear, boss," Harris told him. "One man upstairs, but it ain't Hamilton, or whatever he calls himself."

"Any sign of him or the girl?"

"Not so far."

Delaney dug his nails into the palm of his hand but managed to maintain his composure. He pulled out his pistol from the shoulder harness he always wore on such jaunts. It was a comforting weight in his hand as he climbed the stairs, but the weight of expectation pressed down on him, his chest tightening with every step.

Reaching the landing, he followed a sloping corridor down to the room at the end. There he found a man sprawled on the floor, barely alive and with blood oozing from a chest wound. A discarded shotgun lay beside him. Ahmet stood guard, his assault rifle aimed at the man's head, ready to counter any desperate attempts at a last stand.

Delaney approached the injured man, his face twisted into a malicious grin. "You aren't looking too special, are ya, mate?" he taunted, waving his gun at him. "Where's Beckett?"

The man glared back, defiance in his eyes despite the pain contorting his features. "Go to hell," he wheezed.

"Dickhead." Delaney's fist tightened around the pistol, suppressing the urge to put a bullet between the man's eyes. Instead he squatted down before asking again, his voice now a low, threatening rumble. "Where. Is. Beckett?"

The man pressed his lips together in a hard line, offering no answer. Delaney's patience shattered. Digging his finger into the man's chest wound, he twisted it around in the shredded flesh and burnt tissue. The man screamed in agony, tears streaming down his face.

"I don't know!" he gasped, choking on his words. "He's gone. He left before you arrived. You'll never find him."

"Where is he going?" Delaney asked, still tormenting the wound.

"I don't know!"

Delaney ceased his gruesome interrogation. "Well, ya know what? It doesn't matter anyway, mate. We're tracking the slippery fucker. How do you think we found this place? Dickhead."

He rose to standing and tilted his head to take in the pathetic wretch at his feet. The man was bleeding out. He'd be no use to him in a minute or two. Without hesitation, he raised his pistol and shot him between the eyes. It would do no good in the long run, but it alleviated his stress levels momentarily. The man's body fell limp, blood pooling around his head like a crimson halo.

"Fucking useless," Delaney muttered under his breath. He could still hear that bastard clock ticking in the back of his mind.

"Ahmet, take this." He pulled out the phone they'd been using to track Beckett and the girl and handed it to him. "The signal has dropped out since we arrived at Old MacDickhead's farm, but once we're back on the road it'll reconnect. Let me be clear. I need Beckett found in the next couple of hours. Take Harris with you. I'll head back with Trey and Carter."

"Yes, boss." Ahmet turned and strode from the room.

Delaney watched him go. He had faith in his men. If anyone could find that treacherous bastard, it was them. But right now he needed to get back to London as soon as possible. Time really was of the essence. And as well as finding Beckett, he had some important contingency plans to put into place.

27

Beaumont leaned out from his office doorway, scanning the corridor in both directions. It was just shy of 7:30 a.m. The day staff were yet to arrive, but he didn't want to take any chances. Satisfied there was no one in earshot, he closed the door and returned to his desk, ready to make the call.

"Please pick up," he whispered into the receiver, as the ringtone chimed in his ear.

He'd already tried twice the night before and had been met with an answering machine each time. He'd wanted to keep trying but Martha had come downstairs and insisted he get some rest. He couldn't argue with her reasoning. She was his wife, after all; Martha knew best. The night's sleep had left him revived and able to think more clearly. Plus, it was important to place bookends around the day in situations like this, lest the long hours swam together into one surreal thread. But he'd also wasted valuable time.

"Hello?" a gruff voice answered, finally. "Who is this?"

Beaumont hunched over his desk. "The name's Finch," he replied, using the alias from their previous encounter. "You did some work for me a few years back. Two passports, at very short notice. We were happy with the results and wondered if you could accommodate us again."

A heavy silence followed. Beaumont waited. He wished he had a coffee to sip, something to do with his other hand. He glanced over at the kettle as the voice came back on the line.

"I remember. You need my services?"

"Yes. Same request as before. We need a physical passport as soon as possible."

"When?"

"Within forty-eight hours."

The man on the line made the noise an MOT inspector might make right before he stung you for four new tyres. "That might be difficult."

"We're willing to pay a premium, like last time."

"Well, times have changed, my friend. You know… Brexit. One piece is two-k. You want fullz, it's three-k. You want fresh Brit fullz, it's four."

Beaumont turned his head to face the window. "We don't need… fullz," he replied, adopting the vernacular – fraudster slang for a complete package of stolen information. "We just need one passport." He glanced at his laptop screen; at the photo of Amber he'd found on the government database. Her colouring was similar to Beckett's. "We don't need it to be British but it has to be European. Whatever's easiest. We can do two grand for a quick job."

"Okay, but I only accept crypto now, understand? XMR. Half now and half on delivery."

"Fine. Send the details to this number. And be quick about it."

"All right, boss. Chill. It's all good. I'll be in touch." The line went dead, leaving a tightness in Beaumont's chest he couldn't shake.

He sat in silence, trying to regain his composure. He

inhaled. He held it. He released. It felt as if his mind was so full of thoughts they'd almost cancelled each other out. He considered making a coffee, but as he glanced over at the kettle, he saw movement through the frosted glass panel in his door.

Closing his laptop, he got up and went to the door, just in time to catch Locke heading to his own office, deep in discussion with Bowditch. The relief Beaumont felt on seeing the chief director told him he was doing the right thing.

"Robert," Beaumont called after him. "Can I have a word?"

The two men stopped and turned back. "What is it?" Locke asked.

"Can you step into my office?" he asked. "It won't take long." Locke and Bowditch exchanged glances before heading his way. Beaumont stepped back to allow the men to enter and closed the door behind them.

"We're due to meet with the Foreign Secretary in twenty minutes," Bowditch told him. "What's the issue?"

Beaumont steeled himself. "I've reason to believe the source of the data breach is closer to home than we first thought."

"Where?" Locke asked.

"Definitely Europe, possibly the UK, possibly London itself. One of my top analysts is looking into it."

Bowditch scoffed. "That's ridiculous. It has to be the Russians."

"I'm not convinced," Beaumont replied, eyes on Locke.

"What exactly are you suggesting, Beaumont?" Bowditch asked.

"Nothing. Yet." He grimaced. "But we may have to prepare ourselves for the possibility there's a mole amongst us."

"I see," Locke said, his hand going to his chin as he contemplated the idea. "I suppose it's not beyond the realms of possibility and we have to explore all options. Good work, Beaumont. I want to speak with this analyst. Who is it?"

"Ruth Armitage."

"Armitage?" Bowditch repeated. "I'm not familiar with her."

"She's a recent addition to Sigma Unit," Beaumont said. "She's young but highly competent. I trust her. I'll arrange a briefing as soon as possible."

"Excellent," Locke said, checking his watch. "And let's keep this between us for now. Until we can verify this theory, that's all it is – a theory."

"Absolutely," Beaumont said. "My thoughts exactly."

"Good. Well, if that's all for now, I need to get to this meeting. See what else you can find out and I'll catch up with you on my return."

Locke opened the door and headed out of the room. Bowditch followed him out but stopped in the doorway and turned back.

"Any updates on Beckett?" His eyebrows rose expectantly before his expression drooped. "By this stage, might we assume Delaney has caught up with him?"

Beaumont paused, weighing up his options. "There's a chance he's still active," he said, choosing to play it vague. "Two bodies were discovered in a flat in Pimlico last night and I'm hearing chatter regarding two more casualties in the woods near Sevenoaks. The killings are consistent with Special Forces methods."

Bowditch nodded, managing a smile. "That's promising. I'll let Locke know." He leaned in closer. "You and Beckett are close, is that correct?"

"We've known each other a long time, if that's what you mean."

"Do you think he'll contact you?"

"He hasn't so far."

"But if he does… you'll order him to come in? Immediately."

"Absolutely."

Bowditch's eyes darted around Beaumont's face, but if he was looking for a hint of hesitation or guilt, he didn't find one.

"This situation is beginning to look very embarrassing for us," he said. "Xander Templeton is not happy. Neither are Eastwood and Calder. And don't get me started on the Foreign Secretary. He was apoplectic when I spoke to him earlier. They all want this handled. As soon as possible."

Beaumont narrowed his eyes. *Handled*. He knew what that meant.

"We need to track down Beckett and bring him in before we have an international crisis on our hands," Bowditch added.

"I'm well aware," Beaumont replied. "My team and I are doing everything we can."

"And if Beckett does make contact…?"

"Both you and Locke will be notified immediately."

Bowditch held his gaze for a moment longer, then grinned. "That's all we can ask for. Speak to this Armitage person and we'll regroup after the meeting. In the meantime, keep looking."

"Will do." Beaumont walked him to the door and closed it behind him. "Wanker," he whispered.

Returning to his desk, he pulled his phone from his pocket and set it down in front of him. So, this was it. He was flying solo on this one. Going off book and against orders. It was a risky move, but after the conversation just now, his instincts told him he was making the right choice. He took a deep breath and picked up the phone. He had another important call to make.

28

Picking up his bag, Beckett exited the toilet cubicle, stuffing the handful of balled-up wet wipes into a large bin standing against the white tiled wall. He felt better to have changed his clothes, even if the crude swabbing down hadn't been the most thorough or hygienic of washes. Placing his bag down on one of the sinks, he unzipped the side pocket and took out a tube of toothpaste. He applied a thick line to the end of a travel toothbrush and leaned into the sink, brushing his teeth methodically before spitting out into the bowl. He twisted on the cold tap and scooped a handful of water into his mouth. It tasted chalky but was refreshing enough. Replacing the toothbrush in his bag, he used both hands to splash the cool water in his face, feeling it invigorate him as he'd hoped.

As he straightened, he noticed a man observing him from the other end of the row of sinks. He was around his age, and as their eyes met, he gave Beckett a sympathetic smile. Probably he assumed he was a wayward husband, having to use a service station bathroom to freshen up before work after being chucked out by his wife. Avoiding further eye contact, Beckett picked up his bag and left the bathroom.

Amber was standing in front of a newsagent, casually flipping through a magazine as he returned to the main body of the building.

"There you are," she said, placing the magazine back on the rack as he walked over to her. "I thought you'd left me."

"I wouldn't do that."

She sniffed the air. "Are you wearing aftershave?"

"Just a touch."

She smirked. "Why? Do you want to smell nice for the passport forger?"

"All right, keep your voice down," he said, grabbing her arm and guiding her over to a Burger King counter on the far side. "Let's grab some food. We both could use it."

Amber ordered six vegan nuggets, a small portion of fries and a bottle of water. Beckett opted for two of the largest burgers they had on the menu and a coffee. Out of the corner of his eye, he saw Amber watching him.

"What?" he asked, as he handed the server a twenty.

"No fries?"

"I avoid carbs. Especially this early in the morning."

"Oh no. You're not one of those men who are obsessed with protein, are you? Like all those ridiculous gym bros."

Beckett took the change from the server. He had no idea what Amber was talking about and didn't want to know. He avoided carbs for the simple reason they made him sluggish. Seeing as they were heading back into the lion's mouth, he needed to be as alert as possible. He planned on eating the meat out of the burgers and tossing the bread.

"I don't want anything too heavy," he told her. "That's all."

Once the food arrived, he carried the tray over to a table in the centre of the seating area, positioning himself so he had a clear view of the entrance. A TV screen high up on one wall showed a rolling news channel, which Beckett intermittently glanced at while deconstructing his burgers. But nothing regarding the data breach appeared on the screen.

"What was my mum like when she was younger?"

Amber's question snapped him from his thoughts. He stared at her. "Umm… She was… I don't know… She was Rebecca."

"Oh, brilliant, thanks. You paint such a vivid picture of her." She lowered her chin. "Were the two of you close?"

Beckett took a large bite of one of the burgers. It was greasy and salty, but tasted better than he'd have liked to admit. He considered Amber's question as he chewed.

"We were close when we were young. But she was four years older than me, so when she reached sixteen and I was only twelve we'd grown worlds apart. Then a few years later our father died and everything changed." He quickly shoved the rest of the burger patty into his mouth, eager to avoid further discussion.

"Yeah. It's hard," Amber agreed, her voice wavering, speaking to one of her nuggets. "Losing people, I mean." She shrugged and took a bite.

Beckett studied her. Given everything that had happened in the last twelve hours, he'd expected her to be more traumatised. But after what she'd been through already, perhaps life had already hardened her sufficiently. He couldn't decide whether that was a good or bad thing. The toughness and resolve she exhibited weren't the result of courage but necessity. She'd had to face so much and at such a young age. He wished he could have been there for her when Rebecca died, but circumstances had made it impossible. Now, he was determined to do right by her, whatever it took.

"Did they kill Nigel?" she asked.

Beckett paused mid-chew. "Yes."

She nodded, her expression not changing. She was an

enigma to him, but perhaps no different from any self-obsessed teenager. Regardless, she looked to be thinking hard about it. "Are you sad?" she asked, meeting his gaze.

"Yes. He was a good man."

She scoffed. "Do you want to tell your face then? Because you look as if nothing happened."

Beckett leaned back, resisting the urge to tell her the same thing. Maybe they weren't so different. "What do you want me to do?"

Amber leaned in, whispering. "He's dead because of me. Because of us."

"Nigel was a brave man," he said. "He let us stay knowing the risks involved. I'm sorry for what happened. But you're my only priority."

"Jesus. How can you be so cold?"

Beckett didn't answer. He didn't want to be having this conversation. He knew he often came across as cold and uncaring. But he'd trained himself to be that way. It was the only way to survive in the world he inhabited. He let the silence stretch until Amber turned her attention back to her vegan nuggets. The moment passed.

Picking up a second burger patty, he glanced up at the television screen, which was now showing the weather forecast. It was to be another cold day.

"Are you watching to see if you're mentioned?" Amber asked, turning to see what he was looking at.

"They seem to be keeping a lid on things," he muttered to himself, picking up his coffee and taking a sip. "For now."

"Yeah, I checked while you were in the bathroom. I thought there might be something in the news about Carol and Gareth."

"It might take a day or so." He nodded over to the newsstand in front of the shop where Amber had been browsing. "Even if someone discovered them last night, it's unlikely the news would make it into this morning's papers."

Amber frowned. "I wasn't looking at the papers. I checked the news app on my watch." She extended her wrist, revealing a smartwatch.

Beckett stared at it. "Have you had that on the whole time?"

"Not all the time. The battery ran out, but there was a charging station near the bathrooms over there. I've just… Oh…" She trailed off, a look of realisation washing over her face. "Shit. Sorry. I never thought. There was so much going on and—"

"Give it to me," Beckett said, rising from his seat and extending his hand. "Is it linked to your phone?"

She grimaced and nodded, hastily removing it from her wrist and handing it over. He saw the dawning horror in her eyes as she comprehended the gravity of her mistake. But this was on him. He should have been more thorough.

"We need to get out of here," he told her. "Now."

He grabbed his bag and strode over to the double doors that led to the car park, discarding the watch in a waste bin on his way out. As they reached the car, his phone buzzed in his pocket. He flipped it open and answered. "Beaumont?"

"Yes, it's me. How's it going?"

"It's… going. Any news?"

"I spoke to our man with the goods. We're all set. I'll text you the details once he's made contact. But you'll need to take care of a few things on your end."

"Like what?"

"He wants payment to be made in cryptocurrency. XMR. I've already sent him half, but you'll have to cover the rest when he delivers. You owe him a grand."

Beckett glanced at Amber. "Okay. I'll sort it. And I'll pay you back once this is all over."

"Don't worry about it. But damn – setting up encrypted crypto wallets and memorising intricate keycodes? What does he think we are, spies?"

Beckett laughed. But he didn't have time to mess around transferring money and downloading complicated apps. He hoped he could convince the man to accept cash payment. If charm didn't work, he had other skills. Whichever was quickest.

"Anything else I should be aware of?" he asked, gesturing for Amber to go around to the passenger side.

"Only that the situation is getting more heated around here. I had to let them know you were still at large. Otherwise it would have looked suspicious if they got wind of the intel my analysts are sourcing from the police reports." He sighed. "Nerves are frayed and you know how it goes when people get antsy. Just stay sharp, is all I'm saying. I hope I'm wrong, but you can't be too careful in this line of work."

"You said it," Beckett replied, unlocking the car and watching as Amber climbed in. "And thanks, Jacob. Hopefully I'll see you soon."

"Damn right. Next year in Jerusalem and all that."

Beckett hung up and climbed into the car beside Amber, stuffing his bag onto the back seat. "All right, let's get to London and find somewhere to lie low. But no music, okay?" He attempted a grin, but her expression was solemn, distant. "Hey, Amber. It wasn't your fault. I mean it."

She nodded, but didn't look at him. "Yeah."

"We're nearly there," he told her. "A few more hours and we'll be safe. Hang in there."

She nodded again and this time managed a weak smile. Beckett started the engine.

A few more hours.

Yet something told him their situation was going to get a whole lot worse before it got better.

29

In his grand kitchen-diner, Delaney prowled restlessly, traversing from the bay window with its view of the Thames over to the French patio doors that opened out on the luscious greenery of his city garden. A pistol clenched in one hand, his phone in the other, he paced the full expanse once more as it rang out for a third time.

"Pissing shit."

He glared at the phone screen. Why weren't they answering? He'd tried calling on his way back from Bentworth and every twenty minutes since. It was now a few minutes after 8 a.m. and they still weren't answering. The Consortium were many. There was no way they were all asleep.

He needed to speak with them urgently, get ahead of the chaos and reassure them it was all being taken care of – before they found out from elsewhere that Beckett had slipped through his fingers yet again.

That bastard.

He'd screwed everything up, but the betrayal was also personal. Patrick had been a friend as well as his number one. They'd stayed up together drinking on many occasions. He'd told him things about himself he hadn't even told Miranda. They'd made plans. He'd trusted him like a brother.

Like a fucking brother…

He shook his head, attempting to dispel the thoughts clouding his focus. He walked to the kitchen island, set his gun down on the marble countertop, put his phone on loudspeaker and dialled the number again. As the ringtone filled the room, he resumed his pacing. He felt as if he was going crazy, persistently ringing them like some needy ex-lover, but what other options did he have? The stakes were so much higher now. Hamilton's betrayal hadn't only hurt him personally, but put his career and life in jeopardy.

It wasn't bloody fair.

He'd been so close to getting everything he'd ever wanted, everything he'd dreamed of since his days as a petty criminal in the East End – control of the city, respect, honour, unimaginable wealth. As the acting steward for The Consortium in London, he had savoured a taste of true power and he wasn't ready to let it go. He had to prove to them he was still the man they believed him to be.

The phone rang out once more. With frustration boiling over, he hurled it onto the countertop and smashed his fist down after it. An intense surge of anger boiled up inside of him. He snatched a vase of flowers from the breakfast bar and flung it against the wall, delighting in the chaos as the glass shattered into hundreds of tiny chunks. Yet the action did little to alleviate the pressure in his head and chest. Picking up two wine glasses from the sink, he launched them at the wall too, the remnants of red wine in the bottom of the glasses spreading up the stark white paintwork like blood spatter.

He scanned the room for more things to smash, other outlets for his rage. Violent eruptions like this had once been Delaney's default response to stress, but over the years he'd learned to tame his frenzied impulses.

Not today.

Finding nothing to relieve his destructive whims, he marched over to the bay window with his hand clenched, ready to punch his fist through the glass. At the last moment he pulled back, pounding his fist into his other hand instead. It stung. It didn't make him feel any better. All at once he felt small and insignificant. He slumped against the wall and closed his eyes as memories of his younger self bubbled up in his soul. That angry youth, desperate for power and recognition. He'd come so far. He couldn't go back. He wouldn't. But if The Consortium learned of his failures, he might not have a choice.

He opened his eyes to the sight of broken glass and wine-splattered walls. Fucking idiot, he chastised himself. Now he needed to do something constructive. Anything. Time was running out and unless—

His phone vibrated on the countertop.

It was them. It had to be. No one else knew this number. With his heart in his throat, he walked over and picked up the call.

"Mr Delaney. You've been trying to reach us?"

It was a woman's voice, husky and sophisticated. It was always a different voice; he had no idea how many of them there were.

"Yes. I have," he replied, trying to inject some levity into his voice. "I was beginning to think you were ignoring me." He laughed, but the woman remained silent.

"We want to see you," she said, her tone icy. "Today. 3 p.m."

"I see."

"We'll send a car for you," she told him. "Stay where you are until then."

The line went dead. Delaney stared at the phone display for a moment before tossing it against the wall.

"Beckett!" he roared. "You've fucked me! You bastard!"

A sinking feeling consumed him, spreading from the pit of his stomach throughout his body. The Consortium weren't calling him in for a strategy meeting. They'd found out. They knew. He'd disappointed them and now they needed a fall guy.

Unless he did something, he was a dead man.

30

Locke thanked the driver and stepped out of the unmarked black Range Rover onto the rain-slicked pavement of King Charles Street, adjusting his collar as he took in his surroundings. The Foreign, Commonwealth & Development Office loomed over him, its historic facade and stately architecture an enduring testament to Britain's storied past. The air was cold and damp, a typical March morning in London. Locke checked his watch: 8:57 a.m. Another gruelling day awaited him. He could only hope it went better than yesterday. It couldn't go much worse.

Bowditch joined him on the pavement and they nodded solemnly to each other, a silent pep talk before entering the building. Words had been sparse on the journey over from Nightingale House, the silence broken only by Bowditch relaying what Beaumont had told him – that Beckett was still alive and eliminating Delaney's foot soldiers with ruthless efficiency. This news offered some solace to Locke, but he couldn't shake a nagging thought – that his life would be a lot simpler with Beckett permanently out of the equation.

"Everything all right, sir?" Bowditch asked, unable to hide the wry smile on his face.

There had always been an unspoken tension between the two men, a professional rivalry that simmered just beneath the surface. Locke was well aware of Bowditch's ambition to claim the top spot for himself.

"All good, Bowditch. Thank you."

After passing through security and having their briefcases scanned, they walked together down a long, ornate corridor, their footsteps reverberating through Locke's already busy mind. The news that morning, that six of the compromised operatives were safe and on their way home, had been a relief. Yet the fact that the leak had happened at all threatened the very existence of Sigma Unit. If any whiff of their off-the-books manoeuvres reached the press or the public, it would be disastrous. Not only for him and his unit, but for the government, the country, even the world. Control of the situation had to be regained before it spiralled further out of his grasp.

As they neared the conference room for the briefing, hushed voices seeped into the corridor, prompting Locke to slow his pace when they turned the corner. A large man in a dark suit stood guard in the doorway. He opened the door for them as they approached, muttering a stoic, "Sir," as they nodded their thanks.

The Foreign Secretary was standing in front of a large window on the far side of the room, staring out at the grey morning. He turned as they entered and clapped his hands together.

"Ah, Locke, Bowditch. You're early. Well done."

His face was flushed with the same self-importance as always, but he looked tired around the eyes and his posture was weak. At his side, his aide, a young woman with mousy hair and a boyish figure, barely looked up from her smartphone.

"Shall I commence, Foreign Secretary?" Locke asked, as everyone took their seats. "I should brief you on the developments since—"

Shepherd cut him off with a raised finger. The sound of approaching footsteps echoed from the corridor outside, and Locke felt a draught run up the bottom of his trouser leg as the door swung open. Turning, he saw Xander Templeton striding into the room.

"Mr Templeton, thank you for joining us," Shepherd said.

"I was in the area." Templeton dismissed the offered chair and headed straight for the window. "Morning, all."

"I wasn't informed you'd be attending the briefing," Locke said.

"Not a problem, is it?" Templeton asked, turning to look at him with an imposing glare.

Locke countered with a cordial smile. "Not at all. It saves us going over this twice."

"Robert, why don't you start?" Shepherd said. "You were about to update us on Sigma Unit."

Composing himself, Locke began, confirming that six of the deep-cover operatives named on the leak were now safely on their way back to England, a revelation that brought a chorus of quiet approval. He went on to explain their top priority now was to focus on the fallout from the leak and that, by all accounts, Beckett was alive but remained uncontactable. He concluded by saying he had every confidence in his unit and their ability to contain the situation.

"There's one thing we haven't yet addressed in relation to this clusterfuck," Templeton said, gazing out the window. He turned, his heavy brow casting a shadow over his eyes. "The Consortium."

Locke leaned back in his seat. Beside him, Bowditch bristled uncomfortably. Shepherd coughed and glanced at his aide.

"We've been monitoring their activities as best we can," Locke replied cautiously. "But we don't want to jump to conclusions without solid intel."

"Screw solid intel," Templeton growled. "This situation is getting away from us. Can't you see that?"

Locke pursed his lips as he processed Templeton's words. It was no secret that The Consortium's rise to power had taken them all by surprise, a collective failure of the British intelligence community. Their understanding of the organisation, even six months later, was still irritatingly vague.

"As you are aware, Mr Templeton," Bowditch interjected. "Sigma Unit, along with both MI5 and MI6, have been working together on a joint task force to gather information on the group."

"Yes? And…?"

Templeton's words hung in the air. Bowditch shot Locke a look of distress and he picked up the thread.

"Beckett had been investigating key Consortium members in London," he said. "From what we can surmise, he was making good progress and getting close to uncovering vital information. It's plausible that The Consortium realised this and somehow discovered Beckett was secret service. If that is the case, and they are behind the leak, they're more powerful – and a lot more dangerous – than we anticipated."

"Obviously," Templeton snapped. He moved from the window and leaned over the table, jabbing a big finger down as he continued. "They've caught us all with our pants down. Not just here, but across Europe."

"But it doesn't make sense," Locke said. "If they saw Beckett as a threat, why not eliminate him themselves?"

Bowditch shuffled beside him. "We already know they don't get involved firsthand with anything dirty. They'd have assumed Delaney would have taken care of a mole without hesitation."

"But they weren't counting on that mole being John Beckett," Locke added.

"Ah yes, quite the soldier," Shepherd mused. "What do we suspect Beckett's next move will be?"

Locke clasped his hands together in front of him. "We simply can't predict, Foreign Secretary."

A tense silence followed, interrupted only by Shepherd's aide as she tutted and swiped at her phone screen.

Templeton made a low growling noise before he spoke. "Regardless of Beckett's actions, we must tread carefully in relation to The Consortium."

Locke's frown deepened. "What do you mean?"

"The Consortium are… bad news," Templeton said, choosing his words with care. "We all agree on that. However, they could be a valuable asset. Whoever they are, they have a lot of resources and I'm not just talking money – although, by all accounts, they have more than one billionaire in their ranks. The CIA has reason to believe their scientists are on the brink of developing an advanced AI-based Cyber Defence Module. Once operational, it could predict potential cyber attacks, detect real-time intrusions, and initiate countermeasures to neutralise threats. We also understand it could have the capability of forecasting potential conflict zones, analysing social media and phone networks to highlight threats to life – *before* they happen."

Locke let out a bitter laugh. "Let me guess. You want to get your hands on this technology, and you don't want to upset The Consortium before it's ready. Jesus Christ, I can't believe what I'm hearing. Or rather, unfortunately I can."

He glanced at Bowditch, but his second in command remained silent, his face inscrutable. Shepherd, on the other hand, appeared out of his depth, his eyes darting nervously between his aide and the tough American.

"Hold your nerve, Locke," Templeton told him, his voice

low and controlled. "This could be a real boost for the UK, too. Think about it. You could pre-empt terror attacks, stop political unrest at source."

"And how legal is this system?" Locke asked, already suspecting the answer.

Templeton held his hands out, the wide grin of a used car salesman playing across his face. "Now, gentlemen, let's not lose ourselves in unnecessary details, shall we? We're acting for the greater good here."

Locke gritted his teeth, British stoicism winning out over his mounting anger. He couldn't afford to lose his cool, especially not now. But he also couldn't stay here and listen to Templeton for another second.

"Right, well, if there's nothing else, Foreign Secretary," he said, his tone firm as he rose from his seat, "I must excuse myself. Duty calls."

He hastily collected his belongings and exited the room. As he strode down the corridor, he could hear Bowditch wrapping up the meeting and hurrying after him, but he didn't turn around. He was losing his grip on the situation and what Templeton was suggesting was far too risky. If The Consortium were behind the leak, then doing nothing would essentially mean surrendering control. He couldn't allow that. But if The Consortium did want Beckett dead, how far would they go to achieve that aim? This was getting out of hand. Something was going to blow.

He could feel it in the air.

31

Across town, Beckett was concealed behind an industrial waste bin in an alleyway not far from Kings Cross Station. Having abandoned the Audi in a Camden side street, he and Amber had made their way over on foot, sticking to the backstreets as much as possible. It was a cold morning and the air was damp. The alley stank of urine and rotten food, but it was important they wait. One wrong move and everything they'd gone through up to now would be for nothing.

"Can we not go yet?" Amber whispered. "I'm cold and my feet hurt."

"In a minute," he replied, not turning around. "We just need to be certain."

They'd already spent close to forty-five minutes in the alley so Beckett could scope out the building across the road and wait for anyone who might have followed them to show themselves.

"You said 'a minute' five minutes ago," Amber muttered under her breath.

"Well, this time I mean it."

The building in question was the Queen's Head Hotel, a neglected establishment that had seen better days. Restoring it to its former splendour, if it ever had any, would require more than a lick of paint and a new sign out front. Hotels in this area were notorious for attracting a questionable crowd – prostitutes and pimps, junkies and petty criminals – and that was precisely why Beckett had chosen this dilapidated hotel as their temporary sanctuary; normally it would be the last place he'd take his young niece. He hoped it would throw Delaney off the scent whilst they waited out the clock and secured Amber's passport.

"Okay," he said, satisfied they hadn't been tailed. "It looks safe to proceed."

Gathering his holdall and Amber's rucksack, he led her across the road to the hotel. Up close it looked even more dilapidated than it had done from the alley. The bricks were stained with grime and exhaust fumes, while the windows were streaked with layers of dirt and neglect. A neon sign flickered on the side of the door, casting a pink glow over the entrance. The overpowering scent of decay hit Beckett in the face as he opened the door and guided Amber inside.

The reception area was as uninviting as the building's exterior suggested it would be. Faded wallpaper that looked to have been there since the eighties covered the walls, and a large brown watermark spread out from one corner of the ceiling. The carpet, threadbare and revealing its underlay in several places, had long since lost its original colour. A musty scent – a disagreeable mix of stale cigarettes, old beer, and bodily fluids – clung to the air. The counter was manned by a tall, wiry man with hooded eyelids and a crooked nose. He eyed Amber with a lecherous gaze as they approached, then gave Beckett a knowing smile. It made him want to grab the pervert by the head and slam his face into the counter. Maybe not stop until there was no counter left. And no face.

He made do with clenching his fists until his knuckles burned, maintaining his composure as he addressed the man. "Do you have a room we can take for the night?" he asked. "Perhaps two nights."

"Two nights? Okay, cool, whatever," he replied. "It's a hundred and ten a night. So that's… umm… two-twenty in total. Are you paying cash? Most people do."

Beckett confirmed with a nod, retrieving a roll of cash from his jacket. He peeled off four fifties and a twenty, sliding them across the counter.

The man accepted the payment and slid back a key with '118' etched onto a round plastic tag.

"First floor," he said, pointing towards a white door to his right with a glass panel in the centre. "The lift's out of service, so you'll have to take the stairs."

"Fine." Beckett scooped up the key and beckoned to Amber. "Let's go. You first."

They headed through the door, finding themselves in a low-lit stairwell – a fire escape rather than a primary staircase – with lino-covered stairs and a metal handrail that was once white but was now more rust than paint. As they headed up to the first floor, faint echoes of muffled disputes and unenviable wails drifted down from above.

The door to room 118 was as weathered as the rest of the establishment. Beckett pushed it open, revealing a predictably dismal room. A double bed, its mattress sagging, was positioned against an open window, a yellowing net curtain fluttering in the breeze. Other than the bed, there was a rickety chest of drawers, a worn-out armchair that had seen better decades and a grimy sink unit on the wall facing the door.

While Amber inspected the room, trying the taps on the sink, Beckett tossed his bag onto the bed and retrieved two rolls of fifties and the burner phone from the side compartment. He checked the phone. A recent text from Beaumont revealed that the forger had finished the passport but was now asking for an extra grand due to the quick turnaround. It irked to be held over a barrel in that way, but Beckett had anticipated it. Beaumont's text also confirmed a rendezvous for the pick-up – a Mexican restaurant beneath a railway bridge near the South Bank. He checked the time. He had just over an hour.

Stashing the money rolls inside his jacket, he turned to Amber. "Your passport is ready. I need to go pick it up." Her eyes widened, a glimmer of fear seeping in. She was a bright girl, quick to understand. "I can't take you with me," he confirmed. "I'm sorry. It's too dangerous. You'll be safer here."

She shook her head, open-mouthed. "I can't stay here alone. What if someone bad shows up?"

"They won't. I'll make sure of it," he reassured her, maintaining eye contact. He didn't like leaving her alone, but he'd spent the last hour assessing their options and he was convinced this was the best course of action. It was dangerous enough to be out in daylight, surrounded by surveillance cameras and CCTV, but having to worry about Amber too would only complicate things further. He tilted his head to one side and forced a smile. "Amber, you're going to be fine."

Tears welled in her eyes but she held them back. She was scared, but she trusted him. "I can handle it," she whispered, offering him a shaky smile. It was more for his benefit than hers and he appreciated the effort.

He stared at her for a moment longer. His niece. His only family. Being an S-Unit officer meant suppressing emotions, but he wished he could offer her more comfort.

"I will protect you," he told her, his voice steady despite the turmoil brewing within. "But for now I need you to stay here. Don't open the door to anyone but me."

He handed her the burner phone. "Take this. If anything happens, call the saved number. It'll connect you to Jacob Beaumont. You can trust him. He's a friend, a good man." He squeezed her hand gently, a silent reassurance that he hoped she got.

"But you're coming back?"

"You can count on it. I'll call you on that phone when I'm on my way back to the hotel. Make sure to answer. I'll be the only person who'll call."

"Thanks," she replied, suddenly looking very childlike. "But please don't be too long."

"I won't."

He held her gaze, his eyes softening for a moment. Then he turned and left the room, shutting the door behind him. "Lock it," he whispered through the wood, but she was already there on the other side. He heard the mechanism click and headed down the stairs.

Leaving the hotel, he made his way across the street and back to the alley, taking cover behind the industrial waste bin, his senses on high alert. His eyes, trained to spot the slightest anomaly, scanned the early morning scene. Commuters mingled with locals, jostling for space on the pavements and walkways. Further down the road in front of the station was an old newspaper kiosk, the vendor huddled over a hot drink as he awaited customers. Beckett's ears were filled with the sounds of the city – blaring horns, noisy engines, the hum of a million conversations all happening at once – but none posed an immediate threat. His heart beat a steady rhythm in his chest. He was in control.

The biting wind whistling through the alley barely fazed him. His focus was on the grimy windows of the Queen's Head and the area immediately in front and down the side of the building. Leaving Amber alone was a gamble, a high-stakes one at that. But in this deadly game they were playing, every decision came with an inherent risk.

He waited another thirty minutes in the stinking alleyway, but no one entered the hotel. He gave it a few more minutes;

then, satisfied, he left his post and crossed the road, merging with a group of foreign students and disappearing into the crowds. His destination was the underground station located in front of Kings Cross's main outlet. Descending swiftly onto the concourse below, he found the right platform and saw the next Tube train was due in three minutes. It would take him twenty-five minutes with a change at Leicester Square to get to Embankment and he could walk to the pick-up point from there. The rendezvous was in forty-five minutes. It was going to be tight, but he could make it. He had to.

32

Ruth Armitage zipped up her hoodie, huddling closer to the laptop monitor as her eyes scanned the data on the screen. The central heating had yet to come on, but the hollow chill she felt in her soul was more likely a result of extreme tiredness. She lifted her foot onto the chair, hugging her legs to her chest while her other hand danced across her laptop keyboard.

Beaumont's orders had been explicit – go home and get some sleep, then check in with him once she was back in the office. But how did he expect her to sleep when they were in the midst of a crisis and the origin of the breach was still unknown? Also, she'd wondered if there was an ulterior motive behind the request – that Beaumont was sidelining her to stop her getting closer to the truth. But she'd dismissed this notion almost as readily as it had formed. She'd only been working under Beaumont's guidance for a short while, but she trusted him. He was one of the good ones. Kind, helpful, generous with his time. And Ruth had seen how his eyes had lit up when, at the end of a recent briefing, he'd mentioned his wife. A loving relationship like that spoke volumes about his character.

However, she couldn't extend the same trust to everyone at Sigma Unit. This was a highly sensitive situation and it was clear now that Beaumont didn't want to disclose her findings until definite proof was discovered. Which was why Ruth had decided to work from home this morning instead of going into the office. She'd emailed Beaumont to let him know, citing a migraine for her absence and that she hoped to be back at Nightingale House by the afternoon. It was now 11 a.m. She planned on spending the rest of the morning on the leak and hoped to have solid intel for him on her return to the office.

But she wasn't there yet.

Dropping her foot to the floor, she leaned back and sighed. She knew she was missing something. She stretched her tense muscles and rolled her neck from side to side. The workstation in her room was much more comfortable, but for the last twelve hours the kitchen table had been her domain. It was cluttered with papers and empty mugs, but here she had everything she needed – a fast internet connection, a robust VPN and a close supply of caffeine.

The rest of her flat was modest, with the living room leading into the dining area and then the kitchen. The plain walls were adorned with the kind of typical art prints you saw in most modern rentals – a line drawing of a plant, a pile of rocks, a black-and-white image of an old bicycle. She hadn't yet had the chance to personalise her space – her life having been a whirlwind since joining Sigma Unit – but eventually she envisioned a home adorned with decent artwork, a bookcase brimming with her favourite novels and a couch that didn't look so forlorn.

Ruth rubbed her weary eyes and pushed back from the table, the scrape of her chair against the laminate floor puncturing the silence of the flat.

Speaking of caffeine…

Grabbing her most recent mug, she headed into the

kitchen, filling the kettle at the sink and switching it on. As the water heated, she delved into a cabinet, procuring a jar of instant coffee and placing it down next to the mug. She smiled to herself as she regarded the worn photo on the side, of her and three friends at Marcy's twenty-first birthday party. It all felt like such a long time ago now. She barely even spoke to those women anymore. It was a shame, but people moved on. Life moved on. And right now she had more pressing matters to concern herself with.

As the water in the kettle reached boiling point, she scooped a generous helping of coffee into her mug and added the water. A rich aroma filled the room, momentarily grounding her as she refocused herself on the task at hand. Holding the warm mug, she leaned against the countertop, her gaze flitting back to her laptop. Despite the perspective offered by this break, she hadn't eradicated the knot of unease in her stomach, the nagging feeling that there was something she was missing. It was like a jigsaw piece that didn't quite fit, a note in a song that was ever so slightly out of tune.

"Come on, Ruth. Think," she muttered to herself.

She closed her eyes, replaying the evidence in her mind. A classified document leaked anonymously online and originating from a darknet site shrouded in digital misdirection. Early suspicions had pointed to Russia or China being the culprits, but she now knew differently. She'd already meticulously examined the metadata and timestamps of the document when the leak first happened.

But, what if…?

She paused. Her eyes snapped open. Could she have missed something? Or had she been looking in the wrong place?

Spurred on by a surge of adrenaline, Ruth returned to her laptop. Setting her coffee down, she hunched over the keyboard, her fingers a blur as she typed. She'd been too fixated on the content and origin of the document. But what about its digital fingerprint?

Locating the original document, she ran it through a basic extraction program and sat back, open-mouthed, as it revealed an embedded image file on a hidden layer. Examining this file closer, she saw it was a photograph of the original list of names that someone had inserted into the PDF document.

Saving this as a new file, she ran it through a metadata extraction tool she'd developed during her university years – a handy little program designed to dig deep into the binary DNA of any file. As fresh data populated her screen, she felt another rush of nervous energy. She was getting closer. The last IP address used to access the file glared at her from the screen. She cross-referenced it with the Sigma Unit's database of known malicious IPs, her breath hitching when it came up clean. But that didn't mean a dead end. It simply meant a U-turn was needed. A change of perspective.

She took a large gulp of coffee, grimacing at the burn in her throat as she sifted through the labyrinth of new data, her eyes scanning every byte and bit of information for clues.

The truth was lurking here, somewhere. It had to be.

Her fingers flew across the keyboard, typing commands into her terminal. She initiated a complex traceroute – a digital pathfinder designed to trace the data packet's journey back to its source. It was a daunting task, like finding a needle in a haystack of encrypted data, but nothing was impossible. Not for someone like her.

The traceroute zigzagged across numerous nodes, making several jumps before finally landing on an IP address. She ran this through a geolocation tracking software and felt a cold shiver run down her spine as a London street address flashed up on the screen. She blinked, disbelief and anger washing over her as she stared at the address. It was one she knew well. She travelled there most days.

Nightingale House.

Ruth leaned back, her hands trembling slightly. This wasn't a power play by a foreign aggressor. It was an inside job. A leak from within Sigma Unit. Someone competent enough to cover their tracks, but not enough to completely wipe the metadata clean.

She quickly took screen captures of her findings, detaching the USB bracelet from her wrist and backing up the files. Her breath quickened, along with her heart rate as she worked, swatting away a flurry of intrusive thoughts. Whoever had leaked the document had access to secure government systems. If they'd gone to this much trouble to sabotage their country's security, they were undoubtedly dangerous. But she was an analyst. It was her job to uncover the truth, no matter how unsettling or risky it could be. And she had Beaumont in her corner.

Finishing her coffee, she next examined the Nightingale House server logs. She went through them line by line, taking care not to let a single piece of data escape her notice. The logs were a complex thread of timestamped entries, each entry representing an action taken on the server – some as mundane as a system status check, others as significant as a file transfer. She scrolled through the connection log, searching for more anomalies. Her heart lurched as the realisation hit her. The timestamp. The embedded image file had been uploaded in the middle of the night, well past the normal working hours at Nightingale House.

She dove back into the server logs, now cross-referencing the timestamped entries with Sigma Unit's employee access logs. She was seeking a correlation, someone present at Nightingale House at that specific time. She held her breath as she ran the script, her fingers anxiously tapping against her empty coffee mug. The script shifted through thousands of log lines before finally spitting out a result. One match.

"No fucking way."

Ruth sank into her chair as she stared at the name on the screen. She had found the source of the leak, and it was much closer to home than she'd ever imagined.

"What do I do now?" she whispered into the silence of the room.

The implications of her discovery rippled through her system. This was bad.

This was very bad indeed.

33

The Queen's Walk brimmed with vibrancy as Beckett crossed over the railway bridge from Embankment, racing down the steps to the concourse in front of the South Bank Centre. Street performers, their faces painted in colours as vivid as their performances, danced with exuberant gusto. Tourists, awestruck by the city's grandeur, raised their phone cameras at the carousels in Jubilee Gardens and the London Eye further down the river. Bankers and suits navigated through the crowds, their minds already in the glass-and-steel skyscrapers overhead.

Amidst this lively tableau of urban life, Beckett was an anomaly. His piercing blue eyes, hardened by decades of service, observed every detail as he threaded his way through the crowd, making his way along Concert Hall Approach towards Waterloo Road and the row of restaurants built into the bridge's archways.

El Refugio was the second restaurant on the strip, an unpretentious Mexican place half-hidden in the archway's shadow. In contrast to similar eateries that favoured the bright colours of the Mexican flag for their decor, the exterior was done out in subtle shades of crimson and gold. It looked both classy and unassuming. The perfect setting for a rendezvous such as this.

He pushed through the door, descending into the basement restaurant where the robust scent of spices and slow-cooked meats enveloped his senses. It was early for lunch and the dimly lit room he found at the bottom of the stairs was half empty. A murmur of conversation reverberated off the exposed brickwork.

On the far side of the room, an open kitchen was a hotbed of activity. Chefs in crisp white uniforms worked with a frenzied determination as they chopped and tasted and blended, their immense flame-lit pans sizzling and spitting sparks. A heady mix of smells – chillies, garlic, tomatoes – hovered like a fragrant cloud above them. A pair of young female servers bustled between the tables, swinging trays laden with al pastor tacos, aromatic pozoles, and slow-cooked carnitas. Loud Mariachi music played from wall-mounted speakers, amplifying the lively atmosphere despite the early hour.

The food smells made Beckett's stomach growl, but he had no time to eat. Moving further into the restaurant, he spotted his contact without difficulty. Despite never having met him before, the man was unmistakable. He was of Eastern European descent, his large eyes darting restlessly around the room, bouncing off the aged, sepia-toned images of Mexican landscapes and the colourful sombreros decorating the walls. His fingers drummed an erratic rhythm on the table's Formica top. Upon noticing Beckett, he hesitated, before Beckett gave him a curt nod.

Yes, it's me.

The man averted his gaze, taking a deep breath before standing and making his way to the bathroom in the far corner. Beckett claimed a table near the entrance, offering him a good view of the room and a quick exit should he need one. He waited a minute; then, satisfied all was in order, he followed his contact into the bathroom.

"I thought you'd changed your mind," the man said as he entered.

"Just making sure I wasn't followed," Beckett replied, studying the forger's appearance for signs of a concealed weapon.

"I'm not carrying," he told him, raising his hands.

"Good." Beckett leaned in closer, lowering his voice. "Do you have the package?"

From his jacket, the man produced a small manila envelope. "It's all here. But first I need the rest of the payment."

"No," Beckett said coldly. "First I see the goods. Then you get paid."

The forger held Beckett's icy gaze for a moment before his sense of self-preservation won out and he handed over the envelope. "Fine. Check it."

Beckett unrolled the envelope and slid the passport out from inside. Flipping to the last page, he saw Amber's photo alongside the name Megan Samuels. He inspected the layout and design, running his fingers over the embossed coat of arms, checking the quality of the laminate.

"It's good work," he said.

"I know it is. Now you pay."

"Fine." Beckett pulled out two rolls of notes from his pocket.

"What the fuck?" the forger hissed. "I said crypto. XMR. That's how we do this."

Beckett clicked his teeth. "Yes, I know that was your preferred payment method but I'll be honest with you, I've had a rather eventful few days. Cash is all I can do." He held the money out, not breaking eye contact with the man. "Here, take it. Two grand in used notes. An extra thousand for your troubles."

The man grunted and began to protest, but seemingly lost his bottle. "All right, fine," he growled, snatching the money and unrolling one of the bundles.

"It's all there," Beckett told him. "Are we good?"

There was a moment of hesitation before the man gave a begrudging nod. "Yeah. Sure."

He glanced Beckett up and down, decided against saying anything else, then slipped past him and out of the bathroom. Beckett used the toilet before washing his hands and raking his fingers through his hair. Then he zipped up his jacket and headed back through the restaurant and up the stairs.

Outside, an ominous feeling of being watched immediately pricked the nape of his neck The familiar sensation, which had saved his life more times than he could count, instantly put him on high alert. Without turning his head, he let his gaze drift over the bustling street outside the restaurant. He clocked him immediately, standing at the bus stop across the street. He was wearing dark blue jeans and a brown suede jacket over a black shirt. He wasn't looking Beckett's way, but Beckett's instincts, finely tuned and razor-sharp, screamed danger. With his senses elevated, he set off, walking at a brisk pace away from the restaurant and slipping into the first side street he came to.

Once out of sight, he quickened his pace, moving to the end of the street and ducking down a narrow alley, which opened onto a wide road with traffic going past on both sides. As he got to the end of the alley and stepped out onto the pavement, he glanced back, only to see the man from the bus stop rounding the corner.

Without hesitation, Beckett crossed the street, dodging between cars and motorcycles then sprinting down another side street further along. His feet pounded the cracked, uneven concrete as he tried to put distance between himself and his pursuer. Behind him was the sound of the man's heavy footsteps. Beckett took a sharp right, doubling back and attempting to lose him in another dark alley. But the man kept pace, a relentless shadow matching Beckett's every move. This was a man who knew the game as well as Beckett, a realisation that only added to his unease as he cut across a main road and slowed his pace through a crowded square where an artisan market was in full swing.

Weaving between the stalls, he headed for the far corner and down a narrow passageway that opened onto a deserted backstreet. Turning, he walked backwards for a few steps, alert for any sign of his pursuer. The stakes had never been higher, the dance never more dangerous. He thought of Amber in the hotel room, alone and scared. But he couldn't go back there now. Not until he'd neutralised this imminent threat.

As the man's footsteps resonated down the passageway after him, Beckett stopped. The guy wasn't going to give up the chase anytime soon. It was better to face him head on.

The only way forward was through.

Squaring his shoulders, Beckett moved over to the nearside wall to wait. Whoever this man was, he wasn't going to stop of his own accord. He had to make him stop.

34

Street fights were a good metaphor for life. You only got one chance to make a first impression. Similarly, if you messed up, if you made a fatal misstep, you were looking at a one-way trip to the morgue.

It also helped to get a head start on your opponent.

As the man rounded the corner, Beckett exploded into action. His body was a finely tuned weapon with the power of a striking viper. Before his opponent's brain had fully acknowledged Beckett's presence, he'd launched himself in the air, smashing his fist into the man's nose. He felt the satisfying crunch of cartilage beneath his knuckles, but despite stumbling back, the man remained standing. Beckett, undeterred, sprang forward, but his adversary was nimble, avoiding his advance and stomping down hard on the back of his shin. His leg faltered and he barely evaded a swift kick, feeling the rush of displaced air as the boot narrowly missed him.

And now the element of surprise was gone.

The man wiped blood from his mouth, grinning as he produced a knife from his belt. The steel blade glinted menacingly in the light. The two men circled each other, the air thick with the promise of violence.

The man lunged, slashing the knife in a wide arc. Beckett dodged away, the blade slicing through the space his throat had occupied a split second earlier. But the man was skilled, and as Beckett pivoted, the blade trailed his movement, carving a fiery streak across the back of his hand. Biting back a grunt, he refused to allow the pain to distract him as he retaliated with a savage punch to the man's throat. It was a brutal blow that sent the guy reeling. Beckett followed up with a calculated kick to the side of the knee, causing the man to buckle. He tried to retaliate, but Beckett was quicker, his movements honed by years of experience. Striking fast and hard, he delivered a series of punishing blows, aiming for the vulnerable Adam's apple area. Next, he grabbed the wrist wielding the knife and gave a sharp twist. There was a sickening snap, and the knife clattered to the ground.

Stepping away, Beckett watched as the man clawed at his crushed windpipe with his good hand. He was on his way out; the least he could do was put the poor bastard out of his misery. In one fluid movement, Beckett scooped up the knife and drove it upwards through the man's ribs.

What could he say – he was all heart.

The man gasped and let out a feeble groan, his eyes wide. A moment later the spark of life faded from them and he dropped to the ground.

Beckett assessed the wound on his hand as he caught his breath. The gash was about an inch long but not too deep. The tube of superglue and roll of Quikclot combat gauze in his go-bag would sort it. He knelt beside the dead man and searched his jeans' pockets, finding nothing but a set of keys. Moving onto his jacket, he found a folded piece of paper in the inside pocket. Opening it out, he saw photocopied headshots of himself and Amber. Her picture had been lifted from her provisional driving licence; his was the one he'd provided when he joined the SAS. He was a lot younger in the photo, with fewer lines around his face, but the determined look in his eyes remained unchanged.

Stuffing the paper in his back pocket, Beckett resumed his search, opening up the man's shirt and then leaning back.

"Bloody hell."

The man had a tattoo on his chest, just above his right nipple. It was small and aged, the faded ink bleeding into the pigment of his skin, but was recognisable all the same – a downward pointing Excalibur wreathed in flames. The guy was SAS. Or he had been at some stage.

Cold dread washed over Beckett. Either this man was still Special Forces, or he was now a merc working for Delaney. He knew which option he'd prefer. Confusion and worry twisted in his guts. He needed answers.

Exiting the alleyway, Beckett found an old phone box down the road. He fed fifty pence into the slot and dialled his burner phone, eyes scanning his surroundings through the grimy glass as the phone rang… and rang…

"Come on, Amber, pick up!"

His plea was answered with the hollow sound of three beeps, signalling the call had rung out. Panic surged.

Why wasn't she answering?

He abandoned the phone box and hailed a passing cab, covering his bloody hand with the sleeve of his jacket as he gave the driver the address of the hotel and promised him triple the fare if they arrived within fifteen minutes. The driver set off, muttering something about him 'being on a mission', but Beckett was too preoccupied to respond. As the car weaved through traffic, he played out scenarios in his mind, strategizing how he'd deal with each one.

Twenty minutes later, the taxi pulled up to the hotel. Beckett handed a fifty to the driver, more than triple the fare, before rushing up the steps and into the dingy reception area. Thankfully there was no sign of the concierge as he headed for the stairs, taking them two at a time up to the first floor. On the landing, he stopped. The door to room 118 was ajar. Moving over to the wall, he traversed the short distance and nudged the door open. He waited a beat. And another. Then, fists clenched and ready, he stepped into the room.

No…

The room was empty, a grim silence dominating the space. He checked the windows, checked the wardrobe. There was no sign of a struggle and both his and Amber's bags were still there. There was a possibility she was using the bathroom down the corridor, but he didn't think so. Exiting the room, he walked down there and knocked on the door. No response. He pushed at the door. No one was there.

Back in the room, he lowered himself to the carpet and found the burner phone under the bed. He wondered if Amber had kicked it there on purpose. It would be something he would have done. Flipping open the phone, he dialled Beaumont's number.

His old friend picked up on the second ring. "That you, John?" He sounded tired and somewhat resigned. Like he had the entire world bearing down on him. Beckett knew that feeling.

"Amber's gone," he said, skipping the niceties. "I left her in a cheap hotel room while I picked up the passport. I thought she'd be safe. She was. But someone's taken her."

"Shit. Delaney?"

"I've got to assume so, but I'm not sure…"

"What do you mean?"

Beckett paused, assessing the situation. Beaumont was a trusted ally, but in times like these it was crucial to be wary. Of everyone.

"I was followed," he started. "They tailed me from the

meeting point just now. One man. He was good, but I got the bounce on him."

"Dead?"

"Correct."

Beaumont made that low rumbling noise he often made when he was deep in thought. Cradling the phone under his chin, Beckett moved to the sink, rinsing the wound on his hand under the cold tap.

"Where is he now?" Beaumont asked.

"In a backstreet near Waterloo Station."

"All right, I'll dispatch a clean-up crew. We don't need any additional attention."

Beckett swept his gaze around the room. There was a dip in one of the pillows. Amber must have been lying down when she was disturbed.

"There's more," he said. "The guy had an insignia tattooed on his chest. He was SAS."

"*Was* – because you killed him or because he'd left?"

"I don't know. He could have been Special Forces, but equally he could have been a mercenary employed by Delaney. Unfortunately, it does rather muddy the waters."

Beaumont sighed. "Why would a Special Forces agent be trailing you?"

"You tell me." He zipped open his bag and removed the roll of combat gauze and the tube of superglue, dealing with the wound on his hand as they talked.

"Beckett, you need to come in," Beaumont told him. "You can trust me. I'll ensure you're given proper sanctuary and we'll find Amber together. Delaney might be a loose cannon with the might of The Consortium behind him, but if he's taken her, we'll get her back. Let Sigma Unit handle it. I'll make sure her rescue is properly actioned. But I can't help you while you're in the wind." There was a pause. When

Beaumont spoke again his voice was soft and low. "Come on, son. It's time. You can trust me. It's for the best."

Beckett sat on the edge of the bed, thumbnail scratching at his forehead. All at once he was worried. Troubling thoughts tangled with dark images in his brain. There was a lot to process and he had to play this just right.

"No," he told Beaumont. "I can't. Not yet."

"What? John!" Beaumont spat. "You can't come in or you can't trust me? Because let me remind you, I've been—"

"Both," Beckett cut in. "I'm sorry, Jacob. But for now I have to do this my way. And that means…" He trailed off as another thought hit him. He lifted his head, squinting out the window as he tried to get it straight in his mind. "Who assigned me this mission?"

"What?"

"The deep-cover surveillance operation within the Delaney Crime Syndicate. I thought at the time that it was unusual to deploy an S-Unit officer internally for such a mission. Whose idea was it? Who authorised it?"

Beaumont was quiet for a moment. When he spoke his voice sounded different, like he was trying hard to stay calm. "Locke," he said. "I'm pretty sure it was Locke. Why are you asking?"

"Just a hunch," Beckett replied. "Something that just came to me. The whole thing could be a setup. But I need to find out for certain. So for now – no, I can't come in. And I can't trust anyone. I need to get Amber back my way."

"What are you saying?"

"If Delaney is so desperate to see me, then I'll grant him his wish." He stood and moved to the window. "I've got to go."

"But, Beckett," Beaumont gasped, "going in alone? That's a kamikaze move."

Beckett peered out the window at the pedestrians below.

Beaumont had a point – for some it could be a suicide mission. But not for him.

"I'll speak to you when I can," he told Beaumont. He hung up, then gathered his and Amber's belongings and left the room. He was done with running. It was time for John Beckett to become the aggressor.

35

Beaumont stared down at his phone screen, watching as the vivid image of Martha posing outside a pavement café in Venice, slowly faded to black. He placed the phone on the desk in front of him.

What a bloody mess.

He understood Beckett's reasoning, but to say he was concerned would be an understatement. He scratched at the scar tissue on his shoulder, his old chair groaning in protest as he did. He'd been the first to arrive at Nightingale House that morning, but now the corridors and rooms beyond his office hummed with activity – a constant reminder of a world in motion. Or a world on the brink of disaster. Nothing new there, but some days it could be overwhelming.

Martha had been on his case again lately to retire, or at least to work from home more frequently. She felt he was working too hard, giving too much of himself to the job. And he wasn't getting any younger.

"You're not a field operative anymore, darling," she'd gently reminded him that very morning, her delicate fingers tracing the lines on his weathered face. "You don't have to carry the weight of the world on your shoulders."

But how could he explain it to her? How could he make her understand the grave responsibility that came with his role?

"I'm needed," he'd replied, moving her hand down and kissing her forehead. "People's lives depend on it."

His phone vibrated on his desk, jolting him from his thoughts. He glanced at the screen, his heart skipping a beat as he saw the message alert. It was from Ruth Armitage.

He unlocked the screen and began to read. The message was long but to the point. She apologised for not being in the office, but explained how she'd been working from home. She went on to say how she'd discovered something 'of vital importance' and was hesitant to detail it via text or even a phone call.

Beaumont's mind raced, a sense of foreboding settling over him. From what he knew of Armitage, she was a methodical professional, not given to histrionics. Whatever she'd found must be serious. He read on. Armitage wanted to speak with him urgently, to show him what she'd unearthed. She requested he come to her flat within the next hour and not to speak with anyone until they'd met.

Beaumont glanced at the wall clock, the ghostly shape of its larger predecessor still visible on the sun-faded wallpaper down one side. It was 12:15 p.m.

He composed a brief reply – telling Armitage to sit tight and that he was on his way – and tapped send. Pocketing his phone, he grabbed his coat and headed out, locking his office door behind him. Armitage's flat was over in Kentish Town. He'd take his car. The drive would allow him the opportunity to gather his thoughts.

He had a lot to think about.

36

Overcast skies shrouded London in a blanket of grey as Beckett peered up at the three-storey townhouse before him. He'd opted for the house three doors down from Delaney's property simply because it was the only one on the row that seemed unoccupied this Wednesday afternoon. But it also had a large conservatory – an ideal access point.

With a firm grip, he scaled its robust timber frame and hauled himself up onto the sloping roof. Treading carefully across the expansive glass panes, he traversed to the main building and hoisted himself onto the ample ledge of a second-storey window. From there he could reach a drainpipe that descended from the guttering above. The pipe was made of metal and sturdy enough to take all one hundred and ninety pounds of him. Victorian construction; they don't make them like that these days.

He shimmied up the pipe, hooking an elbow over the guttering and used his upper body strength to pull himself onto the roof. Once there, he paused, his attention sweeping across the rooftops of Victoria and Pimlico, taking in the distinct outline of the Shard in the distance.

He'd driven over here after retrieving the stolen Audi from Camden and had parked a few blocks away, near his old flat. His go-bag and Amber's belongings, along with their passports, were locked in the boot. They'd be safe there. For now.

He'd also swapped his coat for a form-fitting black jumper, better suited for the task ahead, allowing ease of movement. His only weapon was a small knife strapped to his belt – an old thing that had been in his go-bag for years. The knife was a standard-issue MOD survival knife made of carbon steel, with a black handle and sheath. Special Forces doctrine said a knife should only be seen as a tool, not a weapon. But the way Beckett saw it, when the task at hand involved taking out hostiles without alerting others of your presence, it was handy to have a tool that was also sharp and deadly.

The wind and mist made the tiles treacherously slick as Beckett moved swiftly across the roof and clambered over the gables to the next house along. He may have found comfort in the cold metal of the knife pressed against his back, but it was he who was the real weapon here, a predator on the hunt. His senses were sharp, and his body and mind in stealth mode. As he closed in on Delaney's house, his pulse throbbed in his ears and adrenaline flooded his veins, but he was calm.

Delaney's house had a spacious attic room, with a skylight wide enough for him to slip through. With his trusty knife he pried the skylight open, and dropped into the dim, musky space filled with forgotten memorabilia and dust-covered furniture. The air was stale and heavy with the scent of mothballs. He silently crossed to the hatch on the room's far side, its metal hinges offering no resistance as he eased it open.

Directly beneath, he could see the cream carpet and the edge of a tall, slim table with a huge vase of white flowers sitting on top. He waited a few seconds, then lowered his head through the hatch. There was no one in sight, but that was expected. Delaney rarely used the upper floor except for guests. Patrick Hamilton himself had stayed in the bedroom across the landing whilst searching for his new flat.

Satisfied the coast was clear, Beckett grabbed the hatch edges and lowered himself onto the thick carpet below. Once there, he moved over to the railing that ran across the top of the landing, overlooking the stairwell. The first of Delaney's men was stationed at the bottom of the stairs, facing down the corridor leading to the first-floor landing. Slipping the knife out of his belt, Beckett moved down the wooden steps, his movements fluid and silent. He recognised the man as Harris, a nasty East End hoodlum who Delaney had taken under his wing a year earlier and put on guard duty. He was a big guy, but slow and undisciplined.

Creeping up behind him, Beckett clamped his hand over Harris's face, stifling any chance of a cry for help. Harris stiffened, the shock paralysing him momentarily. Before he could react, Beckett dragged the knife blade across his throat. Blood gushed out from the wound as Harris struggled to get away, but Beckett held on, his grip on the man's face unyielding.

"It's all right," he whispered in his ear. "Don't fight it."

Still maintaining a tight hold, Beckett guided the weakening man to his knees, sensing the life force leaving him. He gave it another five seconds, then lowered the lifeless body the rest of the way to the floor.

Stealthily, Beckett ventured deeper into the house, every fibre of his being on high alert. He had infiltrated the lion's den, but the lion himself was still at large. He made his way down the corridor, cautiously checking each room in his search for Amber. He didn't expect her to just be sitting passively in an upstairs room, but it was crucial to rule out all possibilities.

The corridor culminated in a grand first-floor landing, one

side dominated by the sweeping staircase that spiralled down to the ground floor. Opposite the staircase, a garish chaise longue upholstered in zebra hide sat beneath a colossal bronze-framed mirror. Beckett knew the layout well – four bedrooms, two bathrooms, a gym and a study all branched off from this central hub. The door closest to him led through to Delaney's master suite, and as he crept past, he could hear movement on the other side. He left it for now. Confronting Delaney wasn't an option while his thugs were still positioned around the house.

The abrupt sound of a flushing toilet jolted Beckett into alertness and he swiftly retracted his steps into the corridor. Crouching low, he peered around the corner. Another thug in a suit had emerged from one of the bathrooms and was now standing guard at the top of the stairs. Beckett didn't recognise this one, but he was big and bald, with a thick neck that fused into his cranium with no discernible join. He was also armed, the muzzle of an assault rifle visible around the side of his sizeable frame.

With his breath tight in his chest, Beckett glided across the landing, holding the survival knife at arm's length. It might only be a tool, but it was one perfectly crafted for his deadly trade. Once within range, he straightened to his full height and smashed the butt of the knife handle into the side of the man's neck. The blow was swift and heavy and left the big man stunned. Seizing him by the skull, Beckett jabbed a knee sharply into his back and steered the man's body away whilst twisting his head to the right. Utilising the guard's bodyweight to provide the force, Beckett drew the blade across his throat, severing both trachea and carotid arteries in a single stroke. The assault was so rapid and effective, the man never saw him coming and it was over before he knew what was going on. Beckett eased the body to the floor, shooting his attention over to Delaney's bedroom door as he did. He waited. No one came. He moved on.

As he made his way down to the first section of the ostentatious staircase, he clocked Eddie, one of Delaney's favourites, standing by the front door. Beckett had known Eddie as long as he'd known Delaney and he wasn't a bad guy, relatively speaking. But he worked for Delaney and that made him fair game.

The difficulty lay in Eddie's strategic position. Standing as he was, with his back to the front door and a clear sightline of the stairs, there was no blind spot to exploit, no possibility of a covert attack.

Beckett's mind whirred into overdrive. He needed a new strategy and fast. His eyes darted to Delaney's bedroom door. His presence in the mansion had stretched too long already. With every passing second, his advantage threatened to evaporate. His thoughts flickered between rapidly conceived strategies, each dismissed as swiftly as it arose.

Then it came to him.

It was a risky move, but it might work. Drawing in a deep breath, he retraced his steps back up to the landing. He had one shot at this. He had to make it count.

37

Back on the landing, Beckett's gaze was drawn to the assault rifle next to the fallen guard. It was certainly the easy option, but the noise would alert Delaney, and if he had Amber in the room with him, things could go very bad very quickly.

So… not an option.

Instead, Beckett hoisted the dead man under his arm and dragged the body towards the top of the stairs. The term 'dead weight' didn't even cut it, but Beckett was strong and full of adrenaline. Once in position, he shoved the body over the edge, and as it toppled down the first part of the stairwell, he moved over to the railing that offered an eagle-eye view of the lower steps.

The disturbance drew Eddie's attention. "Jay?" he grumbled. "What's going on?"

Beckett heard Eddie shuffling down the hallway towards the stairs. He called out again, but Jay's days of answering were over, and from Eddie's current position, the fallen guard was out of sight.

Whilst Eddie called out for a third time, Beckett climbed

over the top of the railing, perching precariously on the edge of the landing. Gripping the wooden banister behind him he waited, a predator poised for the fatal strike. Below him, the big man hesitated for a moment before shaking his head and stepping up onto the bottom step.

As Beckett's heart pounded a staccato rhythm in his chest, Eddie took another step. "Jay! What the hell's going on?"

The moment came. Eddie advanced, unknowingly positioning himself directly beneath Beckett's vantage point. As he did, Beckett launched himself forward, aligning his body with the force of gravity and cutting through the air like an arrow. Landing on Eddie's back, Beckett immediately wrapped his legs around his waist, absorbing the shock and redirecting it into the larger man's frame, forcing him to bear his weight as they stumbled forward.

Eddie's exclamation of surprise choked in his throat as Beckett's arm looped around his substantial neck, gripping him with relentless pressure. At the same time, Beckett's free hand secured the hold, pulling back to compress Eddie's airways.

The big man thrashed around, his strength surging in a desperate attempt to dislodge his attacker. But Beckett clung on, his grip tightening like a vice. As Eddie staggered onto the stairs, Beckett rode him down, the impact muted only slightly by the plush carpet.

And Beckett kept on squeezing. With the reduced blood flow to his brain, Eddie was fading fast. Twenty seconds was usually all it took to lose consciousness, but Beckett couldn't have him coming around in a few minutes. This had to be a permanent fix. Eddie ceased moving but Beckett maintained a tight hold for a full minute longer before releasing him. He rolled off and checked Eddie's pulse. Dead.

"No hard feelings, old boy," Beckett muttered, as he got to his feet.

It was standard procedure in Delaney's home to have two

men secure the downstairs rooms. One guarding the front door and the other in the kitchen covering the rear. Eddie had been dealt with. That meant there was one more to go.

Tensing his body for what was to come, Beckett crept into the hallway, pressing himself against the wall. Adjacent to him was the entrance to Delaney's large open-plan kitchen-diner, the likely position of the remaining thug. Slowly, silently, he inched closer to the door, knife poised and ready for action.

Once there, he peered around the doorframe. The door was slightly ajar, granting him a narrow view of the rooms beyond. He saw the grand dining room table, set for dinner as always, with full silverware and cut crystal wine glasses. He saw the edge of the worktop, dividing up the kitchen beyond. But he couldn't get eyes on whoever was on guard.

He ran his mind back through those he'd already eliminated.

Trey. It had to be Trey.

He nudged the door open a fraction, readying himself for an immediate attack. A second went by. And another. No one came. He eased the door open another inch. Still nothing. And another. Now he could shift his body around and get eyes on the entire room. As he did, he saw Trey standing at the far end of the kitchen in front of the patio doors. He was looking at something out in the garden and chuckling to himself. A squirrel maybe, or a cat. Beckett wasn't sure what was so funny, but he knew Trey to be rather slow-witted, so he could have easily been laughing at a cloud.

What Trey lacked in brains, though, he more than made up for in brawn. He was a human fortress, his hulking physique dwarfing the kitchen island in front of him. His hair was twisted back into thick cornrows that hung over the collar of a black bomber jacket, underneath which he wore a white t-shirt and black jeans. Beckett studied him, taking in his broad shoulders, his tree trunk arms, the casual ease with which he cradled the submachine gun in his grip. This was going to take all his mettle, but he had to clear all threats before he went for Amber. Both their lives depended on it.

He drew in a deep breath and held it in his lungs, slowing his heart rate in the process. He was outsized and outgunned, but he had the element of surprise. He had to make it count.

Keeping low, he slipped silently into the room, his eyes never leaving Trey as he advanced, utilising the breakfast bar and then the kitchen island as cover. He was almost within striking distance when the floorboard beneath him creaked and Trey whirled around, surprise flashing across his face. Time slowed down as Beckett lunged, his hand snatching for the submachine gun and smashing his elbow into Trey's throat. The blow stunned the guard and he released his grip, allowing Beckett to yank the gun from his hand and send it skittering across the tiled floor.

Trey roared, a bear deprived of its claws, and swung. But he was all raw power and rage against Beckett's precision and speed. Beckett evaded his initial onslaught, dancing around the first punch and ducking under the second. As he moved away, he swiped at the air with his knife, keeping Trey back. He needed an opening. But in the cramped confines of the kitchen, it wasn't straightforward. Stumbling against the island, he took a blow to the ribs, letting out a grunt as the pain radiated through his side. A heavy boot to the stomach sent him crashing back into the wall, dislodging the knife from his grasp. Trey, sensing his advantage, sprang forward, but Beckett dodged out of the way in time.

"Fucking traitor!" Trey snarled in a deep West London accent as Beckett sidestepped around him. "I'm going to end you!"

With both men unarmed, the fight turned primal. Beckett bobbed and weaved around Trey's blows, countering with a series of calculated strikes – a sharp jab to the ribs, a swift kick to the back of the knee, a heavy chop to the back of Trey's neck that sent him staggering into the countertop. Trey, flailing, grabbed the kettle and swung it at Beckett's head. He swerved away from the blow, using the momentum to pivot and drive his fist into Trey's kidney area.

With Trey gasping and off-kilter, Beckett darted towards his fallen knife. His fingers curled around the cool handle, and in a swift, fluid arc he drove the blade deep into Trey's flank.

The big man's snarl froze as his eyes bulged in surprise. He glanced down at the knife lodged in his side, his fingers instinctively reaching for the hilt. Before he had a chance to get it, Beckett ran at him and clambered up his back, locking him in the same punishing chokehold that had taken down Eddie. Trey growled, gnashing his teeth and lurching backwards in an attempt to dislodge Beckett and crush him against the wall. But Beckett held on, adjusting his grip and tightening the hold. He could feel Trey's body start to give – the stumble, the buckling leg, the slackening tension in his shoulders. He tightened his grip further.

Five seconds... Ten...

Trey was losing consciousness. As his massive frame began to slump, Beckett yanked the knife from out of his side and sliced it across his throat. Blood spattered across the pristine white tiles of the kitchen. Trey made a pathetic groaning sound and fell limp.

Exhausted, Beckett staggered back, panting heavily as he glanced around the kitchen. His muscles burned with effort and he could taste blood. A sharp pain radiated from his side, hinting at a possible cracked rib. But his determination remained unbroken.

Delaney's men were dead.

Now he went for Amber.

38

Beckett wiped his knife on Trey's trousers, and secured it in his belt before returning upstairs and crossing the landing towards Delaney's master bedroom. He paused outside the door, attuning himself to the subtle sounds coming from within. He could hear footsteps and muffled speech. It sounded as if someone was parading up and down.

Exercising caution, he moved away to check the other bedrooms first, silently easing each door open and flicking on the lights. They were all empty, the beds made. Even the children's rooms were tidy. It felt strange. Something was wrong.

But no sign of Amber.

He checked the main bathroom on this floor. He checked the study and the gym. Nothing.

One room left.

The footsteps had stopped as he returned to the master bedroom. He closed his eyes, focusing his senses on the sounds seeping through the heavy wooden door, visualising the scene beyond. He heard a faint rustling sound and the echoey clink of something hard hitting porcelain. Whoever was in there was in the bathroom.

Drawing his knife, Beckett silently cracked the door and slipped into the room. A large suitcase lay open on the bed, a pile of hastily packed clothes spilling out from inside. He glanced at the open wardrobe, at the empty rails and bare shelves. Miranda's clothes were all gone. Most of Delaney's were in the suitcase – expensive suits, dress shirts, polos, an array of Italian leather shoes and belts. A cloud of heavy cologne lingered in the air as Beckett crept forward, his muscles tight and his senses burning with anticipation. He heard the hiss of running water from the en-suite bathroom and a man's voice, muttering to himself.

Delaney.

Beckett crab-walked over to the bathroom door and pressed himself against the wall, knife in hand. The water stopped. A moment later, Delaney emerged wearing a navy tracksuit. Beckett watched him via the large mirror hanging over the bed. His face was distorted by intense concentration. He looked worried.

Well, good, Beckett thought. He ought to be worried.

As Delaney walked across the room, Beckett followed him like a shadow. The first indication the man got of his presence was the sensation of cold steel pressed against his throat and a voice in his ear.

"Stop. Don't do anything silly."

Delaney stiffened, his eyes darting to the mirror. "You," he hissed. "What do you want?"

"I want my niece back," Beckett replied, pressing the knife against Delaney's throat, applying enough pressure to spur him into the truth. "So, where's Amber?"

39

It was a few minutes after one in the afternoon when Beaumont reached Ruth Armitage's flat, tucked away in a leafy street in the heart of Kentish Town. Consulting the message she'd sent him, he pushed the intercom button for flat two, stepping back in anticipation of Armitage's voice or a buzzing sound to signal the door was open and he could enter.

Neither came.

He tried again, pressing the button for longer, hearing the distant echo of the buzzer emanating from the upper floor. The intercom system was working. So where was Armitage? The building housed three flats, but despite buzzing each one in turn, no one responded or appeared at the door.

Beaumont reviewed the message thread again. He'd told her he'd be there by one and she'd replied, urging him to hurry. She was expecting him.

A spike of unease coursed through him as he peered up at the first-floor windows. There was nothing to suggest a disturbance.

"Ruth," he called up. "Ruth Armitage. Are you in there?"

Silence. He tested the door handle: locked. He tried phoning, but the call diverted to voicemail after six rings.

"It's Beaumont," he said. "I'm outside your place now, where are you? Call me back as soon as you get this." He pocketed the phone. It was no use trying again. Something was wrong.

He tried the door a second time. Still locked. But shaking it hinted at the presence of a single Yale lock. Scanning the adjacent properties, he noted the conspicuous lack of activity – not entirely surprising for a Wednesday afternoon when most of the residents were likely at work or university.

Armitage's building was separated from the house next door by two adjacent driveways each ending at a garage. The garage for Ruth's building had a white door, which was wide open, revealing an empty space beyond. The other garage had a weathered silver door, but it was firmly closed.

Crossing both driveways, Beaumont knocked on the front door of the house. There was no answer. He gave it another thirty seconds, then hurried to the garage. His instincts told him this was a family home and there could be tools inside, something he could use to gain access to Ruth's building. The door didn't budge when he tried the handle, but the garage was old and the door slightly warped. Getting his fingers under the edge at one side, he was able to grind the door back against its mechanism and open it enough so he could slip under and get inside.

The garage was dark and smelt of petrol and dust. A small window high up on the back wall provided the only light. In the gloom, he could make out a lawnmower in one corner, a workbench with a box of yellowing newspapers on top and a row of gardening tools hanging from the wall. On the lower shelf of the workbench sat an old, battered toolbox.

Jackpot.

As well as a tray of rusty nails and a couple of

screwdrivers, the toolbox contained a claw hammer and a small crowbar – exactly what he needed. Stooping, he backed out of the garage and pushed the door closed before returning to Armitage's front door. Hammering the crowbar into a gap in the door, he leaned on it with all his weight until the wood splintered and the door gave way. Throwing a cursory glance down the drive, he stepped inside.

The hallway was sparse except for a narrow table under an old mirror. A bunch of letters addressed simply to 'The Occupier' lay on top.

"Armitage. Ruth," he called out. "Are you here?"

Knowing her flat was on the first floor, he climbed the stairs and approached the door, which was marked with a faded number two. He knocked and called out for her again. No response. He pressed his ear to the wood. There was no sound from inside.

Employing the crowbar once more, he pried the door open and tentatively stepped over the threshold, brandishing the hammer. The flat smelt of fresh paint. There were three doors leading off from a short hallway, two were closed but the one at the end hung open, revealing a spacious front room.

He headed through. The room was tidy and unremarkable. There was a sofa, a chair, a coffee table, a television stand complete with a large flatscreen on top. The furniture, although new-looking, was of a cheap quality – the kind cheapskate landlords bought in bulk. The front room fed into a dining area and then a kitchen. Beaumont walked over to the dining room table, noting the half-empty mug of cold coffee and the stack of yellow legal pads covered in notes. He scanned the first few sheets of the top pad, but saw nothing of relevance. What was he missing? Peering under the table, he spotted a power pack and a cable that would fit into the back of a laptop.

Standing, he ran his fingers over the table. It was cold, but leaning down he noticed a rectangular patch free of dust. The perfect size for a laptop.

"Ah, shit…"

Leaving the front room, he tried the next door along, which opened to a small bathroom filled with the smell of bleach and air freshener. He closed the door and moved on to the next room, his heart heavy in his chest as he swung the door open.

"Ah, no. Armitage…"

She was kneeling in front of an open wardrobe on the far side of the room, her arms at her sides. Her eyes were open, but the thin leather belt wrapped around her neck and attached to the wardrobe rail had ensured she'd seen her last day on earth.

Beaumont went to her and untied the belt, lowering her limp body to the carpet. She felt so small in his arms. The poor kid. He listened and felt for a pulse, but didn't expect to find one and he was correct.

"God damn it!" he snarled. This was on him. He should have been more cautious and offered her more protection. But he hadn't expected it would come to… this. Someone had intercepted his comms. Someone who didn't want him to know what Armitage had discovered. And if that was the case, the situation was graver than he'd realised.

Standing, he glanced around the room. It was relatively tidy, with no sign of a struggle. Whoever had done this was a professional. That knowledge didn't help the unease blossoming in his chest.

"What the hell did you uncover?" he asked Armitage's lifeless body.

He walked back into the dining room and began leafing through the pile of notepads on the table. Armitage was a good analyst – systematic, shrewd, logical. If she'd found something important, she would have made a note of it, a backup of some kind.

Moving into the kitchen, he pulled each drawer out in turn and rummaged through the contents. He found a couple of USB sticks, but they were old and dusty and one had something brown and sticky in the end. He pocketed them regardless, but wasn't hopeful they'd contain anything relevant. There had to be something else. He looked in the fridge, even in the washing machine, but it felt futile. Whoever had killed Ruth had taken her laptop and most likely any external hard drives along with it.

He was about to give up when a thought hit him.

Of course!

He ran back into the bedroom and over to Armitage's body. There it was, the bracelet, still on her wrist.

Dropping onto one knee, he clicked it open the way she'd done before. The USB connector gleamed in the light as he held it up. This was it. If Armitage had made a backup of her findings, it would be on here.

Reaching over, he gently closed the young woman's eyes and then got to his feet. Once everything was in order, he'd call this in and send a team around to handle it. He'd also find out whether Ruth had family and inform them personally of their loss – as well as how brave she'd been. But that was for later. Right now he had to get back to Nightingale House and find out what she'd discovered. Before anyone else got hurt.

40

Beckett pressed the cold steel of his knife against Delaney's throat. "Amber," he said again. "My niece. Where is she?"

"Piss off," Delaney spat.

"I'm serious, Rufus. Your men are all dead. I won't hesitate to kill you too."

Delaney scoffed. "You fucking idiot. She isn't here."

Beckett's jaw tightened, his eyes boring into Delaney's reflection in the mirror. "Where is she?"

Delaney raised his chin, the skin on his neck taut against the blade. "Listen, mate, you're in control here, don't you worry. But I think you and I need to talk."

"We've said all we need to," Beckett replied. "I just want my niece. Give her to me and I might even let you live."

"Is that so?" Delaney sneered. "I'm not sure that's down to you anymore."

"What do you mean?"

Beckett stepped back, his chest heaving with suppressed fury. The moment the knife's pressure lifted from Delaney's neck, he spun around and drove his elbow into Beckett's cheek.

"You fucking traitor!" he yelled. "You ruined everything!"

The blow knocked Beckett's focus. Before he could react, Delaney grabbed his wrist and twisted until he was forced to drop the knife. Beckett retaliated with a vicious right hook, sending Delaney stumbling into the centre of the room. He followed him, adopting a fighting stance.

"We were good together, me and you," Delaney growled, as he dabbed at his nose. "We could have been the best. You were my friend. My top man. And all along you were a fucking mole. Bastard!"

He launched himself forward, his face ruddy with rage, but Beckett met him halfway, determined to maintain the offensive. He knew full well no one ever won a defensive fight. You had to keep moving forward. Keep hitting them harder than they hit you.

Delaney aimed a low swing at Beckett's ribs, but Beckett swerved, retaliating with a swift knee to Delaney's midsection that left him gasping for air. His enraged, bloodshot eyes widened even further as he glared at Beckett. But Delaney was a seasoned brawler, a thug at heart. He rolled with it and recovered quickly.

With a feral growl, he sprang forward, a sharp elbow catching Beckett in the solar plexus and sending him careening into the dresser by the window. Beckett grunted as a sharp corner dug into his back.

"You bastard," Delaney growled. "I'll kill you for what you did."

Beckett righted himself as Delaney came at him again. They grappled, the room spinning around them as they battered each other against the walls and furniture. Beckett gripped Delaney's collar tight. Harnessing a sudden surge of energy, he abruptly shifted his weight back and flipped Delaney over his hip before clambering on top of him. From this vantage point, he spotted the fallen knife near the bed. He reached for it as Delaney shoved him away and attempted to scramble to safety, but there was nowhere for him to go. Delaney's back hit the wall, and as he struggled to rise, Beckett stabbed the knife into his inner thigh.

Delaney's screams filled the room, his body bucking as he grabbed at Beckett's hand still holding the knife. Sharp nails dug into his flesh, but Beckett didn't falter as he drove the blade deeper. Blood gushed from the wound, staining the pale carpet beneath them. Beckett got up and pulled out the knife, the room reverberating once again with Delaney's agonised cries.

"Where's Amber?" he snarled, grabbing a handful of Delaney's tracksuit top.

"I already told you," he wheezed, his face contorted in pain. "She isn't here, you fucking idiot."

"Then where is she?" Beckett demanded, his knuckles white with the intensity of his grip.

"I don't know! I never had her. You were always one step ahead of me."

"Stop lying!" Beckett roared, slamming Delaney's head against the floor.

Delaney gnashed his teeth, his face flushing red as he writhed beneath Beckett. "She's not here, Beckett! We've been played. Both of us!"

"What are you talking about?"

Delaney coughed, his body shuddering as blood continued to flow from the wound in his leg. It hadn't been Beckett's intention to kill him, not yet at least, but the knife had severed his femoral artery. He was bleeding out.

"The Consortium," Delaney rasped. "They're behind this. All of it. Don't you get it? Jesus, I thought you were supposed to be smart."

Beckett loosened his grip on him. "Why?"

"You were getting too close, weren't you? They must have known who you were. They set it up so that I'd find out too, and kill you. But that didn't go to plan, so now they want me dead as well." He tried to laugh but it came out as a painful-sounding cough. "Looks like they got their wish."

The blood was already draining from his face, pooling out through his leg.

"That's why I was leaving," he continued, gesturing with a shaking hand at the suitcase on the bed. "Miranda and the kids are already at the villa. From there we were going to head somewhere far away. Where they couldn't find us." He looked up at Beckett. "What a fucking life, hey – *John Beckett?*"

He sneered, and then his body stilled and his eyes glazed over. Beckett let go of him and got to his feet.

The Consortium.

His hunch had been correct, but now he was left with more questions than answers. Except he knew one thing for certain. Whoever was holding Amber had no idea who they were dealing with. They'd made a mistake. A fatal one.

They'd messed with John Beckett.

41

In the stillness of Delaney's bedroom, Beckett felt the world pressing down on him. He didn't know who he could trust or where to turn. But he knew he couldn't let the darkness overcome him. He had work to do. Stepping over Delaney's lifeless body, he moved into the en-suite bathroom.

In front of the large double sink unit, he removed his blood-soaked jeans and jumper and turned on the tap. The cold water stung his raw knuckles as he splashed water in his face and dabbed some onto the back of his neck. He straightened up, meeting his reflection in the mirror. His eyes, usually a vibrant blue, had a haunted quality to them that he dismissed as being due to stress and fatigue. After washing the blood from his hands and smoothing his dishevelled hair, a dark realisation hit him. Something he'd not thought of before.

What if...?

No, surely not.

He screwed up his face, trying to make sense of the conflicting theories fighting for precedence in his mind. Everything was in chaos. But maybe that was the point. Maybe that was what they wanted.

He opened his eyes and glared at himself. He needed the truth, but Amber needed him more.

Leaving the bathroom, he rummaged through Delaney's suitcase and found a pair of jeans and a black t-shirt amongst the designer suits and footwear. He knew they would fit; Delaney and he shared a similar physique. As he dressed, he thought back to all the times he and Delaney had spent together, harsh reminders of the underworld he'd inhabited for the last two years.

Beside the suitcase, a Glock 19 lay in a shoulder holster. Beckett checked the magazine was full and slid the pistol into his waistband, giving Delaney's corpse one last look before turning away. He had to get out of this place. Delaney's packing suggested he was expecting imminent company from The Consortium and didn't want to be here when they arrived. Well, that made two of them.

Beckett went downstairs and found Delaney's brown suede jacket on a hook near the door. An expensive brand; he'd been with Delaney when he bought it, and had always admired it. Slipping it on, he exited the house through the back doors. After scaling the garden wall, he found himself in an alleyway that opened out on a quiet street opposite a gated public garden.

Popping the jacket collar, finding respite from the biting wind, he hurried to the end of the alley and took a right, weaving through Pimlico's maze of backstreets towards where he'd left the Audi. In the distance were the muffled sounds of the city – police sirens, car horns, the hum of industry and the buzz of entertainment. They were sounds he recognised, a world he knew, yet all at once he felt exposed, vulnerable, every movement in his peripheral vision a potential threat. As he walked, the streets and alleyways seemed to close in on him, as if the city itself was part of the conspiracy.

Shaking off his unease, he pulled the phone from his pocket and hit redial.

"Beaumont, it's me," he said, as his old friend answered. He crossed over the road, his eyes darting around the scene. "Can you talk?"

"Just about," came the reply. "I've just parked up at Nightingale. There's a lot going on."

"You don't have to tell me that," Beckett replied. "Delaney's dead."

"Shit. You…?"

"Yes. But Amber wasn't with him. According to Delaney, he never had her and I believe him." Beckett was going to say more, but he stopped himself. "What's going on over there?"

From the sound of it, Beaumont was also now walking. Beckett heard the wind whistling over the mic at his end. "It's bad news," he said. "One of my analysts has turned up dead… murdered. But before that, she uncovered something about the leak. I don't know the details yet, but I found a flash drive at the scene. I'm hoping whatever she found, it's backed up on there."

"Shit," Beckett muttered under his breath. "Any ideas who killed her?"

"Not yet. But she must've been onto something big. It was a professional job, made to look like suicide. Whoever was behind it must have infiltrated my comms. It's the only way they could have known." He puffed out a breath. "I'm entering Nightingale now to see what's on the drive. But at this point, Beckett, we can't trust anyone."

"Well, you be careful in there."

"Why do you say that?" Beaumont asked, the tension in his voice palpable. "What are you thinking?"

"I'm not entirely sure." Beckett ran a quick assessment, decided he had to trust someone and continued. "Delaney believed The Consortium were behind the leak, but I think it goes deeper. It's only a theory at this stage, but remember I asked who assigned me this mission? What if The Consortium knew my real identity from the start and wanted me close to Delaney so they could keep an eye on him?"

"Bloody hell," Beaumont exclaimed.

"I know." Beckett crossed the street. The Audi was parked around the next block.

"But for that theory to make sense they'd have to be receiving your intel regarding Delaney's operations," Beaumont said. "The only people who had that information were Sigma Unit."

"Correct." The theory sounded even more troubling out loud, but his instincts told him he was on the right track. "The issue arose when I started investigating The Consortium. That wasn't part of my brief and they didn't like that, so they exposed me, banking on Delaney taking me out."

Beaumont whistled. "So let me get this straight – you're suggesting they knew who you were and were receiving information about Delaney from S-Unit?"

"Exactly."

"But if that's true, it means…"

"Yes," Beckett said. "We have a double agent in S-Unit."

"Shit." There was a heavy pause. "Well, it's not me. Could it be Locke?"

"Whoever it is, they've got Amber."

"Where are you headed?" Beaumont asked.

"I'm coming in. I'll be there in about twenty-five minutes. I'll use the back entrance. Keep a lid on things until I arrive."

"Be careful, Beckett."

"You too."

His steps quickened as he approached the Audi parked in the shadow of a tall building. Slipping behind the wheel, his mind swirled with thoughts of Amber, Delaney, The Consortium, a traitor within Sigma Unit. The enormity of it all threatened to engulf him, but he forced himself to focus. The game was far from over.

He switched on the engine, the low rumble shattering the hush of the still afternoon. As he eased the car away from the kerb, a rush of adrenaline ran down his spine. He was getting closer. He could feel it. But something told him the situation was going to get a lot more dangerous before the day was over.

42

Beaumont was sitting at his desk in Nightingale House, staring at the closed laptop on the desk in front of him. He'd only been here a short time, thirty seconds at the most, but he already felt different, like whatever happened next would rock the very foundations of his world. He rolled his shoulders back. The clock on the wall told him it was 2:15 p.m. He was also wasting time.

His eyes darted across the room at the closed door. He'd locked it behind him, but it didn't make him feel any less exposed. His gaze flicked up and around, scanning across the ceiling and the framed print on the wall – Monet's *The Houses of Parliament, Sunset*. There were no visible cameras, no obvious bugs. He had to presume whoever had infiltrated his communications had employed more advanced techniques than traditional listening devices or covert cameras.

Which was why the first order of business upon returning to control had been to collect an untouched, air-gapped laptop from the storeroom without signing for it. Having never connected to any online network meant there was no chance of ransomware, keylogger programs or other malicious software being present on the machine.

Beaumont eased open the laptop, and once the screen had flashed into life, he retrieved Armitage's USB bracelet from his jacket pocket and plugged it into the laptop's front port. The device promptly appeared on the virginal desktop. Armitage had named the device 'YOU IS BEE'. Beaumont smiled at the clumsy pun, but any amusement it might have brought him faded rapidly. He was doing this for her now. For Ruth. He had to continue her good work.

He ran his hand over the trackpad, opening the external device to reveal six folders. Four of the folders were numbered, one to four, while another was labelled 'stuff'. The final one was titled 'work'. He started there.

Opening the 'work' folder, he discovered two more subfolders, their titles a jumble of random letters. He checked the metadata of each file and selected the one that had been updated most recently – that morning. Inside he found a series of screenshots and a long list of text files. Casting a glance towards the door, he opened the first set of files and leaned into the screen. It appeared to be saved content from a terminal emulator or some other program Armitage had been using. Beaumont narrowed his eyes, scanning the document. Towards the bottom was a list of IP addresses, just random numbers to the untrained eye, but he recognised one immediately – the parent ID of Nightingale House.

"Bloody hell," he whispered at the screen.

Beckett had been correct. The Consortium, the leak… it was all somehow linked to Sigma Unit. He opened up more files, finding a screenshot of a geolocation tracking portal that had yielded the same results and a list of server logs Armitage had pulled from the system. There was also a file showing timestamped entries of Sigma Unit employees' access logs.

The information was useful and painted a damning

picture, but it wasn't the smoking gun he'd been hoping for. What was he missing? What had Armitage discovered?

What had she uncovered that had got her killed?

An idea came to him. Something Beckett had said. Leaning across the desk, he pulled his usual laptop towards him and booted it up. Once past the security screens, he navigated to the secure personnel files. Only himself, Locke and Bowditch, along with Emily Eastwood at M15 and Frank Calder at MI6, had access to these files. It was top-tier information, requiring the highest security clearance.

Locating Beckett's file, he began sifting through the scanned documents enclosed. Much of it was heavily redacted, but after a few minutes of searching, he found what he was looking for – the paperwork relating to Beckett's deep-cover operation within The Delaney Crime Syndicate. It had been originally titled 'Operation Cuckoo', but he didn't recall anyone ever using that name. His eyes darted over the document as he scrolled, finally landing on the signature at the bottom of the page.

"Well, I'll be damned…"

The signature was a scrawled mess of loops and spikes, but the name was legible enough.

Spencer Bowditch.

He was the one who'd signed off on the mission, not Locke. A shiver ran down Beaumont's back, a mixture of anger and excitement. He returned to the air-gapped laptop and Armitage's files, re-examining them through the frame granted by this new information.

One of the text files was a timeline Armitage had created, showing when the original list of names was uploaded, along with when it had been added to the document that was subsequently leaked online. The list of names had originally been an image file and the metadata of the image revealed it had been created at a specific time and location.

The user logs confirmed it. The IP address did too. Bowditch had been the creator of the leaked document. He was the traitor.

"Damn it, Spencer."

Beaumont sat back. There was enough incriminating evidence on the USB to destroy Bowditch's career, but Beaumont couldn't work out why he'd done it, or for what purpose. There was a deeper thread running through this.

He shut down the laptop and yanked out the USB, stuffing the bracelet in his trouser pocket as he strode for the door. Unlocking it, he marched down the corridor towards Bowditch's office. This was probably a terrible idea, but he had to confront the duplicitous bastard. He needed to have it out with him. He needed to know why he'd done what he'd done before he had him arrested and the case was taken out of his hands. The bastard had endangered the lives of seven of their top officers. Beckett's life was still hanging in the balance. Ruth Armitage was dead.

"Bowditch?" he called out, banging on his office door. "It's Beaumont. We need to talk."

There was no answer. He leaned forward, peering through the frosted glass panel. He could make out an abstract rendition of an office, vague shapes and swirls of a desk and a filing cabinet along one wall. But no movement, no human-shaped silhouette. Bowditch wasn't there.

So where the hell was he?

With determined strides, he continued down the corridor towards Locke's office. As he got closer, sounds of movement emanated from inside. He knocked and then opened the door.

"Beaumont? What's going on?" Locke asked, his head darting up from the report he was reading. He looked the older man up and down. "You look dreadful. Have you slept?"

"Not much." He entered the room and closed the door behind him. "I've got news, Robert. Bad news. I've just seen compelling evidence that points to Bowditch as the source of the leak."

"What? Are you serious?"

"I'm afraid so."

Beaumont remained still, scrutinising every micro-movement on the chief director's face.

"Take a seat, Beaumont," he said, pointing at the chair opposite. "Tell me everything."

Beaumont hesitated, but Locke appeared genuinely shocked by the revelation. Reassured for the moment that he could share his findings, Beaumont took a seat, and once settled, briefed Locke on everything he'd discovered – the timestamps and user logs, the metadata on the image file pinpointing Bowditch as the source – the irrefutable evidence he had been seeking. He also mentioned the unresolved issue of Beckett's missing niece and Beckett's theories on The Consortium's involvement. He finished by delivering the grim news that Ruth Armitage had been murdered.

"You think Bowditch killed her?"

"I think he was behind it."

"Do we have any idea where he is right now?" Locke asked. His eyes were wide, as if by staying alert the answers he needed would materialise.

"He's not in his office," Beaumont told him.

Locke pinched the bridge of his nose between his thumb and forefinger. "How do you know all this about The Consortium and Beckett's situation with his niece?"

Beaumont shifted. "Beckett has been in contact with me since yesterday. I've been assisting him remotely."

"What the hell, Jacob?" Locke raised his hands. "Why am I only hearing about this now?"

"Apologies, sir. But it was a highly sensitive situation. We were concerned that—"

"That… what? That I was the mole, the traitor in our midst? Jesus Christ."

"We didn't know what to think. We were covering all bases until more intel presented itself."

"All right, fine." Locke recovered quickly from his outburst. "Our first task is to locate Bowditch. I want to confront the treacherous swine and see what he has to damn well say for himself. Then we need to get word to Beckett and convince him to come in. Can you manage that?"

"I don't need to. He's already on his way."

Locke nodded. "Good. We need to maintain a united front going forward. Shit!" He clenched his fist, looking as if he was about to slam it on the desk but thought better of it. "How the hell have I let this happen?"

"Let's save the self-flagellation for later," Beaumont suggested. "We were all caught out by this. I should have spotted something."

Locke bared his teeth. "It makes Sigma Unit look weak. Probably what The Consortium want. And let me remind you, we were operating on UK soil. If we mishandle this, we'll have a lot of awkward questions to answer. The Ms will be furious knowing we had a mole among us. Not to mention Templeton and the Americans. Shit, I can't even think straight. What do we do?"

"Two things," Beaumont replied, trying to sound steadfast. "We find Bowditch and apprehend him. Then we help Beckett get his niece back. And something tells me it'll be a two-birds-with-one-stone situation."

"You think Bowditch has the girl? Is he looking for leverage?"

"I don't know what's going on in his head. But if he's working for The Consortium, he's a threat to national security – and to the future of Sigma Unit." A silence fell, the implication behind the words apparent to both men. Bowditch had access to every mission Sigma Unit had ever been involved in. He had the receipts. He knew where the bodies were buried. In some cases, quite literally.

Locke steepled his fingers under his chin, thinking. "When's Beckett due to get here?"

Beaumont glanced at the clock. "Within the next fifteen minutes."

"Okay. Meanwhile, we need to track down Bowditch. Check his comms and any digital footprints he might have left in the past few hours. Whatever you can gather."

Beaumont pushed his chair back and stood. "I'm on it."

"Good man. In the meantime, I need to get ahead of this narrative. I'm going to have to inform Calder and Eastwood of the situation. The Home Secretary as well."

Beaumont frowned. "Is that wise at this stage?"

Locke leaned back and threw his hands up. "I don't bloody know! But I'd rather they hear it from me. I was due to brief Jane Isaacs regardless. I'll assure her we have the situation under control and there's no cause for alarm." He got up. "There's a car waiting downstairs. I'll head to Westminster now." He buttoned up his jacket. "Maintain regular contact from now on and let me know the minute Beckett arrives."

"Yes, sir."

They walked together to the door. "This is it now, Beaumont," Locke told him. "All hands on deck. Use whatever resources you need and I'll sign it off retrospectively. Let's get our man back and find Bowditch. For the good of Sigma Unit. And for the safety of the country."

43

Amber drew her knees to her chest, striving to disappear into the corner of the room as the thin man with the gun approached.

"Don't worry," he assured her. "I'm not going to hurt you." His tone was light and cheery, but it came off as fake. It reminded Amber of the way some people spoke to young children.

"Who are you?" she whispered. "What do you want?"

"I've already told you, Amber. I'm a friend of your uncle's. A work colleague."

Amber drew her legs closer, making herself as compact as possible. She'd been naive, she knew that now. But he'd sounded so convincing when he'd knocked on the hotel room door two hours earlier. He knew her name, her uncle's name. He knew where they'd been and what they were doing. Who wouldn't have believed he'd come to help her?

Your Uncle John sent me. He's in trouble and told me to fetch you. I'm going to take you to him…

Those were the words he'd spoken through the door. The words that had finally made her believe his claims. The words that had led to her unlocking the door and letting him in.

She'd realised her mistake almost instantly. She could still recall the fear she'd felt as he stood in front of her, framed in the doorway, his pale, weasely face twisted into a cruel smirk, his eyes hungry and sinister. He was wearing a black overcoat and black leather gloves and reminded her of the child catcher from *Chitty Chitty Bang Bang* – a film she'd adored and been terrified of in equal measure as a child. She'd let out a scream, but one of his gloved hands had grabbed her around the mouth, shoving her onto the bed. There'd been a horrifying moment when she thought he was going to rape her, but instead he dragged her upright and pulled out a gun. It had a long barrel that she knew silenced the bullet sound – like the ones carried by the men who'd murdered Gareth and Carol. He told her he'd kill her if she didn't do exactly as he said.

When he'd asked her if she understood, she'd nodded meekly. Yet a part of her remained strong, and when he'd momentarily turned his back, she'd knocked her uncle's phone off the bed and kicked it out of sight. She didn't know if it would do any good, but it made her feel a little better that she'd been able to think rationally in such a distressing situation. It told her she might survive this terror if she kept her mind focused.

With the gun pressing into her lower back, the man had ushered her down the stairs and out of the hotel to a car parked out front. She'd considered making a break for it, but had no idea where to go and was worried the man would shoot her if she ran. She didn't think so, there were too many people around, but her legs refused to cooperate. Instead she'd let him bundle her into the back seat, where he'd secured a harsh plastic zip tie around her wrists, fastened to the metal rod of the front headrest.

She was frustrated with herself for allowing him to take her so readily, but it was easy to think that way in hindsight and she shouldn't be too hard on herself. It was a terrifying, unfamiliar situation. She had no idea what to do for the best.

The man had driven her to a large house near Islington. It had high walls and a gate the man opened remotely as they approached. If this was his place, he was rich. But if he was rich, why had he taken her? It didn't make sense.

Now, in the middle room of the house, a sort of library-come-study with polished wooden floors and large bookcases lining the walls, she voiced her confusion.

"What is it you want?" Her voice sounded weak and pathetic. She coughed. "You don't have to do this. Please. You can let me go. I won't tell anyone."

The man tilted his head to one side, leering at her as if she was trying to wheedle some great confession out of him. "I've already told you – as long as you do exactly as I say, you aren't going to be harmed."

"My uncle will kill you when he finds you," she blurted out, then a wave of anxiety washed over her as she realised what she'd said. It was dangerous to antagonise a man holding a gun. But rather than provoke anger, her words seemed to amuse him.

"Is that so? Good old Uncle John." He moved to the desk in the corner, swivelling the chair to sit facing her. The gun was still in his hand and he gestured with it as he spoke. He seemed stressed. She felt that was a bad sign. "You do know this is all his fault, yes? If he wasn't such a bloody nuisance, this would be over already. It should have been. But here we are. Now you're going to help me bring him here so I can clean up this mess once and for all."

"Who are you?" Amber asked, keeping her eyes on the gun. "How did you find me? My uncle said it was safe. He checked…"

"Oh, he checked, did he?" He shook his head and laughed.

"It seems the great John Beckett isn't as wonderful as he thinks he is."

His smirk returned. He was about to say something else when his phone rang. The colour drained from his face as he took it from his pocket and glanced at the screen.

"Shit," he hissed, rising and waving the gun at Amber. "You stay quiet. Okay?"

He turned his back to her to answer the call. "Bowditch here."

Bowditch. Had she heard that name before? She couldn't remember. Her eyes darted to the door, wondering if she could make a run for it while he was distracted.

"Everything is under control," she heard him say. "It's only a matter of time." He spun around and their eyes met. Amber relaxed her shoulders. Running was too risky.

Instead she closed her eyes, listening to Bowditch's conversation, trying to make out what the other person was saying. All she could hear was a faint murmuring, but they didn't sound pleased.

"I can handle it," Bowditch told them. "I *will* handle it. I've already done what Delaney couldn't. I have the girl here with me. I know it's not ideal, but I have it under control."

Amber heard the strain in his voice, a sign of fear. Whoever he was talking to, they intimidated him.

"Give me another chance," he continued. "I can fix this. I can make it right."

He fell silent. Amber opened her eyes to see him nodding along to whatever the person on the other end was saying. It sounded like they were giving instructions.

"Yes. I can handle that," he assured them, checking his watch. "I won't disappoint you." He ended the call and seemed lost in thought as he stared at the phone. But by the time he lifted his head to look at Amber, he looked more resolute than ever.

"Who was that?" she asked, her voice barely audible due to her dry throat.

"The people I work for," he said. "They're not very happy with your uncle. But I've reassured them he won't be a problem for much longer."

Amber tried to swallow. "What are you going to do?"

"You'll find out soon enough," he replied, the sickening grin returning to his face. "I've got another call to make. Then you and I are going for a drive."

44

Beckett was driving along Pall Mall on his way to Nightingale House when his phone vibrated in his jacket pocket. Taking the wheel in one hand, he fished it out, flipped it open and answered.

"Hey. I'm almost there."

He was expecting to hear Beaumont's voice speak back. But it wasn't Beaumont.

"John Beckett. What a pleasure it is to hear your voice after all this time."

Beckett lowered the phone. Caller ID: Unknown. "Who is this…? Bowditch?" It sounded like him, but his voice was higher pitched, strained.

"It's Assistant Director Bowditch to you," came the reply. "Where are you, Beckett?"

He glanced in the rearview mirror and indicated left to turn down Haymarket. "I'm en route to Nightingale House," he said. "I take it Beaumont has briefed you on…" He trailed off as the realisation hit him.

Spencer Bowditch. Of course.

Beckett slowed the car. "It was you."

"You know what? I think it was," Bowditch said, laughing joylessly. "And I think I also have something you want. Someone rather important to you."

Beckett steered the car over to the side of the road and switched off the engine as the last pieces of the puzzle clicked into place.

"You treacherous bastard," he growled. "Where are you? Where's Amber?"

"Now, now. Let's not get ahead of ourselves."

"If you've hurt her in any way, I'll kill you. You have my word on that."

"Relax! You're in no position to be issuing idle threats, Beckett. This is all your fault. All you had to do was stay close to Delaney and report his movements. But you couldn't help but act like the big hero. Sticking your nose in where it wasn't wanted."

Beckett gripped the wheel. If Bowditch were in front of him now, he'd rip out the steering mechanism and beat him to death with it. "You risked the lives of all those other operatives just to throw me under the bus?"

"Collateral damage. All for the greater good. It would have thrown up too many red flags for your details alone to be leaked."

"And Beaumont's analyst, that was you?"

"Indirectly. She's another one who should have stuck to her job description."

Beckett fell silent for a moment, fighting a wave of insidious thoughts – images of Amber tied up and scared. He centred himself, focusing on his breathing. He had to stay calm.

"Where's Amber?"

"She's here. And to answer your next question, I haven't touched her." His voice faded as he moved the phone from his mouth. "Say hello to Uncle John, Amber."

Amber's voice, shaky yet unmistakable, echoed in the

background. He gritted his teeth. Something else was bothering him.

"How did you find us?"

"Quite simple, really. I knew you and Beaumont were close and I suspected he might try to get in touch with you. I had one of his analysts pull the call list off his phone. Two calls, made in the last twenty-four hours, were to an unknown number that he'd never called before. I took a chance on it being you. And it was. Beaumont sent you a message and it pinged off three towers near the hotel. The receptionist was more than happy to point me to the right room once I'd greased his palm."

Beckett shook his head. He should have been more vigilant.

Damn it.

"You should've used a more secure network," Bowditch said, echoing Beckett's thoughts. "But I suppose that's what happens when you're stressed and have the largest crime syndicate in London on your tail – you make mistakes."

"And what's your role in all this?" Beckett asked. "You're working for The Consortium now? Just another of their pawns, like Delaney and all the rest?"

There was a pause on the other end. Beckett sensed he'd struck a nerve. A minor victory. Bowditch had always been a repugnant brown-noser, willing to do whatever was necessary to rise through the ranks. After waiting too long in the shadows for Locke's job, he'd traded his integrity for a more drastic career shift.

"The Consortium have instructed me to do what Delaney couldn't," Bowditch said, his derisive tone now gone. "You've only got yourself to blame."

"I have nothing on them," Beckett replied. "Nothing at all. I don't even know who they are."

Bowditch cleared his throat. "Let's just say they're a

cautious bunch. Thorough. They don't want to take any chances."

Beckett's gaze shifted from the rearview mirror to the bustling street ahead. It was mid-afternoon and the traffic was thick, but he saw no immediate threats. He hadn't been followed.

"So what's the deal?" he asked. "I surrender myself and you let Amber go?" His mind was already working on potential strategies, contingency plans and worst-case scenarios.

"Something like that. Meet me at the Barking Riverside development at 4 p.m."

"I know it."

"Good. I'll be in front of the pier. Come alone. And don't do anything stupid. Otherwise I put a bullet in the girl's head."

Beckett heard Amber whimpering in the background. He closed his eyes. "And are you going to kill me yourself, Bowditch?"

He laughed. "It's nothing personal, Beckett. This is bigger than both of us now. It's out of my hands. But it's the only way your niece gets to live."

"All right," Beckett said, restarting the engine. "Barking Riverside Project. I'll be there."

45

Beaumont was waiting on the fire escape at Nightingale House, waiting to usher Beckett down to the basement and to the large meeting room they often used for meetings. Only he was nowhere in sight. He looked at his watch, confirming the time on his phone. It was 2:36 p.m. He should have been here by now.

Beaumont paced the tight confines of the fire escape landing, muttering to himself, willing his old friend to appear. Five minutes went by. Still no sign of Beckett.

Something was wrong.

He was about to give up and go back to his office when his phone buzzed in his hand. He accepted the call before the first ring could end.

"Beckett. Is that you?"

"It's me." His voice was clipped and from the sound of it, he was driving.

"Where the hell are you?" Beaumont asked, glancing up the stairwell. "I'm downstairs at Nightingale waiting to take you down to the basement."

"Change of plan," Beckett replied. "I'm not coming in. Not now. Bowditch is the mole."

"We know that. He's not here. We have our top operatives searching for him."

Beckett let out a bitter laugh. "I know where he is. He's got Amber. I'm on my way to meet with him."

"No, John. Come in. We can sort this together. Locke knows the situation. We can trust him. You have to let us help you."

"There's no time. I have to do this alone."

Beaumont rubbed his hand across his forehead. Bowditch was a slimy prick, but he had a vicious streak too. On more than one occasion, Beaumont had heard him bawling out analysts when they hadn't immediately jumped at his orders – or if he'd failed to explain himself properly and they hadn't shown themselves to be mind readers. He might be no match for Beckett one on one, but if he was armed, if he had backup – and if he was desperate – who knew how this could go down. The Consortium wanted Beckett dead. Bowditch was their stooge.

"You need to stand down, John. Now. That's a direct order. From me and the chief director. Let's do this as a team. As a unit."

"I'm sorry. *Sir*."

"Stand down, Beckett! I mean it! Locke knows the situation. He's on our side. We can handle this. You know as well as I do the reputation of Sigma Unit – hell, its entire future – is hanging in the balance. We have to do this by the book."

Beckett was quiet for a moment. Beaumont could hear the heavy growl of an engine accelerating at high speed.

"There is no book," Beckett replied. "It's gone. I'm grateful for your help up to now, but I have to save Amber. This is the only way."

"At least tell me where you're going."

There was another pause. Beaumont could almost visualise Beckett weighing his options, assessing whether to divulge that information. Eventually he sighed. "Barking Riverside Project. I'm meeting him in front of the pier at 4 p.m. But I mean it, Beaumont. I have to do this alone. It's your turn to trust me."

"But, Beckett, I—"

"Jacob, please. We go back a long way. I need you to manage this. It's a straightforward extraction, the sort I've done multiple times before. Let me do what I do best. I'll contact you once she's safe."

Beaumont glanced around him, at a loss what to do with himself physically. He leaned his forearm against the wall to stop himself from floundering. "Fine. Get her back. But you keep me posted. You hear me?"

"Of course." And with that he hung up.

"Damn it, Beckett," Beaumont whispered at the wall.

He pocketed the phone and headed up the stairs to his office. Despite his assurances to Beckett, the rules of the game had shifted dramatically and the next few hours would decide everyone's future. He couldn't keep this to himself. Not now. Not after everything that had happened. Locke had to be told. After that, it was out of Beaumont's hands.

46

Alone in her office, with her laptop open in front of her, Jane Isaacs was listening intently as Xander Templeton briefed those assembled on the unfolding chaos. She'd already been nervous coming into the meeting – a video conference involving herself, Tristan Shepherd, and the heads of MI5 and MI6. But when Frank Calder had mentioned Templeton had fresh intelligence he wanted to share, a fresh wave of trepidation had overcome her.

This feeling, though, was not unfamiliar to Isaacs. Ever since yesterday morning, when news of the data breach broke, she'd been living on a razor's edge. And with each new development, her anxiety grew. Being fresh to her role as Home Secretary, she found herself in uncharted waters and kept checking her video feed at the bottom of the screen, worried that the uncertainty showed on her face.

"So we're certain?" she asked, her tone hardening. "Spencer Bowditch is working with The Consortium?"

Templeton didn't flinch. "I'm afraid so. It appears The Consortium orchestrated this entire situation, intending for Rufus Delaney to eliminate John Beckett without leaving any trace of their involvement. But your man in the field has proven more difficult to dispatch than they expected." His voice was firm and emotionless. "We're now at a critical point where one wrong step could risk exposing numerous covert operations, both here and in the US."

Isaacs's grip tightened on the armrest of her chair. This world of espionage and double agents, although new to her, was fast becoming her reality. She was sitting at her central meeting table rather than at her desk, and with her back to the door, she felt very vulnerable all of a sudden. She cast a furtive glance at the antique clock on the opposite wall. They were ten minutes into the meeting. To change seats now would look odd.

"So where do we stand?" Emily Eastwood asked.

"I think it's clear to everyone that containment is crucial." Tristan Shepherd's stern face appeared on the screen as he interjected. "The media cannot get wind of this. As I understand it, Sigma Unit's existence has never been acknowledged. To do so now will open a Pandora's Box that has the potential to expose years of covert operations. This is a matter of national security."

Isaacs's head spun with the implications. She was due to meet with the Prime Minister in a few hours. He'd need to be briefed on what she'd learned, but there was so much information to dissect, she didn't know where to begin.

She leaned into the screen. "But we still need to find our operative, correct? This John Beckett person? Now that we have a clearer picture, we need to secure him immediately."

She glanced from face to face on the screen, each a reflection of discomfort and avoidance. No one seemed eager to respond. They looked down at their notes, they shuffled papers, they cleared their throats.

"Why the hesitation?" she asked. "He's a British officer, in clear danger. It's our duty to help him—"

"It's not that simple, Home Secretary," Calder interjected,

his voice low. "This whole incident has only occurred because Beckett went rogue and started poking around in The Consortium's operations. He disobeyed direct orders and has become unpredictable. The fact he's been involved in numerous clandestine activities both here and overseas makes him… well, problematic."

"Problematic?" Isaacs repeated. "Are we not responsible for the safety of our operatives?"

"Of course we are," Xander Templeton barked. "But we must also consider the wider security implications. Beckett knows intricate details of many past operations involving CIA and MI6 personnel. Should he wish, he could create a lot of problems. Despite requests to return to Control, he's refused. At this point, we have to assume he's as much of a liability as Bowditch." His stare was unrelenting as he continued. "And let's not forget, The Consortium are still an unknown quantity. We have to tread carefully, ensuring our operations remain secure whilst protecting ourselves at all costs from potential blowback."

Isaacs couldn't believe what she was hearing.

"So what are you suggesting?" she asked, the fight returning to her voice. She knew exactly what Templeton was implying, but she wanted to hear him say it. She wanted to see the expressions on the assembled faces as he did.

Templeton didn't miss a beat in his sombre response. "We have to wipe the slate clean," he said. "Erase all traces of our involvement. And of those involved."

Even though she had expected it, Isaacs was still taken aback by his proposal and how brazen he seemed. What was worse, no one else appeared to be questioning his suggestion. She stared at the faces on the screen in turn. They could kid themselves all they wanted that this was about national security, but they were just safeguarding their careers and their positions of power.

Weak bastards. The whole lot of them.

But what could she do? This was so much bigger than anything she'd been involved with before; and if she was perfectly honest, Xander Templeton intimidated her. There was something about the way he stared at people, detached and untouchable. Like his soul, if he had one, was made of ice.

"Emily? Frank?" she said, turning to the respective heads of MI5 and MI6. "Are you in agreement with this?"

Both nodded reluctantly. Calder let out a sigh. "National security is our top priority, Home Secretary. We cannot risk exposing our operations."

"Dear God," Isaacs muttered. She was about to voice her dissent when a knock at her office door cut her short.

She turned to see Robert Locke peering around the door.

"I apologise for the intrusion, Home Secretary," he said. "But it's vitally important I speak to you…"

He trailed off as his gaze fell on her screen. Isaacs instinctively reached out to close the laptop, but it was pointless. He'd already seen.

"Home Secretary?"

"Ch-Chief Director Locke," she stammered, as he stepped into her office. "Apologies. I assumed you'd have been in attendance…"

"Yes, so would I," he replied, moving closer, squinting at the faces on the screen. "So why wasn't I?"

The question hung in the air. Isaacs looked at Templeton. Then at Shepherd. She had no answer for him.

"I'm so sorry," she said, realising she was just as complicit as the people on screen. "I didn't know."

47

Locke couldn't believe what he was looking at. Or maybe he could. Maybe he'd seen this coming all along. He nodded a curt greeting at the faces on the screen. Calder and Eastwood at least had the decency to look embarrassed. But the Foreign Secretary and Xander Templeton stared back at him with firm jaws and eyes burning with resolve.

"Robert. We thought you were otherwise engaged," Calder said. "We would, of course, have briefed you on the outcome of this meeting when you were available."

"I'm available now," he said, pulling up a chair beside Isaacs. "What's going on?"

Templeton let out a low growl as if it was suddenly an inconvenience. "You're aware of the situation, Locke. We're discussing how to proceed relative to recent developments."

"I see." There were five faces on screen, but he didn't take his eyes off Templeton. "So you know about Bowditch?"

"We do."

Locke crossed his arms. For the CIA section chief to know about Bowditch meant one of his spooks must have intercepted Sigma Unit's communications. He didn't like that. At all.

"What do you want, Locke?" Templeton asked, fixing him with a hard stare, a silent battle of wills playing out across cyberspace. "What's so important you had to burst into the Home Secretary's office unannounced?"

Locke straightened. "I had to brief her on a crucial matter – involving Sigma Unit."

"Well, we're all here, son," the gruff American replied. "If it's of importance, we should all hear about it, don't you think?"

Locke remained silent. Beside him, Jane Isaacs bristled with discomfort. But despite her unease, he trusted the Home Secretary. What she lacked in experience, she made up for in principles and integrity. He'd wanted to speak with her first, to inform her of the situation and a possible extraction attempt on British soil. It was more a courtesy than him asking for permission, but he believed she deserved that much.

"Let's hear it, Locke," Shepherd urged. "We're all waiting. What's the situation with S-Unit? What can you tell us?"

Locke glanced at Isaacs, but she remained staring at the screen. "I'm not sure I can divulge at this stage, Foreign Secretary. It's an ongoing situation, and until I have more intel, I feel it's best it stays in-house." Despite Beaumont's assertions to the contrary, he'd already deployed four officers, who were currently on their way over to the riverside development in Barking. Their orders were to locate Beckett and Bowditch and hold their position until further notice.

"Come on, Locke. Spill!" Templeton growled. "We need to work together on this."

"If there are things afoot, we need to know about them," Shepherd added. "The outcome of this affects all of us. It's your duty to share any relevant information."

There was that word again – duty. Locke looked from

Calder to Shepherd and back again as he weighed his options. Regardless of the situation, and what he thought of Xander Templeton, he had to respect the chain of command.

"All right," he conceded. "But I want assurances that I have the last word on any subsequent action taken. As I said, this is an ongoing Sigma Unit operation and we can't have counter operations muddying the waters." He glared at Templeton as he said this, making it clear who he was addressing.

In turn, the American stared back at him with an austere expression, his small, piercing eyes all but obscured by his heavy brow. "Fine. What is it?"

Locke inhaled deeply and disclosed everything that had happened in the past hour. He told them what Beaumont had just relayed to him – that Beckett was returning to control but had received a call from Spencer Bowditch claiming he had his niece. He explained Beckett was on his way over to Barking to meet Bowditch.

"Shouldn't we assume The Consortium has ordered Bowditch to kill Beckett?" Shepherd asked. "If so, doesn't that solve all our problems?"

"No," Templeton spat. "It does not, Foreign Secretary. We should have learned by now not to underestimate John Beckett."

"And it still leaves Bowditch in play," Calder added. "We don't know how much he's told The Consortium already about our operations, but we can't have a high-ranking SIS officer disappear into their ranks."

A hush fell as those gathered seemed to grasp the severity of the situation at the same time. Locke's gaze remained fixated on Templeton. He could almost see the cogs whirring behind his eyes.

"So what do we do now?" Isaacs asked, turning to Locke.

"We hold our nerve," he replied. "We wait. I have a team en route. Once we guarantee Beckett's niece is safe, they'll move in. I'm confident we can extract Beckett and Bowditch without loss of life. I trust we all agree this is the best possible outcome.

"Without a doubt," Emily Eastwood agreed. "The ideal scenario. We bring them in, question them and find out what they know, including what they might have revealed to our enemies."

Templeton responded with a scornful laugh.

"You disagree?" Locke asked.

"No, not at all. Sounds like a solid plan," Templeton replied, reclining with his hands clasped behind his head. A smug grin played across his face. "Excellent job, Chief Director Locke. You keep us all in the loop now."

"Yes, thank you, Chief Director," Shepherd added. "Please notify us immediately with any updates. But if that's all for now, I must get off. I have another meeting." With a wave of his hand, he switched off his camera.

"I appreciate everyone's time," Locke said, rising from his seat and nodding at the screen and the Home Secretary. "I'll be in touch."

With that, he excused himself and left the room. Once in the corridor, he released a frustrated groan, his body rigid, teeth clenched.

That bloody man.

He summoned the lift and rode it down to the ground floor. As soon as he exited, his phone began to ring. It was Beaumont.

"Hey. I've just finished," Locke told him after picking up.

"Yeah?" Beaumont sounded tense. "How did it go?"

"Not great." He quickly filled him in as he made his way toward the exit. Once he'd finished, Beaumont let out a sharp hiss. "What is it?" Locke asked.

"That's why I was ringing so soon. I just heard from the leader of the team you dispatched to Barking. Minutes ago, he received a direct order from Frank Calder to abort the mission and return to Control."

"What the—?" Locke exclaimed. "Calder, too?"

"I told the guy to carry out your orders but he wasn't having it. He said Calder was adamant. What's his angle, do you think?"

"I'm not sure. I didn't expect Calder to pull rank and do this," he said. "But I could tell Templeton was ready to act. He wasn't even hiding it. We know he wants to keep The Consortium sweet, given the tech they're developing. He must have persuaded Calder to follow suit. If that's the case, Bowditch has unwittingly handed them the perfect solution. In Templeton's dream scenario, Bowditch eliminates Beckett, and we take care of Bowditch. Yet something tells me they doubt Bowditch's capabilities and have decided to help the narrative along."

"Do you think they'd go to such extremes?"

Locke walked across the expansive entrance hall. "I hope I'm wrong," he said, lowering his voice. "But if you ask me, Templeton called his hit team the second he got off the call just now. With Calder recalling our team, we've got a big problem."

"What the hell do we do now?" Beaumont asked.

Locke stopped. In front of him, the security station was busy, two men in almost identical pinstriped suits were having their bags checked. He took a moment to think.

"Locke? Are you there?"

"Yes. I'm here." But what did he do? Up until a few minutes ago, his loyalty to Beckett and his obligation to protect national security had been at odds. But with Templeton on the warpath and Calder blocking his orders, it seemed the old rules no longer applied. This was his unit, his team. Beckett was his officer. Sometimes you had to overlook protocol and chains of command and do what was right. "Where are you?" he asked Beaumont.

"Still at Nightingale."

"All right, listen. I want you to grab a couple of handguns and some ammo from the armoury and meet me downstairs in ten minutes. We'll take my car."

He could hear the pride in Beaumont's voice. "Yes, sir. I'm on it."

"Good man," Locke replied, hailing a black cab. "Let's bring our officer home."

48

The Barking Riverside development, once a thriving construction site, now lay silent. An hour's drive from the city along the Thames, the ambitious social housing project had once promised a thriving, inclusive community, complete with affordable homes, green parks, and lively shopping centres – a symbol of rejuvenation rising from the ashes of East London's industrial past.

That was, until twelve months ago, when each of the original backers had mysteriously and abruptly pulled out and control of the site had passed to new developers. Since then, the construction machines had ground to a halt and the area had become a ghost town, its terrain scattered with idle cranes, half-built structures and piles of bricks and hardened mortar.

What was initially conceived as a symbol of social progress was now destined to become yet another cluster of luxury high-rises, accessible only to those with fat salaries; a stark reflection of the city's capitalist ethos. The hopeful vision was over, leaving only blueprints and broken promises, casualties of the faceless new backer's insidious influence. Few knew the identity of these new developers. But Beckett did.

The Consortium.

Beneath the skeletal remains of an unfinished residence, he surveyed the desolate expanse, the development spreading out in front of him like a battlefield. On either side, the empty shells of half-built houses – which would soon be torn down to make way for The Consortium's cynical new vision – cast long shadows across the wasteland.

Beckett's focus was on the wooden pier that jutted out into the Thames three hundred meters away. That was the meeting point. His senses were on high alert as he scanned his surroundings, noting possible escape routes and potential spots for an ambush.

His phone vibrated against his thigh – a cryptic message from Beaumont warning him of company. It was no surprise. Beckett had already factored that into his calculations. He checked the time. 3:50 p.m. Ten minutes to go. He ran the best, worst, and most likely scenarios over in his head, mentally rehearsing how he'd react to each one. Every simulation he'd ever run, every extraction operation he'd been a part of, they'd prepared him for this moment.

Arriving early, Beckett had parked the Audi at a safe distance and approached the site from the north, using the unfinished structures as cover in case Bowditch – or his new paymaster's assassins – had arrived early. But for now he was alone.

He waited.

His position had been a strategic choice, providing cover and a good view across the dusty landscape. To his left, an incomplete brick wall and an idle digger could offer additional shelter if necessary.

He waited some more.

While he didn't have a step-by-step plan, he knew trust, self-belief, and adaptability were essential. His tools were experience, stealth and the Glock 19 he'd taken from Delaney, all supplemented by a simmering rage he just about had control of. He'd never liked Spencer Bowditch much anyway, but knowing a fellow SIS officer was capable of such betrayal incensed him more than was healthy. But that was fine. His anger focused him.

It was his fuel.

And his objective was clear: take down Bowditch, rescue Amber, get the hell out of there. Not easy, but not impossible. He'd faced greater odds before in more hostile territories.

More waiting.

He checked his watch.

It was one minute to four. On cue, he heard the distant purr of an engine over to his right. Moments later, a sleek black Mercedes S-Class appeared and pulled up alongside the raised foundations of an unfinished row of houses on the far side of the pier. Beckett's hand moved to the pistol in his waistband. He pulled it out and held it calmly across his chest.

And he waited.

The car remained stationary. A flock of seagulls coming in off the river cawed noisily at each other. Beckett shifted his position, remaining hidden but with a better view of the car and the track it had approached on – most likely Bowditch's escape route. If it got that far.

The driver's door opened and a figure emerged dressed in a dark suit. Despite the low sun reflecting off a pair of large, mirrored sunglasses, Beckett recognised the weaselly features – it was Bowditch. He took a measured breath, readying himself for action. As a trained operative, he had learned to suppress his emotions and anticipate the unexpected. His pulse steadied as he sank deeper into the mindset needed to navigate such situations.

He watched Bowditch move around the Merc and open the rear door, revealing another figure cowering in the back seat. Amber. Beckett tensed as Bowditch leaned in and dragged her roughly from the car. Her hands were bound in front of her, and even from this distance he could see the terror etched on her face. But she was alive. Still dressed in the same dark grey hoodie and black jeans. That was a good sign.

Bowditch slammed the car door and grabbed Amber's upper arm. She initially resisted, her face contorting into a scowl as she yelled something at her captor. But that was a good sign, too. She still had her fighting spirit.

The breeze from the Thames whipped Amber's hair across her face while Bowditch steered her towards the pier. She glanced over her shoulder and across the construction site, most likely looking for her uncle.

"Hang in there," Beckett whispered, as Bowditch pulled a phone from his jacket. Moments later, Beckett's phone vibrated in his pocket.

He answered it. "Let her go."

"That's not how it works, my friend," Bowditch sneered. He scanned the horizon. "Where are you? Show yourself."

Beckett's finger tightened around the trigger of the Glock. "Last chance, Bowditch. Release her or this will end badly for you."

"I don't think you're in any position to be making threats," Bowditch snarled. He talked a good talk, but the nervy way he was scoping out the area, his head jerking left to right like a baby bird, told a different story.

"Fine. Release her. Then I'll come out."

"No, Beckett, I think we'll try that the other way around," Bowditch spat, glancing around some more. He looked directly at the structure where Beckett was hiding. "I'm making the calls here, so just… shut up! Come out where I can see you."

In contrast to Bowditch's volatile panic, Beckett was calm. His experience in high-pressure negotiations allowed his composure to eclipse the rage in his belly. When he spoke, his words were measured and his voice low. "You don't want to do this, Spencer. Let Amber go. She's innocent. You and I can still find a way out of this. You don't have to betray your country this way."

"Betray my country?" Bowditch yelled back. "I'm doing this for my country."

"Are you serious?"

"Of course I'm bloody serious! I'm doing what's best for the future of our nation. I'm a visionary, Beckett, unlike the rest of you lazy, blinkered fools. Working with The Consortium is going to benefit us immensely. Templeton understands. They have power, money, global influence – and the willingness to elevate Britain to its rightful prominence on the world stage. If we work with them and not against them, they can help us make our country great once more. If only people realised…"

"Oh, I see," Beckett replied. "You really believe that, don't you?"

"Yes. Now show yourself." Bowditch pulled a gun from his jacket and held it at Amber's head. "I'll kill her, Beckett. Don't push me!"

"Fine." Beckett pocketed the phone and, leading with the Glock, stepped out from his cover. There were about a hundred metres between them, but he covered the area quickly, his aim never moving from Bowditch's head.

Both Bowditch and Amber saw him at around the fifty-metre mark. Bowditch growled and yanked the girl closer. Amber squealed.

"Put the gun down, Beckett. I'll kill her. I mean it."

Beckett kept walking forward, slow and calm, his aim unwavering. His focus was on Bowditch's hand, the one holding the gun to Amber's head. He gauged the tension in Bowditch's trigger finger. The man was unpredictable, but Beckett knew his background was in the civil service and then counterintelligence. He'd been a suit his whole career, inexperienced in field operations. As Beckett neared, panic set in. Bowditch yanked Amber in front of him, using her as a human shield and redirecting his aim at Beckett. He was losing his nerve and he wanted to stop his advance.

But that was his first big mistake.

"Put the fucking gun down, Beckett! I mean it. I'll kill the both of you!"

A few metres away Beckett stopped. "No one has to do anything stupid today, Spencer. Let Amber go. She has no part in this. It's me you want."

Amber squirmed, but Bowditch gripped her harder. "Let me go. Please!"

Beckett caught her eye. "Amber – are you okay?"

She nodded, and he saw a spark of defiance in her expression, a willingness to fight. "Yes. I'm okay."

Beckett returned his attention to the point between Bowditch's eyebrows, the centre of his T-zone. Applying a little more pressure to the trigger of his weapon, he took in the tremble of Bowditch's hand on his gun, the sweat-soaked desperation on his face. He assessed his stance, the angle of his aim, the likely trajectory of the bullet if Bowditch fired first. He factored in the distance, the wind direction, everything. But Bowditch was erratic, leaning into his gun one second, skittering back behind the terrified Amber the next. Beckett was eighty-five percent certain he could take him out without Amber being hurt, but he wasn't going to risk it.

"Drop it!" Bowditch screamed, once again aiming at Amber. "I swear to God, you're testing my patience. Five seconds and she's dead."

Beckett tilted his head back but kept his aim steady. "Hold on, Bowditch. Listen—"

"One!" Bowditch barked, his face taut. He jabbed his gun into Amber's temple, making her cry out. "Two!"

Suddenly the harsh shriek of tyres filled the space around them, followed by the grinding halt of brakes as two imposing black SUVs skidded to a dusty stop at the far end of the wasteland.

Bowditch's attention wavered, his eyes darting to the unexpected interruption.

It was the distraction Beckett needed.

He covered the distance between them in two strides, slamming his palm into Bowditch's gun with a swift, coordinated strike. Bowditch discharged his weapon, the deafening crack briefly muting Beckett's world as the stray bullet cut through the grey void above them. Off-balance and startled, Bowditch stumbled backwards. Beckett followed him with a strike to the face, feeling the crunch of broken cartilage under the force of his elbow. Bowditch howled as blood sprayed from his nose.

While the doors of the SUVs swung open, and a team of heavily armoured figures leapt out, Beckett barged Bowditch out of the way. Grabbing Amber, he dragged her behind a low wall as the air was ripped apart by an intense flurry of bullets.

"Stay down," he told Amber, pulling her to the ground.

"Who are they?" she yelled over the crack of gunfire.

Beckett risked a glance over the top of the wall, returning a few rounds to hold the men back. He counted six of them, all dressed in black, moving with the precision of a well-drilled unit. They could be working for The Consortium, or even his own people sent to tie up loose ends – no witnesses, no complications.

Regardless, the situation had just turned from bad to worse.

49

As the sound of gunfire filled the air, Beckett fired off a couple more rounds of his own, taking out one of the men with a perfectly placed headshot. Over to his left, Bowditch was huddled against the wheel arch of his car, fear etched across his face.

"What the fuck is going on?" Amber cried out when a rogue bullet ricocheted off the wall to Beckett's left. He dropped to the ground as a cloud of dust enveloped the two of them. Amber's eyes were wild, darting all around, her breaths coming in uneven gasps.

"Hey! Mind your language," he scolded.

She glared at him. "Seriously? You've not been in my life since forever and you wait until now to try to give me life lessons? Are you crazy?"

Beckett crinkled his eyes. No. He wasn't crazy. But he needed to calm her down, and levity was a powerful balancer of heightened emotions. He saw the blind panic receding from her eyes as she stared up at him.

"Never mind," he told her. "Lesson over."

A fleeting glance over the wall told him the armed men

were closing in fast. Another thirty seconds and they would reach Bowditch's car. The treacherous bastard must have realised this too, as his desire for self-preservation had now seemingly trumped his fear. As Beckett watched, Bowditch leaned over the boot of the car and returned fire, but his shots were erratic and ineffective.

Crouching against the cold wall, Beckett turned at the growl of an approaching car. Over to his right, a familiar maroon Jaguar XJ6 was racing towards them, tyres grumbling against the rough terrain. Robert Locke's car. Beaumont was in the passenger seat beside him.

All eyes turned to the Jaguar as it skidded to a halt. A second later, Locke and Beaumont burst from the vehicle, guns drawn and using the car as cover.

"Hold your fire!" Locke called out, but his orders were met with a hail of bullets. He and Beaumont retreated to the rear of the car and returned fire. One of the men in black dropped, a lethal shot ripping through his throat. But that still left four of them.

Beckett and Amber were positioned about ten metres away from Locke's car. They all had cover for now, but the men were getting closer and he needed to act. "Beaumont," he called out. "Over here."

Beaumont, hunkering behind the car, acknowledged him with a quick wave. "Are you hurt?" he called back.

Beckett shook his head.

But what now?

A stream of options raced through his mind. The Audi was concealed behind a shipping container over a hundred meters away. To reach it from their current position would require them to pass through an open area of wasteland that may as well have been a minefield. If they ran in that direction, their bodies would be decimated by bullets in seconds. But the location of Locke's vehicle presented an opportunity. If they reached it, they could use it as cover to trace a direct route away from the gunmen and through the most heavily developed area of the project. There, the maze of unfinished buildings and workmen's huts would provide ample cover as they made their escape.

Beckett leaned around the side of the wall, assessing the situation, working out the angles. He saw Locke calling out to the men once more, trying – and failing – to assert his authority on the situation. The gunmen were like robots, cold and chilling in their lack of response. The remaining four had now broken formation. Two were approaching Bowditch on a wide arc near to the river, and the other two were coming up on the nearside, one approaching Locke's car, one moving towards him and Amber.

Chancing his arm, Beckett reached around the side of the wall and squeezed off three rounds, aiming for the man's legs rather than trying to negotiate his body armour for a kill shot. The man fell to the ground as two of the rounds found homes in his kneecap. He stumbled and dropped, firing a flurry of bullets into the air. As he hit the ground, Beckett closed one eye and finished him with a headshot.

To his left, Bowditch was scrambling like a scared rat amidst the crossfire. Beckett watched him make a beeline for Locke's car, presumably having had the same idea as him. Only, Bowditch's escape was driven by fear rather than reason, making him a vulnerable target in the chaos.

"Bowditch! Get down!" Locke's voice carried over the gunfire while his deputy ran towards him. Breaking cover, Locke fired at the closest gunman as he pivoted his aim, but it wasn't enough and his warning came too late. A burst of shots zipped up Bowditch's centreline, bursting out of his chest like mini explosions and ending with a lethal shot to the back of the head. He jerked forward, spasming in a grotesque dance before his lifeless body fell to the ground.

"Beckett!" Beaumont's voice sliced the chaos. "Now."

He didn't need to be told twice. Using the brief distraction to his advantage, he took Amber's hand and they sprinted towards Locke's car. As they ran, he pushed Amber on ahead of him while firing at the closest gunman. He hit him in the shoulder, knocking his aim as he returned fire and sending the bullets whizzing overhead.

They'd almost reached the car. They were going to make it. Locke had moved down to the driver's door and was scrambling to start the engine. It wasn't what Beckett had planned, but if the chief director could get them out of there on four wheels, he'd take that over running. Five seconds and they'd be clear.

Up ahead, Beaumont sprang forward, putting himself in between Amber and the gunman.

Three seconds...

With a forceful push, Beaumont shoved Amber behind the safety of the car. Beckett was nearly there too. They'd almost made it.

Two seconds...

Beaumont turned to open the car door but stumbled, caught off guard by a sudden burst of gunfire.

One second...

Beckett's heart stuttered as Beaumont jerked violently, the bullets finding their mark. Time seemed to slow as his body slumped against the car and fell to the ground.

"Beaumont!" Beckett shouted, dragging his friend behind the car where Amber was huddled, her face white with terror. More bullets pinged off the car and blew out the front tyres, jostling the vehicle.

"Is he dead?" Locke called back.

Beckett performed a swift evaluation. No, Beaumont was still alive, but he didn't look good. Blood was seeping from the ragged holes in his chest and his left hand was mangled. He stared up at him. "John," he gasped. "Run... Get out of here..."

Beckett turned to Amber. Then back to Beaumont. He couldn't leave him. Not after everything.

On the other side of the car, Locke was still returning fire, holding back the remaining three gunmen. "Beckett, I can keep them occupied," he yelled. "It's fine. Get her out of here. That's an order."

Amber shuffled closer, her eyes wide with expectation. She trusted him. She needed him. Beckett peered through the labyrinth of broken houses and construction materials to where the Audi was parked. They had a chance, but they had to act now.

"Keep your head down and run as fast as you can," he told Amber, taking her hand. "Don't stop until you reach the car, no matter what."

Amber nodded. Beckett gave Beaumont a final nod, then tightened his grip on Amber's hand.

"Okay," he said. "Go!"

50

Beckett and Amber dashed alongside a row of skeletal homes, their roofs partially formed, front and internal walls missing. Gunfire and shouts echoed behind them, but Beckett kept them moving, racing past foul-smelling portable toilets and down a narrow passage lined with scaffolding.

"Was he? Did he…?" Amber's voice wavered as they sprinted past a battered shipping container.

Beckett didn't look at her as he answered. "I don't know."

He felt awful for Beaumont, but he pushed his feelings down like always. In the field there was no time to dwell on such things as grief or remorse. Maybe later. Not now. His sole focus had to be Amber. Only Amber.

Suddenly the relentless gunfire, which had almost become white noise, halted. There was an ominous silence. Reaching the end of the shipping container, Beckett stopped and looked back.

The three remaining gunmen had ceased their advance and were looking at each other, fingers pressed to their ears. Someone somewhere was giving them new directives. As

Beckett watched, they backed away, guns still trained on Locke's car but now glancing past it. It looked as if they were retreating to launch a more strategic pursuit.

"Amber, let's go." He pushed her back into motion and they navigated through the most built-up section of the construction site. Risking another look over his shoulder, Beckett saw Locke kneeling beside Beaumont's body, clutching a phone to his ear. He could hear the low rumble of a chopper off in the distance, and down towards the riverside he saw the three remaining gunmen climbing into one of the SUVs. The vehicle spun around and sped along a dirt track that wound through the site and merged with the road Beckett had approached on. Turning back, he could see another shipping container in front of him and the rear bumper of the Audi peeking out the other side. They were almost there.

But it was going to be close.

With a renewed surge of energy propelling him forward, Beckett rounded the container. He fished the car keys from his pocket, triggering the remote to unlock the doors and mobilising the engine.

"Get in!" he barked at Amber. The revving engine of the approaching SUV was growing louder by the second.

As Amber clambered into the car, the sound of more gunfire cracked the air. Beckett slid into the driver's seat and started the car. The Audi roared into life. Without a moment's hesitation, he steered them onto the road and put his foot down.

"Hold tight," he told his passenger, dividing his attention between the road ahead and the looming threat in the rearview mirror. "This might get a little bumpy."

He drove through the quiet streets of Barking fast but controlled, weaving around slower cars and taking sharp turns to evade their pursuers. But the black SUV was like a shadow, matching their every move. It was still in hot pursuit as they reached the edge of town. He couldn't shake them.

Amber screaming beside him didn't help.

As they hit city traffic, her terrified pleas and reprimands filled the car, punctuated by the blare of car horns as they skirted dangerously close to other vehicles.

"I don't want to survive all that just for you to get us killed in a car crash," she shrieked when Beckett swerved to avoid a van.

"That's not going to happen," he told her. "I'm actually trying to keep everyone alive."

"Yeah?" she said, gripping the handrail above the door. "Do you want to tell that to that old man you almost hit back there?"

"He was fine. I saw him."

She shook her head at him in that way only a sassy teenage girl can do. It was a defence mechanism, he knew that. But snide remarks were better than panic.

"I am an excellent driver, you know," he added. "You need to relax."

"I need to...? You're a... Jesus..." She gasped, peering out the window. "Where are we even going? Do we have a plan?"

"Of course we have a plan," he replied, glancing in the rearview mirror. The SUV was still trailing them. "London City Airport is twenty minutes away. I'm hoping if we can get to it ahead of our friends back there, we can jump on the first available flight out of here."

"Cool. Great," Amber replied, her sarcasm still cutting through the tension in the car. "Any more surprises? You're not going to expect me to parachute out of the plane or anything?"

"It's not on the schedule." He pressed his foot harder on the accelerator. "But the day's not over yet."

Amber threw a quick look over her shoulder. "And what if we don't get there before them?"

"We will."

"Well, that's incredibly encouraging. Thanks."

Beckett chose to ignore her. He leaned forward on the pedal, pushing the car to its limits as they sped past a large industrial estate. Here Amber fell silent and gazed anxiously out the window, but the sudden quiet only brought him mild relief. He thought once again of Beaumont, lying in a pool of his own blood. He thought of Nigel and the Fords and all the other innocent people who'd died because of him. And he shook those thoughts promptly away.

Maybe later. Not now.

The streets of East London became a blur as they drove past schools and housing estates. Bikers and motorcyclists lurched out of their way, and pedestrians scattered like frightened pigeons while Beckett swung the car from lane to lane, narrowly avoiding a collision with a white Transit van.

The black SUV remained a constant presence in the rearview mirror, but when Beckett turned onto Newham Way, the long road leading towards London City Airport, he spotted another SUV in the outside lane.

What the hell?

He moved over so he was in the same lane and tapped the brake, peering into the rearview mirror to identify this new threat. The front windscreen was blacked out, but in the late afternoon light he was sure he recognised the silhouette behind the wheel.

Robert Locke.

A mix of relief and suspicion twisted Beckett's gut. With Beaumont down, Locke must have jumped in the second SUV to join the pursuit. Yet his motives were unclear. The situation had spiralled out of control in the last few hours. Locke would want to contain this as much as anyone. He'd want to bring Beckett in and debrief him at the least. But Beckett couldn't let that happen – not with so many unknowns in play. Delaney might be out of the picture but people still wanted rid of him, and permanently. The Consortium, the Americans, even the British Government – there were arguments for all of them being behind the carnage at the riverside. He couldn't trust anyone. Perhaps at some point further down the line he could afford to reassess, possibly reach out to his former boss. But right now he had one mission – get Amber and himself out of the country.

"Uncle John!" Amber's frantic scream snapped him back to the immediate danger. He looked up to see a large delivery truck cutting across their path. Yanking the wheel over to the right, he swerved the car out of the way but into the side of the carriageway. The Audi clipped the kerb, sending a heavy jolt through the vehicle that made Amber yelp. Steering back into the lane, Beckett regained control and slammed his foot on the accelerator.

"We're going to die!" Amber cried, her voice rising two octaves.

"We're not going to die!" Beckett shouted back. "I was just making sure you were paying attention." His knuckles were white as he gripped the wheel and navigated the snaking roads.

His eyes flicked to the mirror, tracking the locations of the two SUVs as he took a left, crossing over the Connaught Bridge. To his right, the afternoon sun cast shimmering rays on the River Thames. Over on the other side stood mecca, in the form of London City Airport. They were almost there. But when they reached the end of the bridge, a salvo of gunshots shattered the Audi's rear window.

"Shit! John!" Amber cried out, safety glass falling around them.

But Beckett was undeterred. He gritted his teeth, eyes hardening with determination as he floored the accelerator and swerved the car around the corner.

"Are you insane!" Amber yelled, the car nearly tipping onto

two wheels. "I can't take this!" She hunkered down in her seat, her eyes wide as they darted between Beckett and the chaos outside the car.

"It's nearly over," he told her. "But stay down."

He checked his mirrors. The first SUV remained on their tail. Locke, too, was keeping pace, adding another layer to the manic puzzle.

They zoomed past the Albert Dock service station. Beckett's jaw was clenched to the point of pain, his mind working overtime, trying to predict the SUV's next move while simultaneously charting their escape route.

Another barrage of gunshots ripped through the air, the sound bouncing off the surrounding buildings and turning the thoroughfare into a tunnel of noise. Amber screamed louder. "They're catching up with us!"

Beckett's focus shifted back to the rearview mirror as they sped down Hartmann Road, the airport's main entrance coming into view. The SUV was closing in, with Locke keeping pace right behind it. If Locke was here for assistance, it would be helpful if he applied it right about now, Beckett thought.

"Here we go," he said, darting a glance at Amber. She was gripping her seat as if her life depended on it. And in many ways it did.

"What now?" she asked, when Beckett drove past the barrier of the main car park, searching for a spot near the terminal entrance. "We're just going to walk into the airport and jump on a plane?"

"That's the plan," Beckett replied, checking his mirrors. The SUVs were a couple of hundred meters behind, held back by a slow-moving shuttle bus. But they were still coming.

"You really aren't funny, you know?" Amber spat. "What are we going to do?"

Beckett screeched the car to a stop in a space allocated for taxis and jumped out. He was banking on the gunmen's employers not wanting a shootout in a crowded airport full of security cameras. It didn't guarantee their safety, but it tilted the odds slightly in their favour.

"Get out," he told Amber, popping the boot and grabbing the bags. "We need to move. Fast."

He glanced back down the street. The shuttle bus was pulling into a layby, allowing the impatient SUVs to speed around the side of it. He rushed over to Amber and herded her towards the airport entrance. They were almost there, but it wasn't over.

In fact, a gut feeling told him it was far from over.

51

London City Airport pulsed with life as Beckett and Amber stepped through the automated doors, immediately consumed by the rhythm of movement. Moving silently and with purpose, they made their way through a sea of people, following a trail of signs towards 'Tickets and Departures'. The acoustics of the hall amplified their hurried footsteps while they passed a row of shops and a lone coffee stand.

"Over there," he called to Amber, pointing at a ticket desk in the distance with only a few people in line.

He led the way, glancing back over his shoulder as they went. There was no one following them. Not yet. He weaved through the crowds with his head down, blending in as best he could. Amber appeared to be keeping it together, but from the wild look in her eyes, he suspected she was now operating purely on adrenaline and hope. At some point, the trauma of the last few days would hit home, but he hoped they'd be far away by then. Away from England, away from danger, away from those who wished them harm.

"Hello! Welcome to Verano Airlines," the woman behind

the desk greeted them, as the customers in front of them left. "How can I assist you today?"

Her smile was warm and it seemed as if she genuinely wanted to help them.

It was probably the start of her shift, Beckett thought.

"We'd like two tickets on the next available flight," he said, forcing a smile while he unzipped his bag to retrieve their passports and a roll of cash.

"Okay. And where are you hoping to fly to today?"

Unseen by the woman, Beckett slipped the roll of notes into his jacket pocket and placed the passports on the counter. "Anywhere," he replied. "The next flight you have available."

"Oh?" The woman's demeanour faltered and uncertainty flashed in her eyes. She looked at Amber and then back at Beckett, perhaps imagining a tragic narrative – a scumbag father stealing his daughter away from an estranged wife. Or something even darker.

"Yeah, it's a thing me and Dad are doing," Amber piped up, leaning on the counter and giving the woman her sweetest smile. "Things have been tough since… since Mum passed. One of her last wishes was for us to have exciting adventures. So we've decided to go on holiday and let fate pick the destination. If it helps, we only need one-way tickets. Dad's taking a few months off work and we want to travel around – experience the world she didn't get to see."

The woman gasped. The way she now looked at Beckett, with her eyebrows raised and her lower lip protruding, told him Amber's quick thinking had done the trick.

"What a wonderful idea," she said. "And I'm so sorry—"

"Thank you. But we are in a bit of a hurry," Amber continued. "We need to leave tonight. It's Mum's birthday tomorrow and we want to be settled wherever we end up."

"Not a problem. Let me see…"

Beckett felt a surge of pride for his niece as the woman got busy on her computer, her fingers flying across the keyboard. He reached down and squeezed Amber's arm. It was the closest he got to affection, but he meant it. *Good work, kiddo.*

"I can get you on a flight leaving in forty minutes," the woman said, looking up. "It's going to be tight, but security isn't that busy this afternoon. If you head there right away, it shouldn't be an issue."

"Thank you so much," Beckett told her, sliding the passports over. "Where are we going?"

"Faro," the woman said. "A beautiful city."

That was perfect. Beckett had been hoping for southern Spain, but Portugal was close enough.

"And the cost?" he asked, peering over his shoulder as he unrolled the bank notes and counted off four hundred pounds in fifties.

"That'll be two hundred and eighteen pounds for the both of you." Leaning forward, she winked at Amber and lowered her voice. "I've put you on my family discount code and you have access to the executive lounge while you wait. Complimentary food and drinks."

Beckett smiled and handed over the cash. Though he doubted they'd have time to enjoy the lounge, he appreciated the gesture. The woman finalised the transaction and returned their passports, now accompanied by their tickets and boarding passes.

"Do you have any luggage to check in?" she asked.

"No, thank you," Beckett said. "We prefer to travel light."

"Very wise. Me too. Well, enjoy your adventure," she said.

"Thanks. We will," Amber replied. "You've been so kind."

As they moved away from the counter, Amber looked up at Beckett with a self-satisfied grin on her face.

"Okay, Meryl Streep," he whispered. "That was good, but don't get too cocky. We're not out of danger yet."

"Meryl Streep?" Amber hissed back, as they made their

way through the bustle of holidaymakers towards security and passport control. "That's your go-to reference for an actress? You really need to get out more, Uncle John."

He glared back at her. "I mean it, Amber. Stay alert. We're not clear yet."

As if to brutally highlight this point, up ahead he saw a large figure dressed in black weaving through the crowds.

"Damn it," he muttered under his breath.

Amber turned around to look. "Shit! What do we do?"

"We move. Over here."

Keeping his head down, Beckett led Amber over to the side of the concourse. The man had removed his sunglasses and body armour, but it was clear he was one of the men from Riverside. He was tall and broad, with a shaved head and small piggy eyes that scanned the room as he walked. But he hadn't spotted them. Not yet.

Beckett manoeuvred Amber through a line of people waiting to use a ticket printing machine and headed for the wide corridor beyond. A sign hanging from the ceiling read, 'Passport Control and Security'. They were almost there.

But then the man stopped and turned their way.

Recognition twisted his face into a cruel sneer when his eyes landed on Beckett. Time stopped. The airport zoomed from macro to micro. Beckett pulled Amber away, but the man was faster than his size suggested and he closed the distance between them fast. Amber cried out as he grabbed the sleeve of her top and yanked her back.

Beckett's instincts kicked in. His hand shot out to grip the attacker's wrist, his other hand latching onto the back of the man's hand. With a swift, precise twist, he forced the man's wrist back beyond its natural limit. He heard the bone snap; felt it, too, the breaking point of a human body under force. The man cried out, his yells alerting those around him that something was wrong. People screamed. They always did. It was a human response even if they had no idea what the hell was going on. All around them, families scattered in a frenzy of terror, their excited expressions now tainted by confusion and dread.

"We need to move," Amber called out.

But the man in black was still standing. He was still a threat. Without hesitation, Beckett drove the base of his palm upwards, colliding with the underside of the man's jaw. The impact was solid and on target, rattling the man's brain in his skull. He folded like a rag doll, slumping against the wall and sliding to the floor.

"Now we move," he told Amber.

52

Beckett and Amber headed down the gangway towards passport control and then slowed their pace, walking briskly but calmly to avoid suspicion. The danger, however, was far from over. In his peripheral vision, Beckett saw another man dressed in black. This one was even bigger than the one he'd just put down, though completely bald except for a clipped goatee beard, and he had a noticeable scar on his left cheek. Beckett lowered his head, but the man had seen him. His eyes now locked onto them with predatory intent.

"We've got company, over to the left," Beckett whispered to Amber, positioning himself in between her and the man. "Just stay calm. We're almost through."

Up ahead, the walkway curved around the side of a shop selling magazines and books, the racks out front displaying typical airport reads. Beckett scanned the crowds behind him. The man in black was edging towards them, winding slowly but surely through the throng. He was acting casual, just another face in the crowd, but as he stepped around the side of a pillar, the clear line of a gun handle was visible under his shirt

Beckett stood by his assumption that the man wouldn't be so reckless as to fire a weapon in such a crowded setting. But he couldn't be certain.

He pressed on. To his right he noticed a pair of security guards stationed near an emergency exit, with an adjoining walkway leading to more departure lounges. He checked his watch. Their flight left in thirty minutes. Time was running out.

Ensuring Amber was by his side he quickened his pace, blending in with the flow of travellers. He could now see their pursuer just a few metres away. The man's expression was neutral, his pace steady, each stride carefully controlled so as not to draw attention. A professional.

Around the next corner passport control came into view, crowded with individuals waiting their turn to pass through the checkpoints. Security guards monitored the area as people approached the manned desks or scanned their documents. Beckett felt it was unlikely the man had papers with him, but he knew better than to put his faith in assumptions.

As they drew nearer to the checkpoint, the gap between them and the man in black closed even further. Beckett could feel the tension coming off Amber while they shuffled forward. Now it was just a delicate game of timing.

A sudden surge in the crowd shoved them forward. Amber screamed. "Help! Uncle John!"

Beckett spun around to see the man had his arm around Amber's waist, dragging her away. He lunged after them, but was blocked by a pair of indifferent businessmen who tutted loudly as he shoved past. "Get out of my way," he yelled. "Stop! Let go of her!"

"Help!"

Their voices were drowned out by the surrounding chaos.

The man continued to haul Amber away. Panic constricted Beckett's throat as he fought his way through the swarm of people. He couldn't afford to lose sight of them. If he did, they'd be back to square one.

But with each step, the man was disappearing into the crowd, dragging Amber with him. The terror in her eyes as she struggled to get free only spurred him on. With elbows as sharp as his resolve, he fought through the wave of people coming the other way, weaving around families and loved-up couples to get Amber back. He'd almost caught up with them, but as he neared he saw the man's hand move to the pistol sticking from his belt. Beckett stopped. The man tilted his head back, hitting him with an intense stare that said more than words ever could.

Back off… or else.

Beckett held his hands up, running a speedy assessment of his options.

"Okay… Okay… Let's all calm down. No one here wants to cause a scene in a busy airport. Whoever you're working for wouldn't be pleased if an innocent civilian was hurt and it drew unwanted attention." As he spoke he nodded along, positive reinforcement, an instinctive action from years of negotiations. "Let her go. It's over."

Amber was red in the face, still struggling to get free. All around them, holidaymakers were rushing past, seemingly oblivious to the tense standoff.

"You're making a big mistake, my friend. I promise you that." Beckett took a step forward. "Amber? Are you hurt?"

She glared at him. "No. But help me."

"I will," he said. "But you need to help yourself first. You've got this."

She frowned. He nodded. Hoped she understood.

She nodded back. She got it.

As Beckett moved forward, she jerked her head back with force, striking the soft spot between the man's sternum and abdomen. Winded, he released his grip on her. Seizing the opportunity, Beckett pulled her to one side and launched himself at the man, jabbing him in the throat with his fist.

A scream cut through the noise. It could've been Amber. The man wobbled but stayed upright, lashing his arm out wildly, catching Beckett on the side of the head with the butt of the pistol. The world spun around him as he battled a flash of blinding pain. It lasted a split second; it felt like minutes. He shrugged it off, but when he tried to realign himself, a large hand clasped his throat and a weight descended upon him. He staggered backwards, colliding with bodies and something that felt like a railing as the man toppled onto him, forcing him to the ground. The impact was like a body slam that knocked all the air out of him.

"You piece of shit," the man snarled. "You think you're a tough guy. You're no tough guy."

He was American. So that explained it. Xander Templeton had sent the hit squad. The implications were huge, but he couldn't process any of it right now. The man's hand was still around his throat. Struggling to breathe, Beckett reached up and got a thumb in the man's eye socket, but his grip was unyielding. He felt himself fading, the screams and cries of the crowd around them growing muffled.

Hang on in there, old boy.

He shoved his thumb in harder and suddenly the man was falling away, the weight pressing down on his body lessening. He gulped down air, pushing against the bulk of the man's torso and shuffling away. Blinking to regain focus, he saw Robert Locke, red-faced and grimacing, clutching the American in a tight sleeper hold. With the element of surprise on his side, and utilising the acute angle, he was able to subdue him within seconds.

Beckett sat up as Locke eased the man to the ground. Some of the crowd were now backing away; others couldn't take their eyes off the scene in front of them. Locke got to his feet and pulled his wallet from his jacket, flashing his ID badge.

"Everyone please stay calm!" he said, raising his voice over the din. "I'm with the British Secret Service. Please do not panic." He turned and addressed the three security personnel who had made their way over. "Secure this man," he told them, and while they rushed in to take control, he straightened his jacket and turned to Beckett.

"John, it's over," he said, holding out his hand to him. "Let's go."

Beckett stared at the hand for a moment, then got to his feet unaided. Amber hurried to his side. "I'm sorry, Locke," he said. "I can't."

"John! I need you and Amber to come with me. The last few days have been a total fucking shitshow and now we need to do this by the book." He glared at Beckett, his eyes firm but pleading.

But Beckett shook his head. "I'm sorry, Robert. It's not happening." He looked over his shoulder. The people on passport control were still on edge, but a couple of stations had begun to let people through. He glanced back at the security personnel; one of them had his knee on the American's back, another was talking on a radio transceiver. Locke would want to manage this situation quietly, and as long as the security personnel remained calm, he assumed the airport would remain operational. But he had no desire to stick around and test that theory.

"Come on, Amber," he said. "We've got a plane to catch."

"Beckett!" Locke called after him. "I can't let you do that."

Beckett shrugged. "Then you're going to have to stop me yourself."

For a moment, neither man moved. Beckett knew Locke wasn't a bad man, but he was caught in a world of obligation and conflicting loyalties. Even if he could trust him, there were far too many other factors involved. He had to leave. There were no other options.

Guiding Amber towards the checkpoint, he handed their passports to the official at the desk. He knew Locke wouldn't stop him; he didn't even try. As their passports were being inspected, Beckett cast a glance back at his former colleague. Locke remained rooted to the spot, arms hanging loosely at his sides. As their eyes met, he gave Beckett a slight nod – not necessarily in agreement, but of acceptance. In response, Beckett faced him head on and offered a respectful salute. Then, hoisting his bag onto his shoulder, he followed Amber down the corridor towards the security checkpoint – and their flight out of there.

53

Locke watched Beckett and his niece push through the double doors at the end of the walkway and disappear.

"Damn it, Robert," he muttered to himself. "What the hell have you done?"

He shook his head, mostly in disbelief at his own actions and their implications rather than at his former officer. Behind him, the man he'd subdued was now regaining consciousness, arguing vehemently with the security team who were restraining him. All around them, the airport was teeming with noise and expectation. The well-oiled machine of industry, already back to normal after the recent upheaval. Like everywhere in the modern world, the relentless hum of activity never ceased for long.

Locke knew his decision to allow Beckett to leave would weigh heavily upon him. Maybe not today, maybe not until a good night's rest and a few days of leave – but soon. The potential career repercussions and the blowback that Sigma Unit could face were great. Yet, despite these factors, a part of him knew he'd made the right choice. The system had been ready to crush John Beckett. It was only his exceptional skills and never-say-die temperament that had allowed him to survive. Locke admired the man's tenacity, although he would never admit that to another living soul.

John Beckett was a good officer.

He was a good man.

But consequences were inevitable. Calder and Eastwood would demand explanations, as would the government ministers. Locke's mind began forming strategies to mitigate the damage, ways he and Sigma Unit could recover their reputation.

His career in intelligence had been shaped by structure and adherence to protocol. But today he'd chosen loyalty towards his officer over the orders he'd been given, a decision he knew would have significant career repercussions. But amid the turmoil of his thoughts, he experienced a profound sense of relief. Sometimes you had to do what was right over what was asked of you. And whatever happened next, he'd get through it.

He was a good officer, too.

And a good man.

He drew in a deep breath and released it in an even deeper sigh. It felt as if all the stress he'd been carrying with him left his body. It was over. For now.

His contemplation was cut short as he sensed a new presence beside him. Even before he looked up, he knew who it was.

"I take it our mutual friend has departed?" Xander Templeton asked.

Locke turned, shifting his head to look at him but only slightly. Templeton was facing forward, his sharp gaze fixed on the double doors Beckett had disappeared through moments earlier.

"Yes. I'm afraid so." Locke gestured behind him with a flick of his head. "I take it the man in black is one of yours. As were the men down at the Riverside Project."

Templeton didn't flinch, his icy blue eyes devoid of any emotion. "I don't know what you're talking about, Chief Director Locke. I would never meddle in the affairs of the British Secret Service. And certainly not on UK soil."

"Bowditch is dead," Locke whispered. "My chief analyst is in the hospital, being operated on as we speak. It's touch and go."

Templeton tutted and tilted his head to one side. "It's a tragic situation and I'm genuinely sorry to hear that. I hope your man pulls through. I really do."

Locke opened his mouth to respond, but what was the point? The men who'd ambushed Beckett down at the riverside were most likely mercenaries. And even if they were CIA operatives, the way Templeton worked he'd have no way of proving it. The official line would be they were Delaney's men trying to finish the job.

"So… where do we all go from here?" Locke asked.

Templeton, still staring ahead, pursed his lips and whistled. "Well, Mr Locke. The past two days have undoubtedly been disastrous – but lessons have been learnt, as they say. At least now we can all move forward. Get on with doing what we do best."

Locke smiled. "And what would that be? Protecting our own interests? Doing deals with shadowy organisations?"

Templeton turned to face him, his eyebrows furrowing in pretend astonishment. "Protecting the security of our great nations, Mr Locke! Ensuring our citizens are safe and live free from fear and unrest."

"Ah yes. I see." Locke shoved his hands in his pockets, both men staring at the double doors now. Regardless of what had happened today, of the lives lost and the decisions made, Templeton was right. Beckett, The Consortium, Bowditch, even Locke's own involvement, would all be covered up. There'd be debriefings and discussions and planning meetings, and a media narrative would be constructed to protect all involved. Whatever had occurred here would be... contained. Because that's what they did. It was how things worked.

"You don't have to worry about Beckett," Locke said, his voice firm. "He's gone. He won't be a problem."

Templeton made a low growling noise. "Can you be certain of that?"

"Yes, Mr Templeton. I can. I saw it in his eyes just now. He knows the consequences of sharing information better than anyone. And he wouldn't do it. He's a loyal soldier, not a traitor." He looked at Templeton. "The situation isn't ideal, but I have every faith that he's gone for good. A ghost. He's not my concern any longer. Nor is he yours."

Templeton nodded slowly to himself, mulling over Locke's words. "I hope you're right about that, Chief Director."

"I know I am," he said, his voice softer now. "So, let it be. He's not a threat to any of us.

For a moment, Templeton's gaze lingered on the double doors at the end of the corridor, his mind seemingly elsewhere. A woman's calm voice announcing the next Paris-bound flight filled the silence between them.

The gruff American stifled a chuckle. "Yeah. Maybe."

His expression, however, suggested his thoughts on Beckett were far from over. His lips tightened into a thin line as he patted Locke on the shoulder and wandered away.

Locke waited a few seconds more. Then he turned around and followed after him. It was over. Now he needed a strong drink, a hot bath and the longest sleep he could possibly get. In that order.

54

The sun was beginning to set over the Spanish countryside, casting long shadows through the sprawling olive groves down to the south, bathing the landscape in a soft golden glow. Beckett stepped out of the farmhouse and stretched, filling his lungs with the warm evening air. He was wearing a pair of canvas trousers and a thin cotton shirt; buttons open to the middle of his chest. He wasn't wearing shoes. He hadn't shaved in a few days. The sun was warm on his skin. It felt good to be alive. He was glad he was.

Down at the bottom of the garden, Amber was standing in front of her new artist's easel, tilting her head to one side to take in the glorious sunset in front of her. As he watched her, she held up her paintbrush, using it to measure perspective and distance the way real artists did. He smiled. She was doing well. She'd be happy here.

Beckett and Amber had landed in Faro three weeks earlier and had taken a FlixBus to Seville, followed by a train to Córdoba and finally a bus to Lucena in Andalusia. It had been a long journey but had given them a chance to talk. Or rather,

Amber had talked. Beckett had listened mostly. But she was a good kid and, despite everything she'd been through, he felt she was coping okay. She was strong and her teenage resilience shone through the trauma she had experienced. Her name might have been Amber Irving, but she was a Beckett through and through.

In Lucena, she'd wanted to take a taxi the rest of the way, but Beckett had insisted on getting a final bus to take them down to the farmhouse in rural Alora, where they'd been staying for the last two weeks. A taxi driver might remember his passengers, but a bus driver rarely did. In fact, theirs didn't even look up from his newspaper as they boarded, only grunting as Beckett waved the tickets at him.

But now they were here. Safe. Settled. The huge, whitewashed farmhouse nestled in the verdant hills of Andalusia was the ideal sanctuary, far away from the danger and chaos they'd left behind. The property belonged to an old friend of Beckett's – a man called Miguel Santos, who lived in it with his wife and daughter and his elderly mother.

Santos, once a high-ranking member of Spain's *Centro de Inteligencia de las Fuerzas Armadas*, had collaborated with Beckett on a mission seven years ago. They had worked together to gather intelligence on Mexican cartel members establishing trade routes in rural Portugal leading to Spain and the UK. They'd spent five months together and had become good friends. Santos had also fought as part of the coalition in Afghanistan, so they had a shared past. He was a man with a tough exterior but a heart of gold. His wife, Isabella, was a woman of immense grace and compassion, and their spirited daughter, Lucia, just a month older than Amber, was cheerful and friendly.

The family welcomed them with open arms, as Beckett had suspected they would. Amber had fallen a little shy at first, but the family's kindness and generous hospitality cut through any tension fast. The sprawling fields surrounding the farmhouse, the chirping of songbirds and the hearty meals prepared by Isabella began to mend their bruised souls.

And Amber was happy here. She and Lucia had hit it off immediately, their shared laughter resonating throughout the farm. Even her cynical asides and eye rolls were less frequent. Over the last few days he'd even noticed a look of gratitude, and perhaps even affection, when she glanced at him. Only briefly, but it was there.

Despite this, Beckett felt a sense of numbness and unease, feelings not uncommon for him. Having spent a significant part of his life as someone else, he struggled to know where John Beckett began any more. But there was time to change that. There was an opportunity for growth if he wanted it.

And he was now completely free, untethered by duty or command. After so long as a soldier it felt strange, but he'd get used to it. He'd have to. There was no going back.

A week earlier, he'd taken Miguel's car into the next town and used a payphone to contact the hospital where Beaumont was being treated. He was pleased to discover his old friend had made it through two operations and, whilst still critical, was showing good signs that he'd pull through. The poor old bugger would never play the piano again, due to the loss of two fingers and nerve damage in his left hand, but he'd have an excellent retirement plan. And he had Martha to look after him.

Beckett stepped down off the porch and walked through the luscious garden, avoiding the mist of an automatic sprinkler. Amber must have sensed his approach – another Beckett trait – because she turned and waved as he got closer.

"Looking good," he said, admiring her canvas of rich oranges and burnt umber. A sunset, he presumed, although it was rather abstract for his taste. "You really are rather talented, aren't you?"

Amber scrunched her nose. "I like painting. That's enough for now." She smiled. Beckett smiled back, but his was short-lived.

"Listen, Amber. We need to talk…"

"I know what you're going to say," she said. "And it's fine. I understand."

Beckett was a little taken aback. "What was I going to say?"

"That you're leaving. That you have to. And that you want me to stay here with Lucia and her family."

"Just until we're sure it's safe. Then we can look for alternative arrangements." He'd been giving the matter a lot of thought over the last week. Those wanting to bring him in might still try to exploit Amber, so he planned on making a few 'errors of judgement' once he left Spain – nothing major, nothing that could pinpoint his location; a withdrawal here, a phone call there, just enough to divert the attention away from Amber's whereabouts. And Miguel would look after her. Beckett trusted the old Spaniard with his life.

"I get it," Amber said. "I can't really see you as a farmhand anyway."

"No?" he leaned back. "What can you see me as?"

She shrugged. "I don't know. Maybe a fisherman?"

"Wow. Perhaps I'll try it." He smiled. "I'll keep in touch when I can."

"You'd better," Amber replied. "Now sod off, will you? I want to try to finish this while I've still got the daylight."

Beckett opened his mouth to respond, but decided against it. Amber was a good kid. She was hardy. A Beckett. She might even thrive out here. He scanned the dusky Spanish landscape, bathed in the warm, honeyed hues of the setting sun, the endless fields and the Alboran Sea only a short drive away. There were worst places to grow up. And he meant what he'd said – he would come back for her. One day. When the time was right and he could guarantee their safety.

It was a peaceful morning three days later when Beckett stepped out of the farmhouse with a heavy duffel bag slung over his shoulder. The rest of the house was still sleeping, but he'd said his goodbyes the night before and it was better this way. He'd never been one for grand farewells.

He threw his bag on the back seat of the beat-up old Citroën he'd bought off one of Miguel's friends and slid into the driver's seat. As he started the engine, he couldn't help but dwell on the threats that still loomed. Xander Templeton was the sort of man who took things personally. If he had been behind the ambush at Riverside, he undoubtedly would still be after him. Similarly, he suspected Frank Calder at MI6 wouldn't rest until he was brought in. Beckett had seen too much. He knew too much. He had become a thorn in the side of too many powerful people. But they'd never find him.

He'd make sure of that.

As he pulled the car away, a fresh wave of confidence welled up within him. Not cockiness, but the assuredness of a man who knew his abilities and his limits. He'd been trained to evade, to outlast, to survive. This was no different.

But while he could always rely on his training, he wasn't the same man he'd been even a few weeks earlier. With every mile he put between himself and Miguel's farm, between himself and Amber, he could feel the chains of his past falling away. He had changed. He was not a soldier responding to orders anymore. He was a guardian, a protector.

The early morning sun lit his way ahead as he sped on down the dirt track onto a country road, and finally to the highway towards Córdoba. He didn't know exactly where he was going yet. He had a vague idea that he'd cut back through Seville and spend a few days in Portugal. From there he could get a flight to South America, perhaps. See what comes of it.

He settled back in his seat and smiled to himself. There was a sense of poetic irony in his situation. He was a man destined to live in the shadows, away from the light, and yet right now he'd never felt brighter, never felt more alive.

He was carving a new path for himself, one that was risky but necessary. He was turning away from his past, moving towards an unknown future. His survival depended on his ability to remain a ghost, to haunt the darkness on the edge of town. With a determined grip on the wheel, and the image of Amber safe and smiling at her easel etched in his mind, he was ready to embrace his new existence.

And he was more than ready for what would come next.

THE END

WANT MORE?

READ 'THE BECKETT FILES'

To show my appreciation to you for buying this book I want to offer you a transcript of Beckett's top secret interview prior to him joining S-Unit.

You'll also get access to my VIP Newsletter plus an exclusive John Beckett novella (coming soon)

To sign up and get 'The Beckett Files' go here:

https://www.matthewhattersley.com/jb/

MATTHEW HATTERSLEY

GET BECKETT BOOK 2:

WHEN THE KINGDOM COMES

**In a town ruled by darkness,
a storm named John Beckett is coming**

Dive into the gritty underbelly of São Lorenço, where a vicious family reigns and fear is a constant companion. That is, until a lone figure steps onto the stage. As the town's only hope, Beckett's mission won't just be survival but revolution. Uncover a tale of raw courage, defiance, and high-octane danger in this riveting new action thriller.

Get your copy by clicking here

CAN YOU HELP?

Enjoyed this book? You can make a big difference

Honest reviews of my books help bring them to the attention of other readers. If you've enjoyed this book I would be very grateful if you could spend just five minutes leaving a review (it can be as short as you like) on the book's Amazon page.

ALSO BY MATTHEW HATTERSLEY

Have you read them all?

The Acid Vanilla series

Acid Vanilla

Acid Vanilla is an elite assassin, struggling with her mental health. Spook Horowitz is a mild-mannered hacker who saw something she shouldn't. Acid needs a holiday. Spook needs Acid Vanilla to NOT be coming to kill her. But life rarely works out the way we want it to.

BUY IT HERE

Seven Bullets

Acid Vanilla was the deadliest assassin at Annihilation Pest Control. That was until she was tragically betrayed by her former colleagues. Now, fuelled by an insatiable desire for vengeance, Acid travels the globe to carry out her bloody retribution. After all, a girl needs a hobby...

BUY IT HERE

Making a Killer

How it all began. Discover Acid Vanilla's past, her meeting with Caesar and how she became the deadliest female assassin in the world.

FREE TO DOWNLOAD HERE

Stand-alone novels

Double Bad Things

All undertaker Mikey wants is a quiet life and to write his comics. But then he's conned into hiding murders in closed-casket burials by a gang who are also trafficking young girls. Can a gentle giant whose only friends are a cosplay-obsessed teen and an imaginary alien really take down the gang and avoid arrest himself?

Double Bad Things is a dark and quirky crime thriller - for fans of Dexter and Six Feet Under.

BUY IT HERE

Cookies

Will Miles find love again after the worst six months of his life? The fortune cookies say yes. But they also say commit arson and murder, so maybe it's time to stop believing in them? If only he could…

"If you life Fight Club, you'll love Cookies." - TL Dyer, Author

BUY IT HERE

ABOUT THE AUTHOR

Over the last twenty years Matthew Hattersley has toured Europe in rock n roll bands, trained as a professional actor and founded a theatre and media company. He's also had a lot of dead end jobs…

Now he writes high-octane pulp action thrillers and crime fiction.

He lives with his wife and daughter in Derbyshire, UK and doesn't feel that comfortable writing about himself in the third person.

COPYRIGHT

A Boom Boom Press ebook

First published in Great Britain in April 2023 by Boom Boom Press.

Ebook first published in 2023 by Boom Boom Press.

Copyright © Boom Boom Press 2015 - 2023

The moral right of Matthew Hattersley to be identified as the author of this work has been asserted by him in accordance with the copyright, Designs and Patents Act 1988.

All the characters in this book are fictitious, and any resemblance to actual persons living or dead is purely coincidental.

All rights reserved. No part of this publication may be reproduced, stored in a retrieval system or transmitted in any form or by any means, without the prior permission in writing of the publisher, nor to be otherwise circulated in any form of binding or cover other than that in which it is published without a similar condition, including this condition, being imposed on the subsequent purchaser.

Printed in Great Britain
by Amazon